Who Goes There?

Who Goes There?

Susan Evans McCloud

BOOKCRAFT
Salt Lake City, Utah

Library of Congress Catalog Card Number: 94-74313

ISBN 0–88494-973-7

Second Printing, 1996

Printed in the United States of America

1

THEY LEFT NEWCASTLE-UPON-TYNE LATE IN THE AFTERNOON, heading north on the A68 toward Scotland. It was Penelope's fault, really, for she had tarried too long over their afternoon tea and then maddened Laura by dawdling among the cluster of small, crowded antique shops, and in the end making no purchase at all—nothing to justify the expenditure of their time.

Penelope laughed lightly, rather indulgently, at her mother's fussing. "You haven't learned to relax yet. We have all the time in the world, remember? No one to go home to and nothing to hurry us?"

That was one reason why Penelope had insisted on the purchase of the sturdy green, rather homely Morris Oxford. "We can go where we like, when we like," she explained, "and not have to depend on train schedules and finding someone to taxi us from churchyard to churchyard. That would be disastrous, especially at the rate you walk, Mother." Penelope smiled, not unkindly, in apology. "Why, with a car we might even decide to cross the

Channel and winter in Italy. I have a friend at the University who spent a winter in Italy. Wouldn't that be simply grand?"

Penelope was feeling her oats, Laura knew. She did not share her daughter's enthusiasm; she had long since forgotten what it was like to be vibrant and intense about life. Penelope's exuberance was the very reason for her being here, against her own good judgment. How could she grieve properly among strangers in this green and moist foreign land?

A large upright rock stood sentinel at the border with the word *Scotland* scrawled across it. Penelope slowed the car. "Just a moment, Mother," she murmured as she pulled off to the shoulder of the narrow road and went to stand, like any silly tourist, beside the gray stone. It was past ten o'clock and ought to have been dark, but it wasn't. The night was as gentle as a gray cloak about the girl, and the hills of Scotland stretched in soft folds, smoothly flowing one into another. The stillness, as she breathed it in, was as sweet as the night air. *This will be good for Mother,* she thought. *It will be good for both of us. I can feel that it will.*

Laura, waiting, watching her, was more aware of her daughter's youthful beauty than of the beauties of nature around her. She felt the cold pricks of loneliness and isolation play along her skin, and she shivered. It had been a night much like this when she had heard the telephone ring and had run into the dim, unlit hall to answer it, wondering who could be calling at such a late hour, and why the caller was so persistent—

"Mother, I've never seen such a breathtaking sight. You really ought to pop out and take a look." Penelope slid into the seat beside Laura, seeming to poise there expectantly.

2

Laura shook her head. "It's late, Penny. We need to find a place to stay for the night."

Penelope made no protest, but eased the car out and followed the road as it turned into the village of Jedburgh and became a quiet, narrow street. No other cars were out at this hour, only shadows chased one another across the rough, cobbled thoroughfare and gathered in murky pools along the tight front of houses that lined the street.

"There's an inn somewhere near Jedburgh; I know I saw it in the guidebook." Penelope groped between the seats with her free hand. "Where is that thing, Mother?"

There were no lights on the streets, and the darkness was thickening. Penelope slowed the car as she realized the narrow street came to an end up ahead in a wide, rounded curve, behind which loomed a gloomy hulk of a building. She stopped the car and peered out into the gloom.

" 'Rooms to let.' Look right there, Mother. That's what the sign says. Shall I go and inquire? The house appears very clean and—respectable." She had nearly said "cozy," but the building before her appeared very far from that. Its plain stone front, like all the others, rose straight and unbroken, with no adornment, nothing to speak welcome or to betray the sort of people who may live inside.

"Go ahead, Penny, but do be quick. And if it doesn't look acceptable, decline politely and hurry—"

"Yes, Mother." The car door shut softly and Penelope was halfway up the dark path before Laura's sentence was finished. She let the last word end on a long, resigned sigh. She was not much of a traveler—perhaps because she had not traveled much. Young people were different, and Penelope—well, she was much like her father, curious about everything, quick moving and blessed with endless energy. Laura had never been like that; even as a girl she had had a languid air about her. Though, if she remembered right, that had not harmed her appeal. Men in her day appreciated a woman's subtle qualities. Then the Great War had turned everything haywire. The war had—

She stopped herself with an angry gesture and tapped her fingernails against the brittle glass of the car window. She must not think about war and loss and horror; she must not think about either Gerald or Peter, or she very well might go mad. She watched Penelope glide back down the path toward her, and for a moment she felt a sharp stab of envy. How free the girl was still; how free, and how whole.

"It's lovely. You'll like it, Mother." She held the door open invitingly. "You look tired, dear. Just grab that small bag from the backseat, why don't you? I'll introduce you to Mrs. Grant and you can start getting settled while I come back for the rest."

She really is a good daughter, Laura thought as she followed Penelope up the unfamiliar path. *My only daughter, and now she's all I have left.*

Reluctantly she entered the dimly lit warmth of the tall stone house. She was a stranger in a strange land. Her heart was too grieved, too tender for her to reach out and be more.

———◆———

Laura awoke to the sound of rain beating an irregular rhythm against the low roof. Beside her Penelope stretched and yawned, and the cocoon of warmth that had held them slowly dissolved.

After that the day seemed wet and dismal to Laura, traipsing through the damp streets: touring the castle-jail which had loomed a dark and sinister presence the night before; walking through the graceful arched ruins of Jedburgh Abbey and the sixteenth-century house where Mary, Queen of Scots, stayed in 1566—she and Burns, Walter Scott, and Bonnie Prince Charlie. History breathed down their necks here, and she was not yet in tune with it. If she could only push her own feelings aside, as Penelope had hoped she would. Her own history, if one could call it that, pressed upon her with more weight than the centuries of life that were layered around her.

Penelope, on the other hand, unaccustomed to her mother's slow pace, raced ahead in spurts and starts, chafing at the sedate confinement her mother would set. "Mother, come! Oh, Mother, look at this!" She was full of urgings and entreaties, her eyes as open with wonder as any child's.

After a quick lunch of English fish-and-chips at a roadside pub, they drove to Abbotsford House, Sir Walter Scott's country home that sat beside the river Tweed. Laura had not yet ceased to marvel at Penelope's adaptability and fearlessness. She drove aggressively, not merely with confidence, though their first hours in the car, driving on the "wrong" side of the road, unnerved Laura, and she had tensed up every time they passed another vehicle, wondering how two cars could possibly fit together along the skinny, poorly paved pathways the English called roads. But even the roundabouts did not confuse Penelope; thank heaven for that. Thank heaven for everything about the girl just now.

On the English side of the border the tall slopes of the Cheviots are bleak and windy. Yet on the Scottish side the same Cheviots roll in friendly green "knowes" and little woods, crisscrossed by burns and dikes and the deep, often tumbling waters of the Tweed. Penelope, ever sensitive to beauty, was overwhelmed by the sensations and the strange drawing out of herself, as though something deep within her was as ancient, as weathered and wise as these moors and fells, and belonged here in a way the conscious part of her could not understand.

They stopped first at Dryburg Abbey, where Walter Scott was buried amid the graceful ruins, and Penelope fancied they whispered to her of the gentleness and beauty of a day gone by. Death, the silent, numbing effect of death, was all that struck Laura's heart. She could not help it. Even at Scott's fine house, while Penelope immersed herself in the books, the ancient weapons, the countless relics on display in the rooms, Laura was drawn to the sad, serene spirit of the place. It felt to her as though the life that had lived there yet breathed through the space in a sort of resigned acceptance of the demands of the grave, of the changes wrought by time which were forever beyond his control.

They dined in Selkirk at a pub called the Queen's Head, eating finnan haddie and stovies, with fruit-filled bannocks, for which Selkirk was noted, for their dessert. Penelope, though she said nothing, was quite concerned. Her mother was still preoccupied; it was easy to see that. How long would it take? Her father had been dead for just over a month; perhaps she had been hasty in dragging her mother off like this, perhaps it was really too soon. With the impatience born of youth she had believed it to be just the right answer, but perhaps she was wrong. Besides, she felt almost guilty. Enjoyment of what they were doing surged through her veins like a tonic. Some part of her had come home. And that was precisely what she had hoped to achieve for her mother. Three of Laura's major family names hailed from Scotland: her fa-

ther was a Douglas, her mother a Cameron on her father's side and a MacGregor on her mother's. That's
what the trip had been for, to do genealogy, haunt the li-
braries and old kirkyards, in search not only of records
but of some clues to the characteristics of those people
whose names they both bore. Her parents had traveled to
Scandinavia after her father retired to seek out his
Norwegian roots: the Nielsens and the Poulsons. Then
they had toured Germany and parts of France where as a
young man Gerald had served a mission. It was characteristic of her father that he hadn't gotten around to
Scotland. He never meant to be unthoughtful; it was just
that his needs came first. His priorities were the family's
priorities; it had always been so. And it was characteristic
of her mother that she had not told her husband how
much she wanted to go, wanted to see the places her own
grandmother had told her stories about when she was a
child.

I must be patient, Penelope chided herself. *We've only
been in this country one day.* England didn't count. The
time spent in London, the Lake District, and the moor-
lands of the Brontës she thought of as merely a prelude.
Scotland would be the real thing. Scotland would in
some mystical, inexplicable manner provide the key. In
revealing and unlocking the past for her mother, it would
unlock her future as well.

Patience, Penelope repeated to herself. *This will just
take a little patience or, more aptly put, faith.*

She loved her mother dearly. Even during her turbulent growing-up years they had managed to remain good
friends. Now that she was twenty-three and graduated
from the University of Utah she was discovering her
mother as another woman, a whole new dimension beyond the confines of "mother." It was a great pity that her

father had died and left them alone, just seven years after her brother had been killed in the war. But the future did not have to be a tragedy. Her mother could build a new life. This was an adventure the two were sharing—as mother and daughter, as two women who were making their way in the world. That was how she looked at it, and in such light, Penelope knew it was right.

———

For nearly forty miles, from Teddington where the tide ends to Dartford Creek, the River Thames wound its way through the heart of London, carrying on its broad waters barges and lighters, tramps and freighters—the commerce of a nation bound out to the seven seas, merchandise worth millions of pounds; and all under the protection of the Thames Division, the oldest branch of the Metropolitan Police.

Callum MacGregor was proud to be one of the carefully selected men to cover the waterfront. He liked the sights and smells here, the wharves and warehouses, the ships' masts standing stark against the London-gray sky. He liked the scope and variety of the challenges he met here. He had been on the London police force for thirty-three years, serving his stint as a uniformed constable on the city streets, working his way up, learning the work from the bottom upward; there was never any shortcut to promotion at Scotland Yard. As a youth of twenty he had met the exacting requirements with ease: a minimum height of five feet eight inches (Callum measured six-one in his stocking feet); a minimum chest expansion of two inches; good teeth; perfect eyesight, hearing and speech; and freedom from all chronic deformities, defects, or ailments. Now, over thirty years later, he felt in better shape than he had as a kid. Early on he had shown promise in balancing the practical and the theoretical, the physical and the mental. He was a policeman's policeman and had risen steadily in the ranks; until now he did plain-clothes duty as a chief detective inspector along the docks. Which was what he preferred. So when the summons came to report to the commissioner's office he experienced a sensation of unease, a sixth sense warning him that nothing this good could be bound to last indefinitely.

He drove along the stretch of the Thames from Tower Bridge, with the Tower buildings standing square on the north bank, to London Bridge and then on, as the great river passed Battersea Park and flowed beneath the shadow of Big Ben and then of the Yard itself. The first of the buildings, massive and impressive, that housed the offices of the Metropolitan Police was built in 1890, the newer one in 1905. Callum crossed the somber length between them, finding his way to the large, well-appointed office where the commissioner waited.

As he eased himself into a chair he fought the customary grin he always struggled with whenever he met the great man face to face. Commissioner Howe would have failed all the entrance requirements, at least the way he looked now. Callum wouldn't judge his height as over five foot six, and his weight was a good fifteen stone. He was hard of hearing, suffered from high blood pressure, and had a nervous habit of running his index finger vigorously over the line of his hairless eyebrows and the shiny bald pate of his head. One could be deceived into thinking him an almost comical figure, but Callum knew better than that. There was no finer mind this side of the Atlantic than Thomas Howe's, and his spirit had a gentleness about it customarily reserved for women. Callum often wondered how he had survived the cutthroat rivalry he must have encountered as he rose to this place. Perhaps the very rarity of his qualities protected him, boldened as they were by his fierce opposition to evil and the sterling integrity of his own motives and conduct.

The little man smiled at him. "You're not happy to be here," he said matter-of-factly. "But to tell you the truth, MacGregor, I'm happy to have you sitting right in that chair. There are few men qualified to give the kind of help I'm needing."

Callum was pleased; not flattered, but pleased. And he was getting curious now.

"We've a problem that's rising out of all proportion." The commissioner's finger scurried like a long, thin insect along his hairline. "It's these art thefts, you know."

Callum knew. Several of the great houses in the West End had been hit during the past two weeks, burglaries all of them, occurring as they did between the hours of 9 P.M. and 6 A.M. The thieves were masterly, their M.O. seldom varied, and they had gotten away with too much for too long. There had arisen a general outcry of the press and the public at the outrage, for they were hitting not only the very rich but the up-and-coming of the middle class who, for the first time, were accumulating wealth and possessions, and were most zealous to protect them.

"The wretched thing is, MacGregor, that we have so little to go by. From the small amount of evidence we've gathered we know it's two women, and it generally appears that one is older, one younger. We've pretty well ruled out the possibility of it being men in disguise."

Disguise. The word smarted. That was part of the robbers' cunning; they possessed an endless array of disguises and were most adept at donning them, so that even the most watchful were fooled.

"Indeed, this is a bleak one." The commissioner was

watching Callum closely. "And it just so happens that last night our 'lovely ladies' "—so the Force had taken to calling them—"waxed surpassingly bold. They chose Catherine Allen, marchioness of Huntingdon, as their latest victim. It seems that she had purchased a very valuable Laszlo at auction less than a month ago." The commissioner paused, rubbing the line of his eyebrow vigorously. "Do you know this artist, MacGregor?"

"Yes, sir. I believe he is of Hungarian extraction, though he spent some time in Paris. Took up residence here in England in 1907 or 8, some time around there. It's very fashionable to own his paintings—among the rich young set, that is. Does mainly portraits, I think."

"There you go! Very good, man. I thought you would know."

"Our lovely ladies lifted it from her?"

"Only last night."

Callum scowled, and the lines in his well-molded face seemed to grow deeper and more pronounced. "I've heard nothing."

"Good! That's pleasing. We're trying like the deuce to keep this one under wraps."

Callum nodded; the reasons for doing so were obvious. "And me, sir?" he prodded, hoping to draw the commissioner to the point.

Thomas Howe leaned forward in his high swivel chair, giving the illogical impression that he might lose his balance and tip right over. But Callum MacGregor was watching his eyes. They had narrowed and acquired a bright, eager glaze. Callum could feel their excitement reach out and touch him, much the way the heat from a radiator does when one is standing only a few feet away. He felt his own muscles tense; he felt expectancy, like a restorative, race through his blood.

"We have a tip from a reliable source that they've headed north into Scotland, perhaps merely to escape the heat after this last job. Perhaps their plans have altered. I'd like to know what they're up to, I would!" The commissioner scowled, and the expression made him look like an unhappy Humpty Dumpty. "And I'd like to break into their organization. Who are the brains behind it all, who's calling the shots? What fences do they use? These are pretty sophisticated goods they're moving, you know. Has to be a big market for them somewhere. We haven't even fingered one of the van drivers yet—and I'm convinced Reliable Lines delivery, or at least someone in their employ, is in on the scheme."

Callum nodded and met Thomas Howe's scowl with a tightening of his own facial muscles, which lent his features a bit of the fierceness for which he was well known.

"We must get something, and quick. I'm sending you to Scotland. Be my bloodhound, MacGregor, and run the pair down. Who knows what disguise they might travel under? Perhaps something bizarre—perhaps something deceptively simple. Two women—what more have we really than that? But you must find them. Then stay so close to them that they can't help feeling you breathing right down their necks! They'll slip up sooner or later, and when they do, you'll be there." He paused. His eyes grew soft, with an open appeal in them. "You really are my last chance—and my best one. I have great confidence in you, and well you know it, my man."

So that was it! Callum would not have guessed. Mentally he rubbed his hands together. This was a temporary assignment, and if he handled it well it would prove to be a feather in his cap, to put it lightly. But then, it was no small thing the commissioner was asking of him, no light task.

"Yes. Very good, MacGregor. I knew you'd take it, and I know you'll do the job well. Make what arrangements you need to to settle your affairs in the city and report back here. Is tomorrow evening too soon?"

It sounded like a reasonable request, but the wording Howe had used was a mere courtesy; it was really an unquestionable command.

"I'll be ready, sir."

"Very good. Shall we say seven, at my place? I'll brief you and we'll share a dram of good Scotch whiskey before you set out on the road." He chuckled and extended his hand to Callum, who rose and leaned over to take it, surprised as he always was at the strength of the grasp.

"Thank you, sir. 'Til tomorrow, then." Callum turned and walked out of the room, out of the building, across the large mall, chill now with afternoon shadows. He was heading instinctively for the waterfront, and he let his impulses move him at will. It was a gentleman's job he was being handed, and that did flatter him, though uncomfortably. He had clawed his way up tooth and nail, as the saying went, but his taste for the good things of living was real. Music, art, poetry, architecture—being a Scotsman, he was naturally interested in the finer points there. He had a feel for such things, which he had recognized early and cultivated largely in private. He was the private type, a loner by nature, that much was for sure. If Annie had lived longer, he might have been different. But that was all so long ago. Too late to conjecture, to think about; too late to change.

A thick gray mist, like a ground cloud, was rising up from the water. Callum blew on his fingers, then thrust his hands into his pockets. He hadn't been in Scotland for years. No reason to go back there; both his parents were dead. So were Annie's parents. In time, everything changed. Whoever else he might call family were scattered here and there, busy with lives of their own.

Scotland. He paused and squinted his eyes to gaze out over the river. The mist was so thick he could taste it. He would miss this place, but he would be back before long. That didn't concern him. What concerned him was Scotland. Going back. Going home. What would he find—in the place, and in himself? He walked the cold, crowded wharves trying to sort it all out, a shadow among the shadows, picking his way with ease, moving with practiced assurance despite the clinging blindness of the fog.

2

THE ROAD FROM SELKIRK CRAWLED FOR SIX MILES ALONG THE Ettick River past places with names like Dodhead, Gilmanscleuch, and Rankleburn, and at last to a little village called Ettrick Bridge. A few miles up the valley, Mrs. Grant had told Laura, stood Ettrick Kirk, and in the shadowed graveyard she would find many a Douglas buried and sleeping.

Penelope steered the little Morris up the narrow roadway. The morning was chill, as though the sun had not yet found a way to break through the gray mists that trailed like limp tatters and shreds of night's discarded veil. It was gloomier still beneath the great trees of the kirkyard. Laura shivered and hugged her arms to her sides. "I can't get used to this moist cold, Penny. I can feel it clear down in my bones."

"I know." Penelope glanced around her. The square old church with its castellated tower stood as silent as the graves—hundreds of graves leaning and falling upon one another. Penelope could feel their crowding, and a sad curiosity of her own. *These were all human beings who once lived and thought and hoped and dreamed as I do.* She shivered. What had happened to all these people whose lives had once been as hearty and glowing as hers? For the first time since her father's death she saw his face clearly before her eyes. Had he been afraid when the moment overtook him? Had he been afraid and shrunk back? Had he cried out at the blank injustice of it?

She sunk down on her knees beside one of the headstones. What could they find here? Not even a whisper of what had once been! Nothing but rough chiseled names, faint and faded after the ravages of centuries.

"What soul, lass, do ye mourn in this place? What brings you to kneel in our churchyard?"

Penelope looked up into the dimness above her. The voice she had heard seemed to hang in the air, to tremble there, even after the words had been spoken.

"We come from the United States," she heard her mother answer as she rose to her knees and brushed the damp, clinging moss from the folds of her skirt. "My father was a Douglas, and we are here out of interest in those of that name."

The old man Penelope gazed upon appeared as gray and worn as the gravestones, bent and shortened by the storms of many long years as they were.

"And ye carry a grief of your own." It was a statement, but the way the man said it made it sound like a benediction, like a blessing upon their heads.

Penelope stared at him, unable to help herself. "My father died suddenly, only a month ago." She heard her mother draw her breath in sharply. She watched the stranger's profile, for he was turned to Laura and his eyes were on her.

"Aye." The word was only a small sound. "Then this is

a good place for you, here with these quiet spirits who lived such turbulent lives and are at peace now."

He spoke the words matter-of-factly. Penelope wanted to ask, "How do you know they are at peace? How can you state that so surely?"

"Mortality is a rough road for all of us, and it can do many strange and harsh things to a man. These people—" He extended his arm in a wide arc, seeming to encompass all before him, and Penelope was surprised to see the lean, muscular strength of that arm. "These people, men and women, lived by their wits," he continued, and his voice was like a lullaby or the soft sighing of wind in the trees. "They never knew from one day to the next if they would have food to eat or a roof over their heads; never knew if their cattle would be lifted by the reivers, their barns burned, their sons killed in battle or simply for poaching a deer from the lands of one of the great lords." He shook his head. "Such a life could breed love-lessness. But not in this people. They learned to hold life very dear, to cherish each new day their Maker saw fit to give them."

The soothing voice ceased for a moment, and Penelope glanced at her mother. Her eyes were fixed on the stranger's face. They were wide and open, like a child's who is listening to a story and waiting for the next word, and the next word, wishing it never to end.

"You see, in death the burden of their harsh lives was lifted. Their spirits could breathe; they could see freely what the mists of earth life had hidden."

"And what was that?" Penelope bit her lip, amazed that the words had come out of her.

The old man turned his head and his kind eyes rested on her. "The love of God who had sent them here to learn from their sufferings, to become more like him.

17

How sweet life will taste when cruelty and fear, when pain and loss become only vague memories chased away by God's light."

He was saying with his eyes, *It is so for your father. It will be so for me and for you.*

Laura felt the tears rise in her throat. The old man put his arms out to her and she felt both her hands cradled in his, and a sense of warm comfort surged through her—a sensation she had not experienced since she had learned of her husband's death. She had prayed for this peace, but then had forbidden it, closed her mind and spirit to any heavenly assistance in a selfish, childlike fear that in letting go, she would really lose him. Odd that this kind, gentle man—a stranger—should approach her, should somehow know of her grief, know how to speak to her.

"*Chaochail e,*" the man said, looking into her eyes again. "We never say of a person who has died *bhasaich e,* the word 'death.' That is for animals only. Of people we say *shiubbail e,* 'he traveled,' or *chaochail e,* 'he changed.'"

"Yes." Laura understood why he was telling her. She tightened her grip on his hands. Then the moment was over and he was leading her through the worn stone markers, Penelope gliding along in their wake.

"Here lie the descendants of James of the fiery face," their guide said gently. "Many of them dead by the pestilence, others killed by the sword. A powerful family in the Borders, the Douglases. Ye have heard, of course, of the Black Douglas, or James the Good."

They had not heard. They sat on the grass, damp still beneath the pale sun, while he told them the tales, the brave Border legends so filled with courage and pathos. They listened unmindful of time, unmindful of the weak substance of the passing moment, totally immersed in the past, in realities that somehow lessened the tight grip of their own.

They left with reluctance. As they drove out of the kirkyard the world they reentered seemed too busy, too bright. Penelope drove slowly with the windows down, and the Ettrick water laughed and sang beside them. Laura knew, she had been taught all her life the truths about life and death: why we are here and where we are going. But when Gerald died she lost hold. It had been difficult enough with Peter, but then she had not been alone. Now she faced a long corridor of loneliness as the years weakened and destroyed her, and led her at last to the grave. Her grieving for Gerald had been very selfish. Why had the old man's words touched her and struck a chord? For the first time she felt the tenseness within her begin to relax. Perhaps, perhaps . . . she would not hope for too much too quickly. But this was a beginning; at least it was that.

———————

That September evening in the Salt Lake Valley was as mild as June. The man with the narrow beak nose and the thin moustache walked the perimeter of the large brick bungalow for the third time, moving much as a bloodhound moves, his nose and eyes as active, the tilt of his head as intent. There was absolutely no movement, no sign of life or activity within or without. Not even the expectant feeling of someone's return. He knew that feeling, and he knew just as surely that his birds had flown. He walked back to his car and sat in the driver's seat and waited. He waited for one hour, then another. It was not that he was patient; rather, he was methodical and thorough. He was simply doing his job. When a Ford pulled into the driveway next-door he moved quickly and was already on the sidewalk when the middle-aged lady had gotten herself out of the driver's seat and closed the front door.

"Good evening," he said. His voice was low and pleasant. "Lovely weather we're having, isn't it?"

The woman stared at him, unimpressed. "I don't recognize you," she replied. "Do you live hereabouts?"

The man was irritated; touchy old dame. But his stance and expression did not alter in the least; if anything, his smile became a little more relaxed, a little warmer.

"No, I don't, as a matter of fact. I am—was—a friend of Gerald's, a business associate, and I've been trying to get in touch with Laura, but I can't seem to find her at home." He laughed lightly, as though his listener would understand this slight inconvenience and sympathize with him. "Has she gone off somewhere? Vacation, she and the daughter? I thought perhaps you might be able to help me. . . ." He made his voice linger over the last two words, drawing them out into a gentle appeal. It was lost on the middle-aged woman.

"Sorry, but I can't, sir. You're a stranger to me. And what's more, I don't think I like the look of you." She turned her back on him and began walking in long strides toward her own lighted porch. "It isn't my place to give information to a stranger," she added loudly as she walked. Then, turning her head once, she quickly added, "You'd better be on your way."

This was the sort of attention the quiet man shunned. He moved as smoothly as a shadow. The persnickety woman had seen his face. Had that been a mistake, an error in judgment? At best it was sloppy, and he cursed himself inwardly. Close-mouthed and loyal, these Mormons. That much he'd learned already. Well, it was not his decision to make. He got back into his car and drove out of the neighborhood, back to the Hotel Utah where he had a nice room and a private phone.

He reached the New York number on the first dial, then went through a series of connections until he heard the voice he was looking for. He told the facts briefly and accurately as they had happened, the skin of his face stretched tightly across his high cheekbones and nose line as he spoke. But the tenseness relaxed somewhat as he listened.

"I can handle that," he finally said. "Yes, I'll be more careful this time. I'll wait a day or two until the old broad's forgotten she saw me and won't be looking for anything, and I'll go in the dead of night. Ought to be simple. No hitches." There was another pause while he listened and his long fingers fumbled through his pockets in search of a cigarette. "Righto. You got it. I'll call you Wednesday, seven in the morning your time. Yes, sir."

He put the phone receiver back in its cradle and found a match to light his cigarette. This job was a fluky one, very out of the ordinary. He settled into a chair. Time on his hands, and what did a guy find to do in a city like this? Well, that's what he got paid for, and paid very well. He took a long draw on the cigarette and picked out a magazine from the stack that sat on the table beside him. He'd relax for a few minutes with his smoke and then go get something to eat. There must be places in this town that were open past nine o'clock. What a weird place Salt Lake was. What a weird assignment for the old man to give him. He hummed under his breath as he thumbed through the lewd magazine, and in a few minutes he had forgotten all about Gerald Poulson and his widow and the proper, proprietary woman who had gotten herself in his way.

Tweeds and tartans and soft Shetland wool sweaters—
Penelope had never seen such an array. She looked be-
seechingly at her mother, and Laura nodded. She felt
like being indulgent, and the lovely goods were nearly irresistible. Through the years she had never been too free
with Gerald's money, though there had always been
ample, and she had been grateful for that. But now, after
the insurance settlement—well, she had never thought to
see so much amassed, undesignated money in her lifetime. It overwhelmed her a little. And then there were
Gerald's stocks, which he had collected with such zeal
over the past few years. She hadn't even looked into
those yet. So why not let Penelope have a little fun?
Edinburgh was an exciting, impressive city after the quiet
Border villages. It had a strange way of stirring one's
blood. They had rooms in an old red stone hotel called
the George, which was grand without being pretentious.
They planned to spend several days here, and already
Laura could see they would be well spent.

"Look at this, will you? I'll warrant every other shop
on Princes Street is a bookshop, and all of them thrive."
The young man's voice was warm with pride, like an indulgent and boastful father. "Edinburgh is the most intel-
lectual city on earth. Even Paris seems illiterate by com-
parison."

"You love it." Penelope smiled at the handsome
young man walking beside her. "And I don't blame you a
bit."

She called it a stroke of luck that she had met Donald
Ross on their very first day in the city. Since then he had
shown them around: from Edinburgh Castle high on the

rock down the Royal Mile which links the castle with the Palace of Holyroodhouse, where the queen herself stayed whenever she was in town; the old churches and the houses of famous people like Sir Walter Scott, Robert Burns, and John Knox. He was as generous and gracious with Laura as he was with Penelope; a true gentleman, Laura called him, though not out loud. She did not wish her daughter to become too enamored of the charming young Scotsman and let his attentions go to her head. But it was nice to have someone to lean upon, someone who knew what to do. Donald's father was a solicitor in the city and Donald a student at Edinburgh University, which had been founded in the year 1582. Difficult to even imagine anything going on continuously for that length of time. It did put one's own life in a little different perspective; Laura realized that. "They learned to hold life very dear," the old man had said. She could feel that way, too, in such places as this.

———•—•———

He had forgotten. How could he have forgotten the feel of this place? Callum had arrived in Edinburgh long after dark and gone to sleep to the sound of a wet wind rattling in the chimney. Now, up early, the morning he looked upon was breathless and still. The craggy old city, gray with the silt of centuries of living, rose tower by tower and spire by spire above the thick morning mist which still choked the ravine below Princes Street. The faint flush of sunlight was in the air, though the smoke of the city threatened to altogether obscure it; but that was of no account here. This regal capital, this "Athens of the North," was recognized as one of the centers of European intelligence, of art and architecture and philosophy—recognized by men such as Voltaire, Rousseau, and the American patriot Thomas Jefferson, who had declared that, in scientific matters, "No place in the world can pretend to a competition with Edinburgh."

Callum loved it. He was tempted this fine morning to indulge himself in a bit of harmless sightseeing, but he did not give in to the urge. Business first. He had places to check out and people to contact. There would be time for himself later. He would make certain of that.

Their last day in the city was spent largely in shopping, and Laura returned to the hotel with a dull, throbbing headache. Donald had promised Penelope a smashing night out at one of the most fashionable cabarets in Edinburgh with dinner at ten and dancing 'til one, when a floor show every bit as good as the Follies at the Cabaret Club in London would be performed. After that it would be dancing 'til dawn—though not in Penelope's case, Laura assured her. The proprietor at the George hotel knew who Donald Ross was and had pledged his word to the respectability of the boy and his family when Laura questioned him. But their first evening after becoming acquainted with Donald she had still insisted he take her to meet his parents. They had proved to be kind, gracious people, inviting Laura and Penelope to stay for a late tea and showing them around the sumptuous town house they called home. Only then did Laura relax and feel safe entrusting her daughter to Douglas's youthful care.

This evening, though both Penelope and Douglas urged her with genuine concern and sincerity, Laura declined going along. They would enjoy themselves more without her, and she did not relish the noise and bright lights of a dance club, where men and women would be so obviously paired off, so obviously caught up in enjoying themselves. No, she would have a quiet supper in her room and pick one of the dozen books they had purchased over the past week to read.

Donald, when he came to collect Penelope, looked the perfect model of the "bright young thing," with baggy trousers—"Oxford bags," Penelope called them—in a color labeled "sage-green." He had a Valentino haircut, right down to the long sideburns, and since the evening was chilly he wore a Fair Isle pullover and a felt hat that sported a flat, three-cornered dent, worn with the brim turned up in front and down at the back.

"Isn't he divine," Penelope had murmured when he first appeared in the doorway. And Laura had to admit, despite the outlandish clothing, that the boy was a dream. Penelope, if the truth were told, didn't look too shabby herself. She had traded her fashionable suit and her round felt cloche hat for a tea frock, modeled after a Paris fashion—a slinky, clinging sheath affair made up of soft silks and chiffon. She had insisted on plucking her eyebrows to a pencil-fine line and painting her mouth until it looked nearly purple, and at the last moment had decided to wear those horrid long drop earrings that nearly touched her shoulders. But despite all that, she was a vision of loveliness as she swept out the door on Donald's arm.

"I wonder what Mark would say if he could see her right now." Laura spoke the words out loud, into the vacuum of silence left by Penelope's departure. Mark Phillips was the "boyfriend back home." Penelope had dated him nearly all through college, with time off for his mission, of course. He was a good boy, solid and dependable. Penelope's worst complaint against him was that he didn't know how to have fun. But that wasn't true; Laura had seen enough to know better. That was just her excuse to keep a distance between them. Laura believed her daughter was afraid of marriage, afraid somehow of making a commitment, of seeing herself settling down into a real life of having babies and making a home for a man. It was these crazy times and the effect they had on young people. It was losing so many young men so quickly, so helplessly, in the war.

Laura sighed. Peter would have been twenty-seven this year. She could not imagine her son at that age, could not even picture him more than vaguely in a series of images that all blurred and merged. Penny had been sixteen when he went off to the war in the last months of 1918, the very last months! Laura dare not let herself think of it. He had been twenty years old, with black, wavy hair like his father's, and laughing blue eyes. He had been the idol of his sister and her schoolgirl friends.

Laura shook her head, trying to dislodge the old memories, the muffling pain that was beginning to close upon her. Not tonight. Not when she was alone. She looked around for her pocketbook. She would go downstairs to eat in the public dining room, then come back upstairs to read. She would not give in to the black misery that taunted her, beckoned her with an almost macabre appeal.

"Yes sir, that's my baby, No sir, I don't mean maybe, Yes sir, that's my baby now. . . ." The music blared, the saxophone throbbed as Donald whirled Penelope around the floor in the one-step. He was a good dancer and made it easy to follow. She liked the way other eyes watched them; the men looking at her in open admiration, the girls, more covertly, drawn by Donald's open and obvious good looks. She knew it was a Cinderella kind of night she was

having. Tomorrow they would leave Edinburgh and that would be the end of it, and she would put on her old life as she would a worn, familiar piece of clothing. And that was all right. This kind of living wasn't compatible with the life she had been raised for. With a brief rush of excited guilt she let herself wonder what Mark would do if he could see her right now. There was nothing like this in Salt Lake. They had dance clubs, and Mark would take her if she insisted, but there was nothing like this! With a sigh she gave herself over to the bright lights and music, the sense of beautiful people around her. Donald had said that he wanted to write letters, to keep in touch. He would say that. But writing never worked out, and it certainly wouldn't in this case. No, tonight was the night. The magic and the mystery—just like Cinderella. She had told the Scottish boy little about her world. How could she? Let her remain the lovely stranger who came into his life briefly and left a lingering sweetness. . . .

The band had switched to "Sleepy-Time Gal," a new hit. The lights dimmed and the pace slowed, and Donald drew her into his arms. She closed her eyes and let herself lean close against him, savoring the warmth of his embrace and the tangy scent of his skin. It would end, it would end all too soon. But for Penelope nothing existed beyond this brief, trembling moment—nothing at all.

———

Callum had forgotten that in Edinburgh, when darkness comes creeping the ghosts come creeping as well. As he walked down the Royal Mile into Lawnmarket, past St. Giles and into Canongate, he felt them, crowding round him and tugging at his memory. How corroded and covered over that memory of his had been these long years! It awoke now with an ache and a small thrill that had much of fear in it, and Callum MacGregor was not accustomed to fear. He pushed the past from him; nowhere more than in Edinburgh did the past coexist so comfortably with the present. No, not really—not here more than anywhere else in this land of Scotland. It seemed his cells, the very pores of his soul were opening to the spirit of his homeland. And this was not what he had expected at all. He was a London cop, come here to do a job of work, nothing more. He did not wish to be bothered, distracted, churned up with the emotions of the Celt that had slumbered so peacefully within him these many years.

He willed the ghosts back into their old gray court-yards and concentrated his mind on the present. The Rag was the favorite night spot of the fast young set. He remembered it from more quiet days, when it had been a supper club that went by the name of the Dreamer. These were mad, vulgar times—vulgar people hurrying, hurrying, in a wild, mindless flurry, going nowhere at all.

Once inside the club Callum scouted out a small table meant for no more than two, which would provide him with a good view of the dance floor; ordered a bowl of Scotch broth and a stiff glass of whiskey and settled in for the duration. He had long ago grown inured to the effects of "life as usual" going on about him. He was not a part of anything normal or ordinary, safe or solid. With Anne no more than a dim, painful memory he could accept his lonely lifestyle without thinking. At least, most times he could. This was not one of them.

He ordered another whiskey, feeling uncomfortable and restless. It must be the effects of this city. He cursed Edinburgh roundly, though only inside his own head. Nevertheless, it made him feel a bit better. He settled back into his chair and let his eyes rove over the people, picking favorites here and there to watch and go back to. Like that perfect young couple over to the left of the dance floor—"beautiful people," he called them, and they seemed to calculate their every move as though they knew that they were. The boy looked every inch the young university dandy, dressed to the teeth, with a head of thick, wavy hair and a dreamy look in his eyes that Callum believed had to be practiced; such a look on a male was not natural at all. The girl—the girl had an odd look about her. He couldn't quite put his finger on it. She certainly was pretty enough, with a peaches-and-cream complexion and long, shapely legs. Her hair was blonde, not white blonde like a movie star but more golden in color, with a hazy hint of red to it. Thick hair, would be beautiful, the kind of hair a man likes to run his fingers through if it hadn't been cut in that ghastly bob which was all the rage now.

Callum stared as the couple moved smoothly in and out of the other dancers, no small feat in a place as crowded as this one was. On second thought, Callum considered, draining his glass and realizing he still felt thirsty, the girl wasn't really a beauty. Pretty. Just pretty enough. Yet there was something about her. He called a waiter over, ordered another whiskey, then flashed his ID card and asked the waiter if he knew either of the two people. He identified the young man at once: Donald Ross, son of James Ross, a successful and wealthy Edinburgh solicitor. Was this Donald a student at the university? Callum couldn't help asking. Indeed he was. And the young lady with him? The waiter had not seen the young lady before. But that was not unusual. This particular young man was in the habit of coming in with a constant variety of young ladies.

Callum thanked the man and tipped him, and mentally

cursed Donald Ross and other spoiled lads of his type. The girl looked nice. Hoped the young fool treated her squarely. Chuckling under his breath, Callum chided himself for an old fool and downed half the glass in a single swig.

———•◆•———

The shrill ring of the phone startled Laura. She glanced at the bedside clock as she hurried to answer. The hands read 1:45. Good heavens, she had been dozing in her chair for nearly two hours!

Her hand was trembling as it closed over the receiver. But she couldn't help it. An unexpected call in the night—in the dead of night. For a moment as she listened for the voice on the other end, her heart stood still. Then recognition brought with it a flood of relief, followed at once by surprise.

"This is nonsense, Mark," she teased. "You can't miss her so much as to throw your hard-earned money away just to hear the sound of her voice."

Mark assured her he could. And the sound of *his* familiar voice across the thousands of miles that separated them made Laura want to laugh out loud with sheer girlish pleasure. Then she remembered where Penelope was. For a moment she panicked. What should she say? How much should she tell him?

"There was a big party tonight, Mark. It's our last night in the city—"

"I know. I have no itinerary for you past Edinburgh; that's why I called, to see how you're faring before you take off for the Highlands and leave civilization behind."

Back home, looking at it from a distance, he was still caught up in the adventure of what they were doing.

"I'll call back in an hour," he offered. "Surely Penny

will be back in an hour!" He was the only one besides herself who called Penelope "Penny"; everyone else used her given name, except for the times when her father called her "Monkey." He had never stopped calling her "Monkey," even when she was grown.

"Yes, yes, that will be fine. She'll be pleased as punch, Mark."

"All right, it's nearly nine o'clock here."

They synchronized their watches, though that wasn't really necessary. Laura's mind was already racing ahead. After he rang off she sat in the silence for only a moment before deciding what must be done. She would catch a cab and go get Penny herself; that way she'd be assured that the girl would really show up. At first she had thought to merely call the Rag and ask for Penny or Donald. But what if there was difficulty locating them? What if, in the noise and confusion, they misunderstood her message? What if there was an accident as they made their way home? At worst she would be stuck here wondering and waiting while the moments ticked by. No, best to go for them herself and be certain.

She took a few moments to go to the rest room, splash water on her face and straighten her hair. Then, leaving a table lamp on, she went down to the lobby. The man on desk duty found her a cab and directed the driver as to where to take her. It was all easier than she had thought it would be. In a very few minutes she found herself at the entrance of the swank club, with the cabbie himself handing her in very handsomely, making sure she was safely inside. She stood for a moment, adjusting to the din—the rise and fall of voices, the clink of glassware, the play of light and shadow over bare shoulders and glittering dresses. All the bright young dancers looked a bit bedraggled to her, and no wonder. It was past two o'clock, and she hated to think of the pace they must have kept up all night. But the kind gentleman at the desk located the table where Penny and Donald were seated and took her back to it himself.

She hadn't thought how shocked her daughter would be to see her there. For a moment she felt embarrassed, realizing suddenly what it must look like: an irate or overly anxious mother come to drag her poor daughter home. Then, too, there was the awkwardness of explaining in front of Donald. How *did* one handle such things? In the end it was Donald who smoothed things over, ordering her a ginger ale from the bar and acting pleased to see her. *Good breeding,* she thought to herself. When the reason for her visit finally came into the open, he laughed out loud.

"We must get Penelope home, by all means," he said. "By all means. We don't want this determined fellow coming across the pond in search of her."

From his corner Callum heard the laughter and, bored as he had been these past hours, perked up at the sound. It was the university swank and his girlfriend, and— He watched as Laura rose. He hadn't seen this woman before. Older woman. Handsome features, it appeared from this distance, though he couldn't quite tell.

Just then one of the waiters bent over him. Apologetically he explained that there was a disturbance out back between some of the floor show dancers who had had too much to drink. Would he mind? Shouldn't take much to break it up, but—

"Haven't you a bouncer or guard or something of that sort of your own?" he muttered as he followed the lad. As it happened, they did. And, as it happened, the disturbance was nearly too small to bother with anyway. But when Callum went back inside, his head cleared by the fresh night air, the "perfect couple" were nowhere in sight, neither they nor the older woman who had come on the scene. He sought out the management, who told him the young people had gone off in a cab with the lady only moments before. He thanked them politely, but inwardly he was seething. Had he been set up? And if so, for what reason? Two women . . . one younger . . . one older. No, it just couldn't be. They wouldn't be so blatant, surely—wouldn't be seen together. They were on the run. They would never—and yet—

Callum sat down at his table, all his muscles aching. Perhaps he was simply trying too hard. The commissioner's words came back to him: "It might be a deceptively simple disguise." He'd wait half an hour longer, see if one or all of them returned. Then he'd call it a day. Half an hour—he grimaced at his sour whiskey glass—and not one minute more.

———

It wasn't exactly the ending to her evening that Penelope had imagined. When they reached the hotel her mother did have the thoughtfulness to slip out ahead of them and find her own way to the room. But the magic had been broken and things were already different between them. Penelope fancied the whole thing was already winding itself down.

He did kiss her good-bye, and she closed her eyes and let the touch of him thrill through her. Prince Charming. Donald was the perfect model for such a daydream. Yet she had met him here, in the flesh. And it was all that more difficult for her to let go.

———

On the hill, in the dark, the wind whistled with the sharpness of a sword edge, and Callum fancied again that he saw the ghosts—or felt them, gliding through the shadow-choked wynds and closes where the lamps, swinging in the force of the night wind, threw only pale, insignificant circles of light.

He had decided to walk to his room, which was not far from the club. He usually enjoyed having time to himself of a night, time to sort things out in his head; he was used to his solitude. He was also accustomed to London streets. But Edinburgh was different. Edinburgh stirred something in him.

Without warning he slipped into a black courtyard behind a great oak, disappearing from sight with the sudden swiftness of a shadow that has swallowed itself. Those *had* been footsteps he heard behind him! And he had caught, out of the corner of his eye, a flutter of crimson cloth. Then nothing. Only silence and the eerie sounds the wind made in the chimneys and eaves.

He stayed behind the tree for a long time, but nothing moved, nothing came near him. In the end, cold and cramped, he found an exit from the courtyard on the opposite end and walked the long way round to his quarters. He met with no other disturbance, no other sign of life, indeed, beside his own weary self. He was chilled when he turned his key in the lock and let himself in. His head ached and he could think of nothing but sleep. What a deuce of an assignment, this! Was it nothing but a wild goose chase, a willy-nilly wild goose chase? That was the last question that taunted him as he pulled his heavy clothes off and crawled into bed.

3

PENELOPE WAS SURPRISED AT HOW EASILY EDINBURGH FELL behind them. The Scottish countryside, with the rowan trees turning red and the long, graceful ferns wearing a fine, lacy edging of brown, had a dreamlike aspect. And yet the bracing fall air and the brilliant blue of the sky overhead made her feel tantalizingly alive. A sense of well-being; that's what it was. She hoped her mother was feeling it, too. She hoped the peace here would penetrate deep enough into both their hearts that they might be able to carry it with them, that somehow it might last.

———————

Stirling, placed strategically on the River Forth in ancient times, boasted a fortress built on a huge, unscalable crag that faced west over the marshes round the river. They had come to see the castle—residence of Scottish kings since the twelfth century and where, in 1543, little Mary, Queen of Scots was crowned in the Chapel Royal at the age of nine months. They had come to see the surrounding countryside: the battle sites, the deep blue lochs, the gray, quiet graveyards. They had come like two pilgrims, innocent and eager and at the mercy of their own desires and the ageless forces of time and place.

———•——

Callum sat still as stone listening to the young officer explain again, in painful detail, what had happened that night—or early in the predawn hours, when the world was a soothing, dove-soft gray and everything slept under the peaceful gray wing and evil did not seem possible.

"The son of the household was out late the previous evening, but the man and wife were at home. Nothing unusual then. The following morning all three left together—shopping spree in London, I guess, before the lad was to go back to school. That's when it happened. Nothing but servants in the house, and nobody heard a thing. Went right to the MacWhirter landscape Mrs. Ross had purchased at auction three weeks ago."

"Three weeks ago?" Callum allowed no emotion to alter his expression nor the professional tone of his voice. "No changes in the household during that period? No new employees?"

"Apparently not."

Callum thanked the young man and dismissed him. He looked across the table at the Edinburgh police chief, who had already contacted Scotland Yard and had been told by Howe himself to give his man free reign there.

"I'd like to question the family myself. Especially the son. I have reason to believe . . ." *Reason to believe*—the only way to word it at present. No need to reveal his suspicions about the women at the club two nights ago, no need to make anyone privy to his own stupidity in not following up his hunch about them. He was disgusted with himself, and if he wasn't careful, that disgust would get in the way of his judgment.

"This afternoon at three will be fine. I'll be there." Callum thanked the chief and left the office with a sense of relief. The first place he headed was the George hotel. He had already rung up the proprietor of the Rag. The man had indeed remembered the good-looking woman who had entered alone about two o'clock in the morning and had asked for assistance in locating her daughter. Yes, her daughter had been with young Donald Ross, and he himself had been at the desk and escorted her back to their table. And minutes later, when the three left together, he heard the young man ask the woman if she had a cab waiting. When she confirmed that, the young gentleman had grinned at his companion and said, "Fine. I'll ride back to the George with you; then Laura will know she's not going to lose us."

Callum had been elated at the information, which saved him many tedious steps and much precious time. He paid a handsome tip for it, but figured he'd got his money's worth. Now, crossing the long stone courtyard leading up to the hotel, he felt expectation tighten his muscles and quicken his pulse.

Here things went smoothly as well. The clerk remembered the charming women.

"They were from the States, sir," he said importantly, handing Callum the hotel statement with their names on it. "Mother and daughter. Both striking women."

Callum winced inwardly but said nothing. *Laura and Penelope Poulson. What kind of name was Poulson? Scandinavian? An odd choice.* He turned to the young man who was watching him, obviously pleased with the intrigue and too unsophisticated yet to hide that pleasure. "What part of the States? Did they say?"

"'Fraid not, sir. They didn't have much to say to the likes of me, though mind you, they were more than polite. Gracious, I'd call it. Real ladies."

Callum ignored the effusive praise, wondering uncomfortably why the women would want to be remembered, as it would seem from their behavior. Low profile. On the run. This didn't fit in at all.

"Can you think of anything—take your time now—anything at all that was unusual about them?" That was too vague. "Something they wore, something out of the ordinary you heard one of them say or saw one of them do?"

The lad thought for a moment, then shook his head. "Sorry, sir." He really was sorry, wanting to impress the detective, give him something that would help.

"Any questions, unusual questions they may have asked you?" Callum pressed.

The clerk shrugged his shoulders; then his expression altered slightly.

"Anything," Callum urged.

"The mother, Mrs. Poulson, did ask me one morning if there were many Camerons in the area and if I knew an Archibald Ewen Cameron. I reminded her that Edinburgh was a large place and she might try checking the city directories, and she thanked me and told me she would." He paused, and then his eyes lit up. "Oh, yes— they did ask how far it was to Stirling."

Callum rested his hand briefly on the uniformed shoulder. "Thank you, lad. You've been most helpful." He drew a card out of his breast pocket. "I'd appreciate your giving me a call if you think of anything else. I'll be here for another day or two. After that, call this number." He took out his pen and wrote on the card before handing it to the boy. "Ask for Mr. Howe and tell him the message is for MacGregor. Will you do that for me?"

The boy nodded solemnly. "Certainly. Anything, sir."

Callum walked out into the sunlight, amazingly strong for September. He looked at his watch. Just time enough to get to the Ross house for his appointment. He was looking forward to this.

——•◆•——

The law courts in Edinburgh are located on the Royal Mile, which runs between Edinburgh Castle and Holyroodhouse. Ramsay Gardens, a cluster of picturesque buildings built by Patrick Geddes in the nineteenth century, rise elegantly on the city skyline at the very foot of the esplanade of Edinburgh Castle itself.

James Ross owned an impressive two-story flat right in the middle of the Garden, even more elegant in its appointments than Callum had thought it would be. The butler ushered him into a small first-floor sitting room, where he occupied himself in admiring the matching Chinese lacquered cabinets and, ironically enough, the artwork that lined the walls.

When Donald Ross walked into the room Callum was struck anew with the straightforward freshness, even openness, of his good looks and his manners. His mother came in on his arm, apologizing for the absence of her husband.

"He had an important meeting in London which he had to return for," she explained. Then she added, with the mere wisp of a smile, "You see, our trip was not for pleasure alone."

After a few moments' conversation Callum had satisfied himself that these people would not be as difficult to handle as the marchioness of Huntingdon was being. That would make his job much easier. He had already decided not to bluntly state his suspicions of young Ross's newest lady friend, though the lad's replies to his questions did nothing but strengthen his previous misgivings.

"Both ladies were in this house, then? More than once?"

"Laura once only," Donald replied lightly, "when we enjoyed one of Mother's most lovely teas. Penelope several times, but never for more than a few moments. I don't see how—you're not really supposing that *they*—"

Callum brushed the boy's concerns aside and changed his line of reasoning, not getting back to the Americans until he had stood up and was ready to leave. Then he asked offhandedly, "Where did your friend—Penelope?—say she was from, then?"

"She didn't, precisely. 'The West,' she said, 'the great American West! There is nothing about my life so interesting that you should bother yourself knowing it, Donald.' You see, she liked to tease—lovely way about her. And then, I do believe she was a bit—well—" Customary politeness made it difficult for Donald to say what he had started. Callum waited patiently, not crowding him. "She was a bit embarrassed, I believe, being American."

Callum laughed. "And you can't blame her? Well, to tell the truth, neither can I!"

It was just what they needed. He could walk out on a light note and assure them he would keep in touch, and hopefully the paintings would be recovered, and he appreciated their patience, their cooperation, etc. He could do such things well. In this instance there was a lot of sincerity behind it, while in others the surface courtesies ran pretty thin.

Upon leaving their house Callum went straight to the police station and rang up Thomas Howe. He gave him all the relevant details. Howe was silent. One of his gifts was listening well.

"So you think they're masquerading as Americans this time round?" Howe asked when Callum had finished. "Do you believe you can follow their route? Stay on their trail without flushing them out until the right moment?"

"The hotel clerk said they asked how far it was to Stirling, so I think I'll take my clue from that. Otherwise, it's anyone's guess. If they didn't take the Stirling route they could be at one of half a dozen places."

They both knew what that meant, especially when heading into the highlands.

"They could split up," Howe reminded Callum.

"Yes, but for some reason I don't think they will. Can't explain it beyond just a feeling, a hunch."

"That's why I've got you there, MacGregor."

Callum rang off feeling better, feeling good—that was another gift Howe had. As he walked out of the building he remembered one thing he had omitted. Had it actually slipped his mind? That night after leaving the Rag he had thought someone was following him. Oh, well. If it was his "lovely ladies" then they knew he was here, probably knew who he was. Hadn't stopped them from pinching some pretty precious goods right from under his nose. Mayhap they were waxing not only bold, but cocky. Maybe he was the sauce to the meat that had grown stale and tasteless. Too easy. Maybe that was it. Maybe more than a deterrent he would act as an impetus, an irresistible challenge. He'd wait and see. It would certainly be interesting to learn the answer to that one. He chuckled under his breath as he thought about it, yet at the same time a chill ran along the surface of his skin and lifted the hair on his arms, bringing back the tense, high singing in his head that he both hated and loved.

It had been easy as pie, child's play, really, to break into the bungalow. With a low-voltage, very dim flashlight the stranger walked through the rooms. This was a quiet neighborhood; no late parties, no comings and goings. The neighbors were sleeping soundly, with no reason to be suspicious. He moved with unhurried ease, opening drawers and closets, looking through stacks of magazines, household bills mixed in with cards and letters of condolence at the death of Gerald Poulson—darned discourteous thing for the man to do, die that way, all things considered.

He was finding nothing and getting a little impatient when he stumbled across the upstairs office. He hadn't thought to find a man's office in the bedroom section of the house. That's what it looked like, a converted bedroom. This was a pretty modest setup compared with what he was used to. He searched every inch of the room: the drawers, the closet—piled high with stacks of cardboard file boxes carefully marked. He opened each one, even if the labels did read "Family Trip to Yellowstone, 1911," or "Gas & Auto Expenses, 1920–1925." Labels meant nothing in his business. He had to be thorough. And thorough he was, down to pulling the drawers out and looking behind them and under them, ripping out the baseboards and, at last, the cushions and stuffing of the two armchairs which sat facing the long desk. Angry now, he did the same thing in the bedrooms, then went through the kitchen cupboards, leaving a terrible mess in his wake. He was ready to go out the way he had come, empty handed, when he spied, in the stack of bills and cards and advertisements, a brochure for a vacation in Scotland. He picked it up and thumbed through it. Certain places were marked with stars, and the address to write to for further information had been circled in red.

He put it in his pocket and took it with him. This was one thing, at least. At least he had a pretty good idea where his two dames were, which meant he wouldn't have to face the full force of the boss's wrath. And which probably meant he would be taking a little vacation to that wretched country himself.

He was right. When he called New York and gave his report he held the telephone away from his ear for ten minutes while the old man raved on and on. Finally he said, "Relax, will ya? He was bound to have a box in a bank somewhere. Even he wasn't that stupid. We have to find the women, anyhow, don't we? So don't give yourself a heart attack."

He drew a deep breath and listened for another minute, fiddling nervously with his thumbnail. "Yeah, yeah, I know it. I'm on my way, boss. Course I know what to do. I'll keep in touch, though that won't be easy going where I'm going."

He paused again to listen. "Take who along? That bozo? You gone off your rocker, boss?" His face was taut with anger, and the skin, pulled tight over his angular nose, made it appear even more beaklike, so that he looked very much the predator. "I work better alone! One's company, two's a crowd in this business, boss."

He listened again unwillingly, his face drawn out in lines of anger. "Yeah, yeah. All right, I'll see you tomorrow. Sure. Have a good one yourself."

He slammed the phone back into its cradle and reached for his cigarettes, mumbling and cursing under his breath. *Stupid business, this. And it's the boss's own doing.* His mouth tasted stale and his anger left him feeling powerless, and there was no place he knew of in this city where a man could go to get properly drunk. At least there would be plenty to drink in Scotland. He chuckled at the thought. But the sound was deep in his throat, and gravelly, devoid of all mirth.

———•◦•———

"Lady of the Lake . . ." Penelope murmured the words as a rivulet of water ran from her cheek down her neck and under her collar. She wrinkled her nose and laughed out loud. "We are certainly wet enough to be ladies of the lake, Mother! I feel as if I have emerged dripping wet from that endless gray expanse."

It was true. They had come over the Duke's Road, built in 1820 by the duke of Montrose, to visit Scott's Lake Katrine, the inspiration for his great novel *The Lady of the Lake.* As usual, the heavens were weeping. Rain is common in Scotland, everyone told them. Especially this late in the year. It had chased off most of the tourists, what few were left in September, and they had the quiet stretch of shoreland to themselves.

Laura felt the age-old peace settle upon them as did the mists from the skies; not the peacefulness of quiet living and quiet ways, but the peace that comes from living wholeheartedly, from coming to grips with life and all its vicissitudes and never once becoming so discouraged as to give up or give in. She closed her eyes and the pleasurable feeling increased. The people who lived here had led harsh and turbulent lives. She remembered the stories her grandmother had told her of the Scottish heroes and of the common men and women who struggled for sustenance in the thin highland soil, who suffered treachery and cruelty at the hands not only of armies but of warring clans, who buried their bairns—their wee babies—on the hillsides, and then bore more. Who buried their husbands and their tall, promising sons beside their little children, and then went on alone.

Somehow . . . somehow . . . why couldn't she be like that? Why was she so frightened, so weak, so filled with self-pity?

"Mother, I'm beginning to shiver. Can we go now?"

Laura started as Penelope interrupted her thoughts. "What of the cemetery? Beside the old church we drove past?"

"Do you want to stop there?"

"Yes, I do."

"All right by me." Though Penelope was soaked to the skin, she was pleased by her mother's decision. Her mother was quiet still, but Penelope could sense some changes in her. Surely all the sensations of this land and its people, living and dead, must have its effect on her.

They stood outside the small kirk in the rain, walking through the wet grasses to read the names on the gravestones. There were some Camerons and even a few MacGregors.

"These could be some of your people," Penelope said.

"Yes, they could," Laura agreed. She bowed her head to them slowly, almost ritually, and in her mind said a prayer for all those brave, quiet lives that had gone before hers.

Back at the inn they took tea in their rooms—tea being hot Postum with milk and sugar—and changed into dry clothes. It felt delicious to be warm and cozy and out of the weather.

"Let's leave early, Mother, and start for Loch Lomond tomorrow. What do you think?"

"Yes. I've seen enough of Stirling. I want the quiet of the lakeside. There are too many people in Edinburgh and Stirling to make any proper connections, especially for a genealogist as poor as myself. I don't know what happened to my Great-Uncle Archibald after his father and brothers left for America, but they had a sister, you know, who married a Campbell and is supposed to have lived in a little village outside Oban."

"Then the sooner we get there, the better."

Laura smiled at her daughter. She felt warm and tired, and almost content.

———————

They had nothing to hurry them, nothing to hamper them, no schedules to keep. Laura was beginning to feel it, to respond to the freedom in which Penelope was already reveling.

In the clear light of the autumn morning, with the green hills beyond the loch stretching into the distant blue of a cloud-flecked sky, Penelope could truly believe that the soft green banks of Loch Lomond were indeed the bonniest place on the earth.

"Twenty-four miles the loch stretches," she read from the guidebook. "And this lake marks the entrance into the Highlands of Scotland." A delicious shiver passed through her.

"There are so many islands," Laura mused. She thought they looked like shimmering green jewels strung along the placid blue surface.

They stood on the east bank of the lake, ready for a boatman to carry them over to the island of Inchcailloch, called "the Isle of Old Women" in legend. The man was uncommonly silent, almost dreamy, as he rowed. Laura was aware of the pleasant slap of his oars in the water. She followed the flight of two wild ducks who had dipped low over the lake, cutting the water with their feet as they passed.

In no time at all they reached the damp, sandy soil of

the island. The silent fisherman grounded his boat and helped them alight. Penelope was grateful for the straight, knee-length skirt she wore, glancing at her mother ruefully and wondering for the thousandth time why she insisted on wearing the longer dresses of two years ago. Whenever she tried, even gently, to question her about it Laura would become not only immediately defensive but abusive as well.

"Skirts will go down again," she would argue. "Reason will dictate it. My goodness, child, the clothes designers are making fools out of you. Your waist is down to your hips, you have no bustline at all—I read in *Harper's* last month that a woman's ideal vital statistics for today would be a pathetic 30-30-30." She would always grimace at that point, which usually made Penelope laugh and give up. At least her mother knew how to make herself look attractive, whatever she wore. She possessed a natural feminity Penelope had never quite mastered, and a certain presence—but perhaps that came with age. She could still turn a head or two, and that delighted her daughter, especially now as they traipsed across Britain, two women alone together. She thought, with a surprising ache, of Donald Ross. What a dreamboat he was, and such a gentleman, too. And wealth—she had never seen such solid, all-pervasive quality as in his parents' town house. Her father had not been a poor man; one would call him "well-to-do" by Salt Lake City standards. Yet his tastes were always so modest, so dull. He had seen no need to buy a large, fancy home once he had the means to do so.

"There are only the four of us," he used to say in that preoccupied way of his. "We've more than enough room here."

It was not only the room, it was the little niceties: they

spent no money on expensive furniture or expensive clothing; they did no traveling to speak of, no entertaining. His only concession to wealth was the new Cadillac he drove, but even that was a conservative "older man's" car.

Penelope was preoccupied with her thoughts, though she did not realize it, as she stumbled across the rough island terrain. Laura walked like one in a dream—one who had accidentally strayed through the portals of a long ago world. She felt and nearly saw the ghosts of the MacGregor women who had come here to bury their heroes and mourn their dead.

This island is sacred to the MacGregors, Laura thought. *I am a MacGregor. There is so much that is sacred to me, more so now that Gerald is gone. It seems all I once took so lightly is now sanctified: my marriage vows in the temple, the births of my children, their baptisms, the day Gerald was ordained a bishop—even the time Penelope fell off her bicycle and got a severe concussion, and Gerald placed his hands on her head and I felt the Lord's healing power.* She pushed through the tangled brambles, sharp and dense, that protected the ancient burial ground. A high, gentle sound, like that of faraway singing, came to her ever so faintly. She thought of the spirits who slept here. Did they rest uneasily, or had they found peace? Did Gerald rest well on the slope of City Cemetery? Was his spirit at peace? He had been taken so quickly, so unexpectedly; no time to instruct her, to put his affairs in order, to share a farewell. No time! No idea of what he was thinking—what he felt when he went!

———

On the shore of the lake a chill little wind had risen, irritating Callum into buttoning up his jacket and pulling his hat down over his ears. He adjusted the high-power binoculars and trained his gaze once more on Inchcailloch. Why in the deuce had his women gone there? What were they up to? It seemed they were just playing games with him. Did they know he was here? If the phantom he caught sight of in Edinburgh was indeed one of his ladies, then they must know what he was up to, must know to be careful—and yet they had been far from that; they had been, one could say, almost blatant. He feared they were staging a contest, pitting their skills and nerve against his. And was this part of it? This monotony, this wearing tedium which seemed to lead no place at all?

They were posing as Americans—American tourists. Perhaps this was part of the ruse, visiting all the expected tourist attractions. But for whose benefit? Maybe they weren't yet on to him. Maybe that shadow in the streets had been something altogether different, had been nothing at all. And why Inchcailloch? That certainly fell out of the class of the common. Tourists did not visit the wild, overgrown island. Especially in mid-September. It made no sense, it made no sense at all. There were too many holes, too many unanswered questions. He did know one thing for sure. He heartily disliked this cat-and-mouse game. It was not his style. The uneasy sensation of being pursued as well as pursuer gnawed at him the way he had seen rats gnawing at damp, rot-eaten rope on the waterfront.

He put the glasses down and walked up and down the beach, with the noisy wind skittering at his ankles. The activity warmed him up some, but the prospect of the day ahead was a sodden and gloomy one, and he hadn't the strength of will or self-persuasion to pretend otherwise.

4

When the ringing of the phone jarred him into consciousness, Callum reached for it automatically, only half awake, moving more from instinct than anything else. As he listened a terrible rage built within him, and it was all he could do to temper his reaction for the benefit of the Stirling police inspector on the other end of the line.

"I'll be there before you can pour yourself a hot cup of coffee," he growled, already sitting on the edge of the bed and pulling up both his pant legs.

He looked for his watch, buried beneath the clutter from his pockets. He winced when he saw what the hands read: half past four in the morning. In an estate outside Stirling, the police inspector had told him, a maid up with the toothache had taken it upon herself to light a lamp and sit in the best parlor with her hot tea and medicine. She had discovered that the painting was missing. But no one had heard the burglars. It was only by this chance that the theft had been uncovered so soon.

"Less than six hours ago," Callum fumed as he drove through the cold, sooty darkness, "less than six hours ago I tucked those two scoundrels into bed!" He swore softly under his breath, the only way he was accustomed to swearing, even when he was alone. He had waited outside the inn where they were staying, watching the light from their window go on right about the time that tea, served in the parlor for the guests, was over. He sat in the shadows in his cold car, watching that square of light that grew more and more golden as the wet darkness of the lochside deepened. He sat for an hour, another hour. He had seen both of the ladies enter the house, and from where he was stationed he could also watch the front door. There was no other public or even accessible entrance to the building. As he watched, no one came out; no one went in. After a few minutes more the light flicked off. He sat staring at the darkness for roughly another hour; then he sought his own room and the tardy warmth his whole cramped body was craving. It was true he had toyed with the thought of a stakeout that lasted 'til dawn, but he hadn't believed it necessary. For some reason he had thought, *Not here, not by the lochside. Mayhap if they head for Glasgow or even Oban, up into the Highlands* . . . Again he had acted the fool. Again he had somehow underestimated his antagonists, misread or failed to read any signs or signals.

He took time to drive all round the inn before heading back to Stirling. The green Morris sat exactly where he had left it, with no sign of having been driven, no fresh mud or dirt on the tires. Perhaps there was an accomplice, someone who came round to collect them; perhaps they had walked to some rendezvous point— perhaps—perhaps—

Callum pulled into the constabulary in Stirling and

shut off the car engine. To think like the criminal mind was one thing; he had trained himself for years to do that. To think like a woman—there was the rub in this case. That posed the biggest challenge to a bloke like himself who was extremely rusty where women were concerned. Not since his Annie had died had he had much to do with women; not purposefully so, that's just the way things had worked out for him. Nevertheless, it left him at a grave disadvantage now. Well, he had identified one of his major problems; that was a beginning, at least.

He climbed out of the car and headed through the black, empty parking lot. A fine mist blew into his face; he watched it settle over everything like invisible soot. *I need more than beginnings,* he reminded himself ruefully; *a whole lot more.*

———————

What's the deal? the young desk clerk wondered uneasily. He didn't feel much like answering the homely man's questions. He had a rude manner about him, and when he said the words "Penelope Poulson" he made them sound somehow unsavory. Why all this interest in the two American women? The police—the police he had to cooperate with. But not a viper like this one. Those women were too decent; anyone could tell so. No sir, he wasn't saying one thing.

"You don't know where they came from, you don't know what they were doing here, and you don't know where they've gone? Is that right?"

"That's right."

The man with the beak nose reached out. He was lean and quick. His fingers closed over the clerk's starched collar—what he wanted was to double his fist up and plant it square in that smug little face. His companion stopped him, laying a firm, pudgy hand on his forearm. "Take it easy now, Corker. That's not what we're here for, remember?"

The tall man removed his grip, but with a shove that sent the desk clerk sprawling. When he'd picked himself up he found he was staring into a fistful of money that the short, unkempt man had thrust out at him. He clenched his teeth and shook his head. The man smoothed the bills and began thumbing through them. There were an awful lot of pound notes there. He could feel he was going to weaken . . . so much money . . . so much . . . Then the sweet young face of Penelope Poulson, like an old-fashioned vision, flashed in front of his eyes. This was a bribe. He could go to jail for this! And all for what reason? To do harm to one of the sweetest girls he'd ever set eyes on.

"I don't want your dirty money," he blurted. "You two clear out of here now, before I—"

The slim man held his hand out. It was a warning gesture. "Hey, suit yourself, kid. You help us, we'll help you. That's all we meant. See you round, sucker."

He turned on his heel and walked across the lobby, the little man shuffling after him like a pudgy, misshapen shadow. His insolence hung in the air, making Davie Mathie shudder. "The nerve of the guy," he muttered. But his hands were still shaking when a guest came into the lobby and asked for his keys and Davie had to locate them on the large numbered board and hand them over as though nothing out of the ordinary had happened, nothing at all.

———•◦•———

Davie Mathie worked the day shift at the George Hotel. The night man was older, more experienced, more in command of himself. When the man with the beak nose approached him, he scratched his own nose with a well-manicured nail and paused to consider. His eyes appraised the stranger while at the same time sending the subtle message: *What may be in this for me?*

———•◦•———

Corker, as the tall man was called by his friends, recognized that signal and understood at once that he had won; it was merely a matter of time now, of reaching that rather delicate point of agreement where both parties would feel well satisfied with the subtle, careful exchange made between them. When Corker and Willie strolled out of the lobby they were sittin' pretty, as Willie would say. They knew that Laura Poulson and her daughter had driven to Stirling two days before. The night man knew what they looked like, and he knew they were driving a new Morris Oxford. A green Morris Oxford with two fashionable ladies in it. Ought to be easy to spot. Corker literally sauntered from the hotel. Now they were cookin'. The fact that his pocket was lighter by several pounds meant nothing at all. The money wasn't his—and he had plenty of it. He had gotten his money's worth and more, he figured; he was ready and anxious to get on with the work at hand.

———•◦•———

Laura and Penelope stayed two days on the shores of Loch Lomond enjoying the peace and the breathtaking scenery. Even the rain, when it came, was soft, and no longer seemed to hamper them the way it had in the beginning. They could go out in it now, carrying umbrellas if there was no wind or wearing slickers over their dresses, and fare very well. Laura found she liked to walk in the rain, even when the air gathered thick and dusky around her with the first mild approaches of night. She felt a certain freedom from her past, even from herself at such moments. Amid the clouded gloom of the elements she could shed all pretenses. The quiet weeping of the rain, the sighing of the wind seemed to purify her, to wipe clean the stains, the dark, musty accumulation that life's sufferings had deposited within her own soul. She said nothing of this to Penelope; how could she explain to another something which she only half understood herself? It was enough to experience it, to go day by day, moment by moment—from one small step of faith to the next.

Callum couldn't figure it out. What were these two crazy dames up to? If the hoist had been theirs, if they had indeed pinched the Constable from the estate outside Stirling, would they be sitting by the lochside still, enjoying the scenery and sipping their tea?

It had been a simple, clean theft, as most of theirs were. The painting of Hadleigh Castle, broken and forlorn against a backdrop of storm-churned sky and empty moorland, had simply been lifted from the spot where it hung in the front drawing room. Nothing else had been touched. No fingerprints. No sign or disturbance. No living soul to witness what had transpired; only the house, dark and ancient, filled with echoes and shadows—and now one more secret to add to its store.

Before he left Stirling, Callum set a series of tasks for the local constables: first, find out where the picture came from and if it had been purchased recently—though in order to do that, indeed, to carry out any of his orders, they needed to run down the family, who were on holiday in the south of England. There followed the usual: had there been any recent changes in household staff, anything out of the ordinary in their usual routine—even any new tradesmen with whom they had begun dealings? The same old nonsense, tedious and ineffectual.

When he returned to the lochside the afternoon was waning and the ladies were gone, off on some walk or excursion, no doubt. Callum wondered how much time he had. He knew the painting was by now well on its way to wherever it was going. But there might be some little thing, some shred of evidence, some slight clue, and he felt justified in searching for it in this rather unorthodox way.

It was easy to slip into the inn through the servants' entrance, a low, swollen door set in the stone wall at the back of the building, nearly hidden from sight by the long-reaching arms of a rowan. So much the better for him. He found the right room quickly enough, but as he had feared, the door was locked. He bent down on his haunches. It took no time at all to pick a simple household lock such as this one—that is, if no one came by—if he could be granted two minutes . . . ninety seconds. . . . In the silence he could hear the house clock ticking from where it stood on the landing of the staircase. He could hear a creaking of floorboards somewhere in the house. He worked steadily; thirty seconds more, perhaps only twenty, and he'd be safely inside. He heard a voice from somewhere deep in the building, a woman's faint laugh . . . as insubstantial as an echo. By now he could hear his own breathing, and it sounded as loud as the clock.

The door turned easily, with no sound. He slipped inside and pulled it shut behind him, then straightened and slowly took his first look around.

Somehow he hadn't expected the lovely ladies to be so tidy. The first impression he got was one of beauty and order, and the subtle fragrance of a very costly and tasteful women's perfume that clung in the air. He moved cautiously, careful to disturb nothing, touch nothing. His hands still encased in the close-fitting leather gloves he had worn while opening the lock, he began methodically opening drawer after drawer, noting their contents with care: gloves and stockings in that one, fine lingerie in another, one crammed with a hodgepodge of expected tourist purchases: tartans and shetland sweaters, little plaid boxes, plaid stuffed Scottie dogs, plaid-trimmed hankies. It made him sick. He searched through the silk-covered box filled with scarves and jewelry; nothing too costly here. Without thinking he lifted one of the filmy things and buried his face in the fabric. That same heady smell, delicate yet drawing, enveloped him. He stared at the patterns of the scarves for a long time, trying to store them firmly in his memory. Most were incongruent flows or patterns of color. Two he especially liked; one of a gray and sea-green foulard pattern—or was that shade really blue? The other was a design of butterflies; muted, delicate spinnings of gossamer against a background as subtle and shifting as the sky itself, in shades of indigo and cobalt, with the rosy blush of the sun over a gentle aquamarine. And scented with—what was it? He turned the bottle on the dressing table so that the label showed. "Fantasy." Now, that was a fitting fragrance! It brought him back to himself, to what he was doing here. He checked out the closets, the luggage—a new, finely appointed set made by Samsonite—an American product which could be purchased in several of the best stores in London.

He was finding nothing, nothing at all. He had been

inside the room for six, close to seven minutes. He was pushing it now. He checked the pockets of the dresses and coats that hung in the closets; he checked inside the shoes, under the beds, behind the curtains, inside the tank in the bathroom where the toilet water was stored. He was looking for anything—a letter, a tool, a note of instruction, a bit of glass or wire, a key, even one of those fancy pamphlets they printed up for tourists illustrating all the attractions of the Highlands which perhaps might give their route away, or have some telltale marks on it. Anything! He'd take any little thing. But he kept coming up empty. And now his time had run thin. With one last glance of pained frustration he moved to the door and opened it a cautious inch. Then another. The long, dimly lit hallway was clear. He listened, not just with his ears but with his whole body. Every muscle was taut. Yet he moved with the grace and ease of an animal, and the door when he closed it made the merest sigh of a sound.

In a matter of seconds he was down the stairs and around the curve of low-ceilinged hall that led to the working quarters. The low, swollen door creaked on its hinges, but that mattered little. He was outside and safe. The tightening in his chest eased a little as he climbed into his black Magnette and felt the familiar leather seat fold round the contours of his body. But the exhilaration he usually felt at such moments, acting like a shot of pure adrenaline in his bloodstream, was sadly lacking this time. He sighed deeply, aware of a dull pain at the back of his neck and of just as dull a feeling sitting like a weight on his brain. He backed the car with his usual care and headed out on the road toward Stirling. He had just enough time to confer with the inspectors there to see what they'd come up with, if anything. Then it was back to the loch to sit up all night keeping watch on his charges, like some blasted nursemaid. With a grim set to his mouth he pushed down on the accelerator and drove as fast as the engine and the narrow, winding roadway would bear.

——————•◦•——————

Penelope and her mother arrived late and tired, just in time for the last comforting tea of the day. They took it in the parlor with the other guests, few as they were; and the sound of other human voices, ordinary and friendly, felt good after a day of solitude. With the sinking of the sun behind the far mountains the day had turned cold and the light wind had grown wet and noisy.

When at last they went up to their room, both were sleepy; the warm, lulled lethargy slowed their thoughts and their movements. As Penelope was getting ready for bed she replaced the long pearl beads she had worn that day, her fingers finding the familiar compartment where she kept them. But in the space of the quick glance required for the routine task she noticed, inconsequentially, that her scarves in the square silken box where she kept them were out of place. She was certain of it. She had her own odd way of arranging them, and always the butterfly scarf, her favorite, sat third from the top— within easy reach, but protected from any possible harm by the layers of the other two. It was silly, she knew. But the gypsy-colored cloth, airy and light, sat neatly folded on the top of the stack. Had she drawn it out and left it on top accidentally? Probably so. Obviously so. And yet, as she drew off her earrings and bracelets and set them on the dressing table—it seemed silly to even notice— her bottle of Fantasy was turned so that the label was only half showing, and therefore the little spout through which the spray came was turned away. She made a point of always leaving the spray nozzle pointing directly forward—one of her many idiosyncrasies. She laughed at herself a little as she adjusted it. *I'm behaving just like an old grandmother,* she thought. *What in the world will I be like when I'm Mother's age?*

She gave it no more thought. As soon as her head snuggled into the soft, down-filled pillow she fell asleep and dreamed of islands rising out of a gray mist, surrounded by a cold, sunless sea. And the only inhabitants of the windswept islands were a race of tall men—tall, dark men with blue eyes and strong cheekbones—and each, as she saw his face, looked like Donald; a procession of tender, smiling Donalds that seemed to pass endlessly, all night long, through her dreams.

———————

"Are you quite certain, Mr. Ross?" Callum MacGregor drummed the eraser end of his pencil against the desk where it made a muffled rat-a-tat sound.

"Oh yes, entirely certain. I not only checked with my mother but hunted up the receipt for the painting—purchased at Crandall's Auction right here in Edinburgh the twenty-fourth of August. That would be roughly three-and-a-half weeks ago."

"Did your mother purchase anything else at that auction?"

"She did. A rather large Jacobean sideboard and a pair of Staffordshire dogs—red ones, with baskets in their mouths."

"Yes, yes, well . . ." Callum wasn't interested in the dogs. "Can you tell me what company delivered the merchandise to your home?"

"Hold on a moment, will you?"

There was a brief pause, during which Callum wrote

down his guesses: Reliable Lines, Peerless Movers, Scots Guards . . . There was a muffled shuffling on the line, then young Donald Ross's voice came over the receiver.

"That was Ranald Scobie & Sons, sir. Crandall's uses them almost exclusively."

"Yes, well, thank you. You've been very helpful. I'll keep in touch, then."

"Please do. And if you see Penelope give her a wee hug for me, sir."

The young scoundrel was teasing him, baiting him. Callum chuckled despite himself as he hung up the phone. What a lot these rich people were. Nothing better to worry about than a stolen painting. And it was his job to pander to their feelings! Now, blackmailers, thugs, and murderers—he was accustomed to dealing with them, especially since he had taken up the waterfront beat. He was beginning to sincerely wonder why Thomas had chosen him. He was out of his element here, and he was beginning to feel the rub.

One of the young inspectors had located the family who had been relieved of their new John Constable painting. People by the name of Maclure. The inspector was on the line from Anglesey. Callum lifted the receiver, scarcely daring to ask.

"Yes, sir, the folk bought the painting at auction. An Edinburgh firm called Crandall's, just over three weeks ago."

Callum swallowed against the dryness in his throat. "This is most important. Do they know who delivered the painting?"

"Didn't get that yet, sir. Sorry."

"Well, get it. And ring me at this number."

He gave instructions and felt a bit easier as he hung up the phone. If the dice of chance rolled him a double, then he'd be back to Edinburgh to check out this Ranald Scobie firm. Meanwhile, his lovely ladies needed looking after. They were proving as time-consuming as two spoiled pets. It was time to bring in some of the locals to assist him.

He drove back to the lochside and set up his lonely vigil outside the dark, silent inn. Like two little pigeons he imagined them; heads tucked into their soft under-feathers, cooing and resting, unmindful of him. He was beginning to itch for the time when he could flush them out and bring his unsuspecting prey swiftly and firmly to ground.

———•◆•———

"Margie, I'm always thinking of you, Margie, I'll tell the world I love you, don't forget your promise to me . . ." Penelope sang along with the melody as it came over the wireless. She pulled a matching jumper over the simple navy serge suit she wore. She was beginning to dress more casually without really intending to. In Stirling she had purchased two pair of thick-soled, low-heeled country shoes, and now all the tramping they did had become almost a joy to her. Laura already wore heavy, practical shoes, but she was not by nature a walker; there was nothing brisk or de-termined about her at all. She glided from place to place. Her voice was low-toned—honeyed, that's what Penelope called it, but not in any assumed, put-on way. She looked the very picture of the delicate, feminine woman who needed nurturing and protecting. Perhaps that's what her father had set out to do, love and nurture her, and had only ended up, quite by accident, overwhelming and overriding her the way he had done.

———•◆•———

The little village where Archibald Ewen Cameron's sister had settled with her Campbell husband was Inverary on the edge of Loch Fyne, ancient hereditary seat of the Campbells of Argyll. And the most picturesque way to get to it, their hostess at Loch Lomond assured them, was through the lonely mountain pass called Glencoe.

Laura wasn't sure. "We should go the easiest, safest route," she argued.

"You're still worried about my driving," Penelope teased. "But it's become second nature to me by now. I don't even think about it anymore when I climb in the 'wrong' side of the car and reach for the steering wheel—really. Let's see it, Mother. Let's see everything we can while we're here."

Laura sighed, which was her recognized form of acquiescence. Penelope wondered, a little guiltily, how many times her mother had given in during the long years of her life. She headed the Morris onto the A82 highway, a modest road roughly a lane and a half in width, as most of the British roads were. Penelope had grown used to that, too. Up ahead there were sheep, so she shifted down to first gear and putted along, watching the fleecy white creatures bound in starts and spurts across the roadway. She was in no hurry. The morning was fine. No rain as yet, though the gray massing clouds in the distance promised some before nightfall.

In no time at all they had passed through the village of Crianlarich, for distances were shrunk in this country which, put all together, was not even the size of Utah. Now they were heading up toward the mountains that rose in massed heaps above them. The moors, rough and steeper here, were beginning to be scattered with loose rocks and boulders which had tumbled down from above. For a while as they drove the pass was in sunlight, and the wild, reaching extent of its beauty filled them with awe. Tough knots of grass dotted the boggy land they drove through. There was no sound at all but the distant rushing of water. Sharp gullies, like gashes in the great rocks, harbored gaunt, thin trees whose backs had been bent by the weight of the high winds and who seemed to be shrinking, hiding from the force of the elements, seeking even the merest of shelters.

Penelope felt her mother shudder. She glanced over. "Are you all right?"

"Those trees looked like the shapes of men, huddling in the shadows and frightened. Like the men in the massacre."

"Is that what happened here?"

"Yes! Didn't you read the pamphlet or listen to a thing Mrs. Grant told us?"

Penelope felt a shiver tremble along the surface of her skin. The sun was no longer in view, and the pass had grown instantly menacing, bleak, and lonely. "Tell me the story," she said.

"Right now? Right here where it happened? I don't think so."

Penelope eased her foot off the accelerator and loosened her grip on the steering wheel. "Mother, please." A strange fascination had hold of her. "I want to know what it is that I feel."

Laura sighed. "It was the winter of 1691 when all the Highland clans were required to take an oath of allegiance to William III. The old chief of the Clan MacDonald had held out 'til the end. Then he set out through the bitter snowdrifts to swear allegiance before the proper magistrates."

"And did he get there in time?"

"Yes and no. He went first to Fort William, but there they sent him to Inverary—"

"The little town where we're going."

"Stop interrupting, Penelope." Laura felt uneasy telling the story. No, she felt more than that. She felt overcome with a terrible lonely sorrow, and she did not know why.

"The clan had enemies who were angry that the old man had yielded. They wanted to wipe out the clan. One of them expressed his delight that the season was winter, the proper time, he said, to maul them in the cold, long nights."

Laura looked out the window. The gloom of the gray day engulfed them. They were shut in on each side by enormous black rocks, streaked and pitted by centuries of wear. But on her side of the pass there were scores of small glens, high and precarious, where a cottage might perch, prey to the rough caress of the elements.

"John Dalrymple, secretary of state, erased Mac-Donald's signature from the records and ordered that the clan be destroyed as 'an act of charity.' That's what he called it."

Penelope shuddered. This was more than she had bargained for. "Go on, Mother," she said.

"In February 1692, four weeks after the oath had been taken, a detachment of military men under the duke of Argyll entered the MacDonald fastnesses and were accepted with that hospitality which is almost sacred to the Highlands. The people took them into their cottages, fed and clothed them, treated them with deference and kindness, while all along the men were planning a vicious attack.

"According to orders, at five o'clock one dark winter morning the signal was given and the foul deed was begun."

Her mother really was a very good teller of stories; she always had been. Goosebumps were pricking Penelope's skin as she listened, yet she could not call a halt. This was not merely a story, this was a vivid retelling of history, of something that had really happened. In the high, keening moan of the wind she fancied she could hear the voices of the condemned women and children frightened out of their sleep when the soldiers broke fire and shattered the sacred confidence which was bound up with the honor, the very existence of this ancient race.

"You can picture the rest. I don't know how many were killed, but it was the senseless sacrifice of innocent people, done by their own kind, for political reasons." Injustice always distressed her mother; drove her wild, really. And this had been injustice as well as cruelty.

The bare cliffs stood firm, almost crowding. In some of the deep, etched crevices white water ran in thin clear rivulets against the iron-gray rock. The wind carried a thousand voices, all mingling, all lamenting through the vast secluded mountains which concealed their secrets, which had borne both man's suffering and shame and survived impervious—oblivious to mankind, it seemed; unaffected, unchanged by the little dramas and tragedies played out over and over again. And yet, in this light—an eerie grayness tinged with white and shot through with green rays—Laura could believe that the mind and spirit of only one man, one solitary mortal who had lived and breathed here, worked and struggled, feared and dreamed, contained more power and mystery within it than all the grand, wild expanses before her. And on these rocks, deeply engraven, seeping deep into the pores, lay the record of every life that had touched here during its mortal wanderings. Why did she feel a part? As though what had happened those hundreds of years ago had happened to her?

She closed her eyes, but the oppression threatened to crush her. "Drive faster, Penelope," she said. "I want to get through this place, I really want to get out of here."

Penelope did as she said, aware that her mother had never once delivered such an instruction to her and likely would never do so again. But she offered no argument, no protest; not even a tease. She, too, felt the need to escape the immense shadow of rock and sky that hung over and closed round them, that seemed to breathe with a life of its own that was dark and menacing, harboring the indomitable shades of the past, more intense, more irresistible than any force she had ever felt in her life.

———◆———

Stirling was not a large place by Corker's standards, but big enough—big enough that it took them two days to run down the American tourists, the pretty women who drove the classy green Morris. Those two didn't stay in any spot long, flittin' round the country they were on their old man's money! Too bad he had to knock off like that, though maybe they didn't think so. Well-heeled they were for the rest of their lives—even without what was rightfully the boss's.

Thank heaven these dames were friendly and talked a lot. Otherwise he wouldn't have a clue as to where to go next. But they had told the old lady they rented rooms from that they were driving down to Loch Lomond to stay at the little inn there. Easy pickings, these two. And working conditions couldn't be better. They spent their last night in Stirling, he and Eddie, that fat, sloppy creep the boss had pawned off on him, in the nicest pub they could find, drinking tall glasses of strong, unblended malt whiskey, getting gloriously warm and happy and drowsy, and drunk.

———•—•———

Callum was elated. The young constable had rung him to report that the Maclure family had used the delivery firm of Ranald Scobie & Sons. At last! He'd have to get on this at once. It may be too late already. If there was a plant in the firm he may very well have dropped out of sight after that last heist. But Callum's ladybirds had flown again, and it was his job to follow them. Reluctantly he dialed the constabulary in Stirling and asked for the chief. He would have to rely on him to begin the questioning of the owners of Scobie and hopefully the drivers—and hopefully one driver in particular. Meanwhile, if his birds would alight once more he'd set the local boys on them and go back for the fun stuff himself.

The woman on Loch Lomondside told him the two were headed for Inverary—but by way of Glencoe? That made no sense at all. They would have to double back a considerable distance, and for what purpose? When he stated the obvious, the old woman shook her head at him, as though he were the one gone daft.

"They're tourists, they've all the time in the world, don't you see, lad? 'Twas my Jamie talked 'em into taking the mountain road; they were so keen on such things."

"What things, ma'am?"

"Well, seeing the country, listening to all the old legends about the various clans. Now, I'm a MacDougall myself, though me mother—"

Callum coughed into his handkerchief and very obviously checked the hands on his watch.

"Sorry, sir. As I was saying, the dear things didn't mind the detour. 'Everything's so close together here, anyway,' the daughter said, 'compared to what it's like where we come from.'"

"The young one, you mean? Did they say they were mother and daughter?"

His listener was offended. She drew herself up, her full gray hair bristling as surely as any collie's ruff.

"Course they were mother and daughter! The resemblance was obvious to a blind man. The wee one has such pretty eyes! She reminds me—"

Callum thanked the woman with as much courtesy as he could muster, then took the main road through Oban to Inverary. He parked his M.G. Magnette along the fine curved street that skirted the loch, lined with tidy whitewashed Georgian buildings. He didn't have long to wait. In less than half an hour the green Morris swept gently around the curve from the other direction and into his sight. As he started his engine and pulled discreetly out of his parking slot, he watched it take the turn onto the main street of the village, a wide, hilly road lined with modest shops and houses. Their friend at Loch Lomond must have recommended a place. In a moment the Morris slowed and came to rest in front of that distinguished old hostelry, the George Hotel. Well, well, that was a safe place to install them; he could not have selected better himself.

———————

Several days passed before young Davie Mathie had occasion to speak with the night clerk; then only briefly, at their regular shift change. But the older man, generally so stiff and proper—unfriendly, even—could not refrain from showing off his new pocket watch and the fancy gold chain looping ever so properly just below his vest pocket.

"How'd you manage that?" Davie blurted. It looked expensive, beyond the means of a night clerk supporting a family of five growing children.

"I came into some little money," the man replied, a bit huffily. Then he turned his back on Davie rather abruptly and began to busy himself behind the tall desk.

Davie stood still. A thought was working up slowly inside him. No! His emotions wished to reject it. But something in his head rang clear as a bell.

"You talked to that bloke what was here, didn't you? The evil-lookin' one with a nose like a hawk?"

The man looked up and Davie could see the lines in his smooth face contract, and a look came into his eyes that he could not completely cover by his haughty rejoinder. "I have no idea what you are talking about. And what I do is none of your business, any way you may look at it, lad."

Davie knew. "You told them two about our ladies— the American ladies. Didn't ya see they couldn't be trusted?"

He was disgusted. When the older man turned his back on him again and refused to reply, he stomped out of the hotel much the way a petulant child would who had suddenly been denied a greatly anticipated favor. He muttered under his breath as he walked the block and a half to his underground station. It just wasn't right! Those two could be up to anything—you just imagine it and they'd be sure to do it! And no one to protect his poor ladies.

Then, like a light going on, he remembered what that nice inspector, Mr. MacGregor, had told him. *"Call this number if you get anything at all that might interest me."* He had kept the number tucked inside one of the cubbyholes in his grandpa's old desk.

When he got home, as soon as he had taken off his overcoat and scarf he looked for the slip of paper. Sure enough, it was right there where he had put it. But what to do now? Did he really dare call such an important person? *"Commissioner Thomas Howe—tell him the message is for Chief Inspector MacGregor. . . ."*

Davey carried the paper into the kitchen with him and propped it on the table while he fried up some potatoes for his dinner. Did he dare? Would they laugh at him, or worse, become angry? Would the inspector think him a fool?

On and off throughout the evening he mulled the matter over. What if the tall man and his disgusting companion were merely policemen following up on the inspector's investigation? They had seemed too hard, too evil. But then, hadn't he heard the stories?

When he went to bed some hours later he was still undecided. In the morning he found himself in a hurry to get ready in time to catch his train. But he took the number with him, tucked into his pocket, and the first chance he had he sat down and dialed it, though a weak, sinking feeling came into his stomach.

The number rang six times, seven . . . on the eighth ring he began to remove the receiver; he had decided it was best to hang up. Then he heard a click, and a woman's voice said, "Commissioner Howe's office. May I be of assistance?"

Willie found he had to swallow before he could speak. "I have a message for the commissioner. Is he in?"

"Oh, I'm sorry. The commissioner's out of town until Thursday. Would you care to leave a message?"

Willie ran his finger under the tight line of his collar. "No, oh no. That's all right. It's not important. I mean— thank you, thank you very much, miss."

Well, that's that, Willie thought. He crumbled up the small bit of paper and tossed it into the waste can. He felt better about the fact that he'd tried. *Message probably wouldn't reach the inspector anyway,* he reasoned. After a few minutes he felt lighter, as if a weight had been lifted. He whistled as he copied the names from the ledger of guests who would be checking out that day and needed their bills. He began to hum snatches of a song under his breath, one of those songs the pretty young American girl had always been singing: *"Rose Marie, I love you, I'm always dreaming of you, No matter what I can't forget you. . . ."* The words played pleasantly, over and over again, inside his head, and kept him company as he went about his routine tasks.

5

Inverary, sitting like a quiet jewel on the pretty curve of land that thrusts itself into the blue waters of Lake Fyne, was the seat of the powerful Campbells of Argyll. Penelope was impressed by the snug old-world atmosphere of the George, ironically bearing the same name as the grand Edinburgh hotel they had stayed in; and by the calm loch, the picturesque shops, the old courthouse, and the gaol. But Laura was not. For some reason she could not help remembering what depths the Campbells had stooped to in order to maintain their power, their influence over the people. When she said something to Penelope, the girl only reminded her mother that all the clans had violent, less-than-noble threads woven into their histories. "They were always warring with one another over lands and privileges, Mother."

Laura knew that. But somehow forthright contention, even open hatred, seemed acceptable compared with the cruel treachery and betrayal that had taken place at Glencoe, a betrayal of all the Scots had held most sacred in human relations since ancient times. That was why now, nearly a hundred and fifty years later, a MacGregor would not speak to a Campbell nor shake his hand; why in their hearts they could not, or would not, forget. And for some reason Laura was unable to explain or understand, neither could she.

———•◦•———

"That's about it, lads," Callum concluded. "We'll set a series of watches on the George Hotel and the movements of our ladies. Mr. Jones will have a schedule ready for you in a couple of hours, right?"

Oban's chief constable nodded his round head vigorously and beamed back at Callum, who winced inwardly. He had given only a brief overview of the situation to these locals, no more than they needed to know. He disliked working with men in the provinces; they usually possessed no concept of life outside the narrow confines of what they knew. Not to say that evil could not and did not exist everywhere; Callum knew that. But as for the fine-tuning required to gain access to the criminal mind, opportunities for that were totally lacking in places like Oban, under whose authority Inverary fell, and which stood as it did on the rim of the great Highland fastnesses, where the refinements of intellect and civilization were still unknown.

Earlier he had asked the chief to assign one of his top men to act as Callum's assistant and more or less head the local operation, organizing involvement.

"I have just the man for ye," Jones told him now, pride evident in the thrust of his square barrel chest and the warm look in his eyes. "Young lad, trained in Edinburgh, more competent than most of my men."

"Good. Send him over to my place late tonight, after

eleven. I'll be in Stirling 'til at least that hour. But I may have to return there tomorrow, and I want to see your man before then."

It would be a long day, but Callum was eager to learn for himself the results of the questionings that were right now taking place. First thing he did when he arrived at the office was to familiarize himself with the record of those interviews which had already been done. If they didn't prove satisfactory, he'd reinterview each man himself. There was a skill to interrogation which could make the vital difference between a breakthrough and darkness, between extracting something and getting nothing at all.

The local manager of Scobie & Sons had already stated that a new driver by the name of Thom Dennison had been hired some six weeks before. He had proven to be a quiet man, competent at his work, bothering no one, but then one morning he had just disappeared. It did not surprise Callum to learn that the man vanished on the morning after the robbery had occurred.

They were now questioning everyone who had had anything to do with the alleged Thom Dennison, though Callum was certain the name was an alias. He sent a man to check out the address on Dennison's employee form, and it proved to be just what he had suspected—a vacant lot.

Meanwhile, Callum interviewed the few remaining employees who knew anything of the stranger. One was a mechanic who worked in the repair shop that serviced the trucks. He knew little at all, nothing that had not already been stated and repeated a dozen times. Callum had a complete enough description to call the Criminal Record Office in London and see what they could find for him. But that was a hit and miss, lengthy procedure.

He was hoping for something more. Near the end of the questioning Callum leaned his elbows on the table so that his face was close to the face of his listener. He asked the same question he had already asked the man twice before. "Tell me, is there anything, anything at all unusual or out of the ordinary you remember about Thom Dennison? Take your time."

He drew back and watched the man's face. Callum had long ago learned that memory is a capricious and powerful force that disdains our control. A man could respond to a question sincerely believing that what he said was the truth. But then suddenly the steel-like portals of the memory would loosen, open wide, and reveal their jealously kept secrets. He had seen it happen time after time.

The man opposite him had already begun to shake his head when he paused, and a strange expression came over his face. "There was something," he said.

"Yes . . ."

"I remember one day in the barn when Dennison helped me change a flat tire. I noticed it then—a strange tattoo he had on the inside of his wrist, you know, where his cuff would usually cover."

Callum ground his jaws against the excitement that was building in him.

"It was a tattoo of a little black terrier," the man continued, scowling at the memory, "carrying a rat in his teeth."

Callum's expression revealed nothing of the elation he was feeling. He had mastered that painful but invaluable control long ago. "Thank you, sir. You may have been of some help to us. Thank you for the use of your valuable time."

He ushered the man out. He needed no help from London. That one bit of information positively identified

Thom Dennison as the character known to the police as Willie Spanvill; known to his friends simply as "the Terrier."

Callum didn't have to look up the Terrier's file to remember that his list of crimes included blackmail, petty theft, some drug involvement, and, in the last while, armed robbery. This meant his ladies were playing in a pretty serious league, treading places where ladies usually feared to go.

Before he left he organized a squad of men to check out all the known associates of Willie "the Terrier." He was sure to have gone underground. But the police had their contacts, there were always some poor sods who owed favors . . . there would be ways. . . .

As Callum drove back to Inverary the darkness folded around him like the soft layers of a blanket; the night was unseasonably warm. He drove slowly, with the windows open to draw in the sweet air. He had forgotten the taste of the Highlands; the years in London had obscured it or perhaps only buried it beneath layers of city soot and gray river fog. He felt relaxed despite the pressures that were on him, and though the hour was late there was no dull, throbbing ache at his temples, something he had grown accustomed to after a long workday in London.

Perhaps, as his old father had always claimed, there was no place in the world like Scotland. As a boy Callum had known only hardship and poverty, and he had remained unimpressed. He thought sleepily, as the car purred through the still, hilly countryside, *It would be ironic surely, strange indeed, if an experience such as this were to change my mind.*

"All right, Fraser, I believe that's all. If you'll watch for me tonight so I can get a wee bit of sleep, I'd appreciate it. Tomorrow I'll be in Stirling again, so make certain all the watches report directly to you."

"Yes, sir. I understand. Keep my eye on the ladies, something I've always enjoyed doing."

Fresh young puppy! Callum groaned inwardly at Constable Jones's choice. He'd seen this type before: groomed and spiffy and dressed to the nines, the detective novel image of what a policeman should look like, too good for the old school, the hard, driving ways.

Hugh Fraser, watching MacGregor, knew precisely what he was thinking and decided it was best to get the whole thing out in the open. "Yes, I come from the privileged class," he said. "You have me well pegged, sir. But I am good at what I do, and don't you doubt it." His eyes said: *I can hold my own, you bloke, I'm as good as any of your London professionals.*

Callum said nothing, and Hugh Fraser was impressed by the calm, appraising look in his eyes. He certainly was the image of the burly, well-muscled officer with the set square jaw and a face deeply lined—good, strong lines that spoke well of the will and wit of the man. But it was his mouth that gave him away; Hugh had long since decided that the mouth often betrayed a man before his eyes did. MacGregor's mouth was full and soft, and the lines around it were gentle, belying the harsh nature of the life he lived.

"Your father is . . ." Callum couldn't help himself. His curiosity was overcoming him, and the lad seemed so cool.

"A mere viscount, if you can believe it. Do you know, in the old days a viscount was nothing more than a deputy to a count or an earl. But it makes us noblemen, not lowly commoners." He flicked a piece of thread from the lapel of his jacket. He spoke nonchalantly, but his eyes held a sparkle which enhanced his attractiveness. "And as you well know, that's all that matters, isn't it?"

"As you well know!" Callum glowered at the little upstart, and Hugh Fraser could see that his words hadn't come out right.

"Look here," he continued, with the same disarming indifference, "I'm the youngest son, all right, who'll inherit nothing but the good family name. Very impressive, but it doesn't put bread on the table or pay the rent."

Callum should have liked him, but the class differences between them rubbed an old sore spot of his. It was all well and good; the boy had never had to really prove himself, to go it alone. With assured wealth, assured status, assured opportunity, the lad could indulge in uncommitted criticism of his own kind. From his insular place he could afford to make concessions to uncomfortable realities and that way appear very much a man of the world, giving the impression that he and MacGregor, from their enlightened vantage point, held the same disdainful opinion of his father and their kind. The ultimate egotism, that!

"Will that be all, sir?" Hugh could feel the older man's antagonism and resentment wash over him like a cold blast of wind.

"That will be all, Fraser. I'll contact you soon as I get back tomorrow."

"Right, sir. Good hunting then, and good night."

———•◦•———

Hugh Fraser breathed a sigh of relief as he shut the door behind him and walked out into the night. The lake stretched like a dark stain beyond the curve of buildings. He could catch the scent of the water on the swell of night air.

He crossed the street from MacGregor's lodgings and headed toward the George, passing the old courthouse and the dank, well-lit Boar's Head, where a few men lounged lazily just outside the pub door. A pleasant night, with the cry of an owl in the distance and a cool wind among the high trees.

So my assignment is to watch two beautiful women, he mused. *I've had many a worse job than that.* Besides, he was well fitted for his work. He had long been aware that though his guarantee of blue blood came through his father's line, the money needed to enjoy the privileges of rank and station came from his mother's. And for as long as he could remember he had cultivated her goodwill and that of his two stern maiden aunts. He appreciated women; he even understood them a little. After all, he had practiced manipulating and courting women all of his life, from the time he took his first step and spoke his first word.

He looked up at the black bulk of the George and the bank of windows lit by the moon's slanting rays, appearing as thin, delicate sheets of beaten silver, shimmering islands in a sea of darkness. In one of those rooms slept the lovely ladies who, for the next few days or the next few weeks, were to become the major, the consuming concern of his life.

"There are only two kinds of people in the world, you know, lass."

"And what might those be?" Penelope's eyes twinkled at the seriousness of the old man who rolled his *r*s so delightfully.

"Why, the Scots, my dear—and those who wish they were Scots!"

Penelope laughed out loud. Here, on the edge of autumn, the whole world seemed poised, breathless with its own beauty. The grass at their feet harbored late corn daisies and the sweet, wild gelder rose, and the far fields were stained with the last remaining pink of the heather that was the glory of Scotland.

These last days had been mild, yet braced by the crisp, clean air of the Highlands and the cool morning dews. Here in the peace of the ancient kirkyard Penelope believed she could feel the earth's pleasure, feel the harmony of creation trembling through the soft air. High above her spread the massive arms of a Spanish chestnut said to have been planted by the monks who once lived in the ruined priory nearby. Penelope leaned against the broad, twisted trunk of the tree and closed her eyes.

Laura, coming up, would have called out to her, but the old caretaker put his hand on her arm. "Leave her to her dreams. You and I know how short is the time of youth's dreaming."

She heeded his advice, wondering why it was she always met wise old Scotsmen in ruined kirkyards. Was it her, or was it the place?

She followed him to a section of low wall that was shaded by the fruit-laden branches of the chestnut and gratefully leaned against the cool, rough surface. "I'm searching for information about my ancestors," she confided. "But I'm not much good at it, I fear." She laughed lightly, unaware of the musical notes in the sound. "It might help if I knew what I was doing." It felt good to express her inadequacies aloud.

"Have you tried the recorder's office? There's a wee one tucked next to the courthouse on the main street of town."

"No, I hadn't thought of that."

"If you have names and records, they ought to be able to help you."

"Thank you so much. I'll go there, I'll go there at once."

Laura sighed and gazed at the beauty around her: the far stretch of blue lake and green hills, brushed here and there with streaks of vivid crimson and gold. Closer by, the gentle waving motion of green and brown ferns sketched a fairy tracery above the darker shades of the grass. And beneath the heavy, trailing covering of the chestnut, lost in a gentle spell, rested her own daughter, who contained all the beauty of the world in her soul.

———◆———

The slight, middle-aged woman who sat behind the tall desk in the recorder's office hefted the heavy volume and began leafing through it. "Archibald Cameron, you say?"

"Yes, and a Helen Cameron who married a Campbell."

"Here we are." The woman pointed a long finger at a spot on the ledger, and all at once the endless squiggles of writing formed themselves into words. When Laura saw the familiar names—familiar as her own name—an unexpected excitement coursed through her. It was illogical, she knew, but for the first time these ancestors seemed real to her, existing in some framework other than their limited relationship to her. She dragged the big book to a table in the corner and read the dates: "Archibald Ewen Cameron born 1831 in Dalmally"— Why, they had seen signs for Dalmally on the road from Loch Lomond! "Married Agnes Fife, 1856. Son, Archibald Ewen, born in Oban, 1858." So there had been yet another Archibald Ewen to carry on the male line and the firstborn son's name. And a daughter, Helen, born two years later—Laura's heart gave a painful little jump. The date of Agnes's death was the same as the birth of her daughter. Laura looked up to find the village recorder watching her.

"Looks like she died in childbirth."

Laura blinked up at her. The words she had spoken obviously had no meaning to her at all. Facts and figures, nothing of flesh and blood about them.

"Looks like Archibald came here in his later years to let his sister take care of him. See here—the address is the same."

In another number the woman had looked up the name of a Kenneth Campbell married to Helen Ann Cameron in the year 1859. On a map she located for them the piece of property Kenneth Campbell had lived on, not owned. Laura remembered that the bulk of property here was jealously owned by the privileged few.

She looked a bit further. Archibald died in Inverary in the year 1899, passed away with the worn-out century that had borne him.

"You can go look at the house," the recorder was saying. "It's standing still."

Penelope took the rough map the woman drew and wrote down her sketchy directions.

"Do you think you can find it, Penny?" Laura asked as soon as they were out of the woman's hearing.

"I'm willing to give it a try." She smiled at her mother. "I suppose you want to go right this minute?"

"That's right."

Laura turned so quickly that she ran square into a young woman coming from the opposite direction. The girl was garishly dressed, with blonde hair to her shoulders and a pouty mouth smeared with thick red lipstick.

She uttered a rude, unsavory oath under her breath as Laura's shoulder smashed into hers.

"I'm so sorry," Penelope intervened. "My mother does this at times. Doesn't watch where she's going very well when she's excited about something."

The stranger disdained to reply, but as Penelope gently urged her mother across the road the girl stood stock still, staring after them. A strange look came over her face. She stood there a long time, so that other passersby had to go round her. "I don't believe it! I don't believe it!" she said once or twice. She stood watching until the two women reached the green Morris and climbed inside, and by this time the expression on her face was so hard and unpleasant that it would have sent shivers down Penelope's spine if she had happened to look up and see.

As Penelope guided the Morris out of the parking slot and onto the road Laura asked, "Did you hear what that woman said, Penny?"

Penelope shuddered. "Yes, I heard. I'm just glad that you didn't." She followed the winding road up, in the direction of the woods and the graceful castle with four flanking turrets from which flew the standard of the house of Argyll. The smooth green hills stretched away before them in fold upon fold, closing in their view and dictating their direction.

A little way back on the road a sleek gray sports car repeated their pattern of turns and curves. When the main road, climbing still higher, widened to accommodate a lane leading off to the left and one to the right, Penelope slowed the Morris and took the turn to the left. The driver of the sports car downshifted into second and pulled off on the shoulder, where tall ferns and thick bushes nearly concealed the low car. He turned off the engine, settled back into the soft leather seat, and prepared to wait.

———•◆•———

After just a little distance the narrow path on which Penelope and Laura traveled ran itself out and widened into a yard where the tough grass had been tamped down by tires and was covered with a thick, fine layer of dust. But beyond the dust was a section of green grass that bordered a house, a thatched cottage with leaded windows and a wide front door, and late hollyhocks drooping beside the doorway. Penelope stopped the car.

"Go see if anyone's there, Mother," she said. Then, seeing Laura's expression, she quickly amended, "I'll go knock on that pretty blue door myself. The people who live in such a nice house can't be too terribly frightful."

Laura watched her bounce and skip up to the entrance, saw the wide door open, but Penelope blocked her view of anything further. But after a few moments the girl turned and waved enthusiastically, her expression saying, *It's all right, Mother. Hurry. Come on.*

With her heart beating hard against her tight chest, Laura walked to the small porch. The man who held the door open for her looked to be about her own age, in his mid- or late forties. He was clean shaven and wore a thick, woolly sweater. Laura could see inside to where a woman sat in a rocker beside a long, deep fireplace. Her fears somewhat abated, she smiled at the stranger who held the door for her and followed her daughter inside.

———•◆•———

What in the devil could those two be doing in there? Hugh Fraser checked his wristwatch. Half an hour—no, all of forty-five minutes had passed. What could they be up to, after all, in broad daylight? Perhaps he should have arranged for backup before he followed them, but there hadn't really been time. It was either go with the lovely ladies or lose them. They were lovely, too, especially the young one with her thick, shiny hair and her shapely legs. There was something about her face. . . . He'd give them another hour, though he prayed to heaven they wouldn't take it. The late afternoon sun was hot on his thatch of black hair, and he was growing drowsy. He tapped his fingers against the leather-wrapped steering wheel and began to whistle every tune that he knew, starting with "Sweet Georgia Brown," which was his favorite right now.

———•◆•———

"I was a young man nearly full grown," Angus Cranston was explaining, "and eager to be out on my own. But I stayed for a spell to help my father, whose health was poorly. We lived in that wee house up the hill, above that stand of ash trees."

Laura nodded. "So that's when you knew Helen and her brother, Archibald."

"Aye, 'twas about then when the old fellow came to stay. A gentle soul he was, with the kindest eyes I've ever seen on a man. Him and I used to get into many a conversation on a fine summer's day. I do b'lieve much of himself had died—inside, you know—when his young wife died. Gave his all to raising those two bairns of theirs, then when they were off on their own—well, he didn't have much reason for going on after that."

"Was he ill?" Penelope asked.

"That he was, lass. Cancer of the lungs. He didn't fight it. He just let himself waste away. No struggle at all, and no complaining came from that one. Chopped and hauled wood and tended Helen's vegetable garden until the day he took to his bed. After that, 'twasn't long."

Laura wondered what it would be like to be ready to die, worn out by life and hungering for something beyond. Her Peter, standing on the verge of his manhood, had not been ready. And certainly Gerald, with no warning, no preparation . . . She started to rise.

"Tell them, Angus, before they leave, of the old man's favorite drive. They might like to go up themselves and take a look at the view."

Sheila Cranston spoke shyly and the color rose to her cheeks. Angus exchanged a gentle look with her, which excluded all others.

"First time I took Sheila up that mountain, you see, was when I asked her to marry me. She was so taken by the beauty of it all that she was lulled into answering aye—and I've never let her go back on her word."

———•◦•———

The light was seeping from the sky, drawn upward by some invisible hand, and the empty expanse was left flaccid and gray. Hugh fidgeted in his narrow seat and put the high-power binoculars once more to his eyes. Nothing. Nothing inside but the farm couple and his ladies talking and drinking tea.

But as he watched he saw the older one rise. Perhaps they were leaving at last. He slid down in his seat so that his head was below the line of the window, letting relief and anticipation spread through his tired body and mind.

———•◦•———

The road through the woods wound up sharply and was crowded with trees on both sides. The slender trunks of the ash and beech stood out in stark black-and-white relief against the darkening sky. Immense oaks rose out of the ground mist like sentinels, stolid and still. Rising along the skyline were belts of dark firs and limes, thousands of them crowded into the long stretch that shouldered the sky. Penelope and Laura got out of the car and walked through the wet ferns where the mist rose and crawled up to their knees. The solitude of the setting was as overwhelming, as absolute as some ancient spell.

Laura tried to picture Archibald on this hill, lonely, perhaps even frightened. Did he ever wonder what had happened to his father and brothers who had left him to seek their fortunes in America, a land so far away? *"You go your way,"* he had said to them. *"Do what you must. But I was born a Scotsman, and by heaven, I'll die as one, too."* Laura had heard the story of his stubbornness and defiance dozens of times. Now she wondered what it had been like for him, what sorrows he had struggled with, what regrets.

Here, where such peace enfolded her, she wondered, too, what it would be like for her when her time to die came. Would she be left on earth, without Gerald, long enough to grow tired of life? To grow old and sick and weary—to want to let go?

She closed her eyes. In the floating mist and the gathering darkness she offered a prayer for Archibald Ewen Cameron and for all those he had loved and left behind.

———•◆•———

They drove back down the mountain wrapped in a silence they were loathe to dispel, occupied with thoughts that were solemn and sweet. They did not notice the small gray car that followed so close behind, that slowed, as they did, by the George and crawled into the shadows where the night mist was deep and the silence was fractured by the sounds of the night, restless and uneasy, and lonely beneath the ebony sky.

6

MacGregor was touchy when Hugh told him what little had happened and insisted they search the route the two ladies had driven, while he himself questioned the farm couple. Hugh thought he was carrying things a bit far. There was probably nothing to discover in this direction—but MacGregor was boss. *Probably feels as thwarted as I do,* Hugh thought, and decided to postpone any conversation yet awhile.

Nothing came of any of their efforts. No shred of evidence, no sign of disturbance, no hiding places were located, and from what Callum could judge, Angus and Sheila Cranston knew nothing at all.

"They were working on their family history, they said. Come from Stateside someplace, don't recollect where exactly," the man offered.

Callum was sure of one thing. They did not come "from Stateside someplace"; they were not Americans. One consistency was evident: They were careful to never mention just where in the States they came from.

"Gentle folk—they were lovely ladies, the both of them," the Scotsman continued. "There was nothing wrong there, sir, I'm certain of it."

Callum smiled, a tight, controlled expression; necessary, but difficult for him to muster.

This Archibald Ewen Cameron. Callum questioned Angus Cranston about him, but since the man Cranston had known by that name was long dead, he felt himself going round and round in a senseless circle. The name must, obviously, be a cover for something—a password, perhaps? In that case, the innocuous-seeming Mr. Cranston could be part of their organization; not a fence, surely, not anything so specialized. But perhaps his cottage up here in the middle of nowhere was used as a cache. He could obtain a search warrant, but what profit would that bring him? There were no goods to put the finger on now.

As he drove back to the village the thick darkness assailed him like a living and breathing thing. And with that sense of darkness came shadows, and strange night sounds, and doubts.

He stopped at the chief constable's home before going to his own rooms and gave instructions that a search warrant for the premises of one Angus Cranston be prepared and on hand, just in case. In the morning he would call the Criminal Record Office in London and see if anyone there could find anything at all on a fellow by the name of Archibald Cameron. Just in case.

He went to bed early but found himself tossing and turning uneasily, so he switched on a light and read Agatha Christie's latest, *Poirot Investigates*, for an hour. If it were only as simple as her stories made it seem! A case sprinkled with clues and odd, even exotic, happenings, and a sense of mystery and mission woven subtly throughout. More often, in his experience, the work was drawn out by tedium and blind frustration, as it was now. And mission? He'd once had a sense of mission, but it was a delicate commodity, easy to lose sight of in the day-to-day press of things. How dapper and persuasive Poirot was, a most charming hero. Hero, my eye! There were no heroes in this work. But it made raging good reading; he'd grant it that.

Callum fell asleep to the sound of Poirot's voice, with its soft Belgian accent, asking him most graciously where the paintings were hidden, and if he knew the identity yet of Archibald Ewen Cameron, and just what place in the wide Americas did the lovely ladies call home.

It was murky, the sky well covered with dense clouds that lowered the ceiling of night. No wind stirred the shadows or broke the silence. Maggie Simpson opened the door to the great empty house with practiced skill; Glenda slid in easily behind her. They moved through the dark interior and reached the first-floor drawing room in a matter of seconds. The only sound that accompanied their passage was that of a long, gentle sigh, as though the walls were faintly breathing in the stillness. They moved without light, as though they walked with the ease of familiarity; but this, too, had been learned.

They both moved to the far wall where the painting was hung and Maggie switched on a small light, which she held cupped in the palm of her hand. Glenda drew in her breath.

In a tall, wing-backed chair to the right of them dozed a small, white-haired woman, slumped over the tea she still held in her lap. Her eyes fluttered open. "Who's there?" she called, and her voice was as thin as the china.

The women looked at each other, too well trained to cry out or even speak. The old lady rose slowly, resting her weight on the upholstered arm of the chair.

"What mischief are you up to?" she demanded, and began to lunge forward. Just then Maggie turned off the light. The room was plunged once again into darkness. The old lady let out a cry and fell heavily, bringing some heavy object down with her and creating a great deal of noise. In the stillness that followed the very air seemed to vibrate.

"What was she doing here?" Glenda hissed.

"I'd like to know! But I've got the painting, Glennie, so let's get out—and quick!"

The younger woman bent over and began to feel around in the darkness. "Give me the light a minute, Maggie, just to see how she is."

"Don't be a fool!" Maggie returned, but the narrow golden glow snapped on again, revealing the limp shape of the woman crumpled on the floor.

"She struck her head on the corner of this table!" Glenda moved closer. "Maggie, I think she's dead!"

"Damn! She wasn't supposed to be here. Come on, Glennie! Quick!"

"Before the light blinked out Glenda caught up the small wasted hand; it felt like dry paper against her own. The ring slid easily off the thin finger and onto hers, the most beautiful ring she had ever seen, glowing with deep, sea-green lights—burning, shimmering, begging to be taken.

She rose, a mere shadow stirring through the restored darkness, and followed Maggie outside.

The car was waiting; a milk delivery truck with its lights cut. A man jumped off the tailgate and took their burden from them, wrapping it deftly, quickly in a big piece of canvas and disappearing inside. The women melted back into the shadows. Seconds after the truck pulled away a car with no lights came out of a side road, slowed, and two shadows slid inside. It moved off in a different direction from the milk truck. Somewhere a cat cried into the lonely silence and a breath of wind stirred the brittle, dry leaves. Then the night settled down again, and inside their houses, the people slept.

Penelope could scarcely see the road. She leaned low over the steering wheel and peered through the curtain of rain. Laura shivered despite the heavy wool wrap she wore; the cold was so moist here that it seemed to cut through to the bone.

"Perhaps you ought to pull off the road 'til it stops, dear."

"And maybe sit here all day? No, I'll be all right if I take it easy."

Laura sighed; she wouldn't bother to argue once Penelope had made up her mind.

"It isn't far to Oban, Mother, really. Sit back and relax."

Laura tried to. But the day around them seemed as murky as night, and the elements appeared indifferent, unfriendly even. She felt herself an intruder again and wondered, fleetingly, what she was doing in this strange place.

Oban, the great port for the Western Isles, is one of the most beautiful coast towns in Scotland. On a bright, sunny day it has the look of the Mediterranean about it. But now, slashed by rain, it appeared chilly and uninviting. The main street, flanking the harbor, was called George Street, which made Penelope laugh. "Are we never to escape that name, Mother?" Driving through the wet streets they found a house with a "Rooms to Let" sign and made up their minds to stay there. It was a fortuitous decision, for they were given a small drawing room of their own on the second floor, where the guests always stayed. That and a very large bedroom where a fire was lit, as though somehow they had been expected.

It was really too wet to go out. Laura decided to catch up on her letters. She found it difficult to write to her friends, unless she settled for the bright, empty tourist descriptions of the things she had seen. Perhaps that was just as well, for how could she begin to tell them what she had experienced here, the changes that had been wrought in her, the tentative opening of her spirit to all that was lovely and true? Penelope found it difficult to write something to Mark. She had left him behind with the flippant disregard of a schoolgirl. But she knew she had changed. She could not say quite how, but this country had altered her in some deep, essential part of her being, and she was no longer the person Mark had known and admired. And that in itself was a betrayal she had not anticipated nor planned.

Only the late papers carried the story. The headlines screamed it: A valuable Bellini stolen while the family was away. Mrs. Mary Gow, a well-respected Glasgow matron visiting her daughter outside Oban, killed by the thieves and robbed of her family jewels.

It was no more specific than that. But it didn't need to be. The whole population of the British Isles was shocked and aghast. The people in London and the northern cities were secretly relieved, of course, to learn that the trouble had shifted to Scotland; nothing up there mattered much. But murder? These thieves had been a nuisance before, but it had never come down to this. People shuddered. Those in certain positions called the police. One or two of particular influence called the commissioner himself.

In the hills above Oban, at the scene of the crime, MacGregor prowled with a dark face and gaunt, red-rimmed eyes.

"How could they have done it?" he asked Fraser. "How could they have slipped out right from under our eyes?"

Hugh didn't know, but he had his own theories, and he had an idea as well.

"All right, what have you got on your mind, Fraser?" MacGregor's voice had dropped down to a growl. A strong voice, strangely rich and resonant; the voice of a singer, Hugh thought. But oddly accented, a unique blending of English byways and London streets, and some strain distinctly Scottish—Glasgow, perhaps?

"I have an idea, sir. I wondered if you'd—listen."

Callum would listen. He led the lad into a small, private chamber. Callum was willing to listen to just about anything right now.

"It won't work," Callum pronounced half an hour later. "It's a bold plan, I'll admit, but—"

"Of course it will work! If you have the guts to do it the way I've suggested."

Callum stared back at the young man who sat watching him defiantly. What he had suggested was rash, but it was brilliant as well. Heaven knew he needed something—something drastic—something right now!

"Perhaps if—"

"No! I can see why you hesitate, but it must be my way. Sir, I know—"

Callum waved him to silence. Fears were nagging at him that he did not want to admit. Yet if this worked, it would work splendidly! And he had nothing better—he had nothing else.

"All right. You sure you can make the arrangements?"

Hugh rose, and Callum could feel his eagerness like a force in the room.

"I can, sir. I've no doubt of it."

"Very good. Then we'll meet tonight."

"This afternoon, sir. The sooner the better. Say four o'clock."

"Four o'clock," Callum grunted, and nodded a curt dismissal to the lad, who flew from the room as though suddenly released from a tight spring that had held him.

Callum felt a tightness in his gut, even in his muscles, a sensation he had seldom experienced since he was a young man himself. He didn't like it. He had too much on the line here, and if this thing didn't work he would go down, and perhaps take everyone with him.

Feeling the tightness creep into the muscles of his shoulders, he walked out of the room in search of the sandy-haired Emily Ferguson, lady of the house. Despite the fact that her home had been violated and her mother found dead, Callum was forced to ask her for favors. What a wretched job, this! Did he have any chance of charming her, of appealing to her pity? Perhaps he should have kept young Fraser here. Women flocked to him, Callum had noticed; women of all ages, all types. What did the boy have that was lacking in other men? Callum didn't know. But he certainly felt he could use a large dose of it himself right now.

There came the woman herself, moving toward him, her face white as a sheet and a kerchief held up to her eyes. Cursing the fate that had ever attracted him to police work, Callum walked toward her with a purposeful, yet somehow respectful, stride.

———•◦•———

The rain had stopped, but the sky hung heavy and low, and the air seemed still drenched with water. Penelope, going out to check the weather, walked back into the house with a sigh, and at that moment the gray day grew darker. Their kind landlady, Bess Brodie, who had seemed to so thoroughly anticipate and understand their every need, came in from the kitchen wiping her white hands nervously on a long towel.

"I'm sorry, my dears, so terribly sorry, but my daughter who lives in Glasgow just rang. She has fallen and broken her arm, and I must go to her at once, her having four wee bairns to take care of and no one to help her at all—her husband being off on the shrimp boats."

Penelope blinked at her; Laura looked up from her book. "I'm so sorry to hear that," she murmured in sympathy.

"This means I must close up the house, and I was greatly looking forward to your company, Mrs. Poulson."

"Oh yes, as was I. But we'll find something else, and you musn't worry about us with so much else on your mind."

The poor woman appeared truly distressed. "Well, we three shall spend the night here and start off fresh in the morning."

"I feel like eating some fresh fish-and-chips, don't you, Penny?" Laura asked, rising and laying her book aside.

"There's a grand place right through the block," Bess Brodie suggested, and gave them the simple directions they would need before she bustled upstairs to pack things she would need for her trip.

"We shall bring back a little something for you to eat as well, Mrs. Brodie," Laura called after her. Then, bundling up against the damp weather, they went out into the night.

Laura could taste the moisture in the air and could feel it, like thick fog, penetrate through her skin, down to the core of her. When Penelope opened the door to the pub the released warmth and odors of fish and herbs reached out like long fingers to draw them inside. The eating room Bess had suggested was just an enlargement of the old pub; Laura had learned that there were very few real restaurants in the British Isles, with the exception of the very exclusive and very costly, which were mainly attached to hotels. The pub was the local answer to man's need for food and drink and warm comradeship. At least with the extended space they would be a bit removed from the bar and the smells of liquor and cigarette smoke. Penelope guided her mother to an empty table, where Laura sat down with a sigh.

"'Tis a pity, Mother," Penelope complained after they had ordered—not fish-and-chips, but kidney soup to warm their insides, and venison pie. "We were so comfortable at Mrs. Brodie's."

"Yes, I know, dear." Laura was more disappointed than she wished to show Penelope; after all, she was the mother and must be the more wise of the two.

When the dark, rich soup came they sipped it in a rather gloomy silence. And when the stranger approached and spoke to them both were startled; Laura unconsciously put her hand to her throat.

"Excuse me, ladies." He stood close and his eyes scrutinized Laura's face. "My mistake and I do apologize. I thought you were—well, you look like someone I know, someone I haven't seen for a long time."

Laura smiled; she couldn't help herself. The man's eyes were kind, and she sensed his sincerity. It fascinated her to think she may look like a person who was well known and obviously well esteemed by this stranger who bent over her.

"Lord Forbes." The waiter who approached them was obviously nervous, or perhaps it was merely his obsequiousness which made him appear so flustered. Had he said *Lord* Forbes?

"Your usual table is occupied, sir. I can fix you—"

"No need, lad." The man waved him lightly aside.

On a sudden impulse Laura did not take time to analyze, she found herself saying, "There's room at our table. You're more than welcome to share it."

At first he began to wave away her kind offer as well. Then he visibly paused and gazed at Laura again, as though trying to make up his mind about something.

"If you really mean it," he said suddenly, "I do believe I just might accept."

The waiter beamed and sighed audibly, then hastened to pull out a chair for "m'lord," who seemed used to such deferential treatment and received it with his own casual courtesy. The waiter seemed to know what the great man would order and scurried away to his tasks. Lord Forbes leaned back in his chair, obviously at ease and relaxed. But Laura's throat felt tight and constricted as she swallowed her spoonful of soup, and she was forced to stifle a cough in her hand.

"I should certainly introduce myself," their guest said. "I am Thomas Forbes, earl of Seafield and Lochmont."

He inclined his head a little, and Laura, swallowing hard, said, "I am Laura Poulson and this is my daughter, Penelope."

Lord Forbes nodded in Penny's direction, and she nodded back.

"No Scottish name that," he said. "What brings you to Scotland?"

"My mother is a Cameron and a MacGregor on her mother's side and a Douglas on her father's. We've come to search out our ancestors and to see the country," Penelope supplied.

"Och, aye. I see." The man's expression softened, and so Penelope added, "My mother's always wanted to come. When my father died suddenly we decided this would be a good remedy, and so far it's been wonderful—for both of us." She knew how awkward she sounded, and wondered what had made her tell this strange man of her father's death.

Laura sat silent, distressed by her daughter's forthrightness, yet strangely comforted by the stranger's presence and unstated sympathy.

"And where is it you come from, then?"

Penelope glanced at her mother and answered, with an air of apology, "Salt Lake City, in the state of Utah. It's way out on the American desert. You wouldn't know it, of course."

Lord Forbes nodded, and just then his soup came and for a while they said nothing more to one another than the usual polite dinner chatter. Then, in a little lull, after the bread and the gentleman's whiskey had been brought, Penelope suddenly asked, "Who is it my mother reminded you of? Does she really look like someone you know?"

"Oh, very," the lord said, glancing up from his soup. "She appears about the same age . . . perhaps a little younger than my friend . . . a little prettier . . ." A gentle look softened the sculptured features of his face, and Laura felt he was not merely flattering her.

"It has been years since we met. I asked her to marry me when I was a young, rash lad, but she knew better than to accept me." There was merriment in his eyes, but beneath it a sadness that he could not quite hide. "Her husband was a banker and he took her away with him to London; since then we've only met two or three times, on social occasions. But I'd heard that her husband had died, and wondered—when I saw you—"

He took a hearty drink of whiskey, as if to end his long, perhaps painful statement. Penelope asked gently, "Did you ever marry, yourself, sir?"

"Yes, yes!" He smiled at her naivete. "Happily married these twenty-five years, with three sons, good lads, all; but no daughters, I'm sorry to say."

Penelope smiled with the same artlessness, and the earl added hastily, "My wife died last year. The big house has been wretchedly empty without her." Then, as on a sudden thought, he asked, "How long have you been in Oban? Where are you staying?"

Then, of course, their story came out. But before Penelope had fairly finished the sad recital, the earl interrupted enthusiastically. "Say no more! We are well met, the three of us." He leaned back in his chair and spread his arms out in a gracious gesture. "Please, come stay with me. I would be honored." Laura was shaking her head at him. "It would be no trouble at all. It's a big old castle of a place I've got, you see, and the last two summers, to tell the truth, we've actually let rooms to the public. My factor handles the details."

He looked a bit embarrassed. Penelope had been listening. "He means it, Mother," she said.

"Yes, I mean it." The earl assumed an air of casual command, as though Penelope's statement had somehow settled the matter.

"I wouldn't be comfortable there," Laura admitted, hardly aware that their waiter had come again and brought their plates of steaming pie and vegetables.

"You don't know that, and I would take a bet that you are wrong, ma'am." The earl was hungry and ate with a heartiness that made the food appear even more appetizing. Laura tasted hers and was pleased with the moist, flaky crust and the flavor.

"What had you at Mistress Brodie's?" Lord Forbes asked suddenly.

Penelope colored slightly but answered, "A large bedroom to share, and a drawing room, sir."

"I believe we can match that at the castle," he answered, and everyone laughed. After that, there was no more discussion concerning the matter until the earl got up to leave. "I'll send my man over in the morning—say, ten? He can carry your things and you can follow in your car to the house. Will that be all right?"

"Yes, and thank you, sir," Penelope answered for the both of them.

With the now-familiar gesture he brushed her gratitude aside. "You are doing me a favor, if you only knew it," he responded. With a few gallant words he thanked them for their company and then left them as abruptly as he had seemed to come—with the abruptness of the unexpected, the amazing.

Laura stared after him. "I don't know what to think."

"Do you ever, Mother? You're just too timid. Did you get any bad feelings from him or about what he suggested?"

Laura sighed and admitted that she had only good feelings.

"Then for heaven's sake, Mother, relax!" Penelope spoke the words with her usual strong emphasis, but there was a tenderness behind them that Laura was grateful for. "What an adventure this will be for us! Can you just imagine trying to tell Sandra and Marion and all your friends back home? They won't even believe us—Lord Forbes!"

They laughed together and finished their meal and went back to tell Bess Brodie what had happened to them at the pub.

7

GLENDA SAT BENEATH THE GLOW OF THE FLOOR LAMP, THE only light in the room. In the palm of her upturned hand, cradled there like the precious thing it was, sat the old lady's jewel, throbbing against her skin, almost as if it were some live thing.

"You gotta get rid of that, Glennie." Maggie came up behind her. Glenda couldn't see how dark her face was, but the tone of her voice was enough.

"Sure, sure! You know what the Terrier said when I talked to him—too big, too hot. Nobody we deal with will touch it."

"Throw it down a drain somewhere then! It could hang the both of us."

Glenda shuddered and ran the fingers of her free hand through the short, thick thatch of her hair.

"Why'd you do that?" Maggie was being shrewish about every little thing now; she always got that way when she was afraid.

"What? Cut my hair?" Glenda moved her hand back

and forth so that the lights of the gem sent piercing stabs of emerald and saffron and even violet into the drab, colorless room.

"I already told you why I did it, Maggie! I look like her—that girl I saw in Inverary. A mother and daughter, I'd bet anything on it. And the police are following *them!*"

"I think you're crazy."

"I don't care what you think. I know what I saw. I saw them drive off and another car drive off after 'em. If we could get out of here right now—"

"We can't. Willie has one more job for us."

"That's right. So when we do it, I'm gonna go in lookin' like her. Help convince those conscientious police that they're on the right track. Then, when we light out of here for France, I'll go as a black-haired beauty—throw 'em right off our tracks."

"And what about that thing?" Maggie indicated the ring with a disgusted snap of her head.

"You're beginning to irritate me, Maggie! I'll take care of it; I told you I would."

"The Terrier's angry, Glennie. He's making threats. He's never done that before."

"That's 'cause he saw that London cop in Edinburgh and knows they're onto him. He's walkin' scared, though he won't admit it. We'll be all right. Do this last job while the cops wander about after our stool pigeons. We can get clean away before they figure out they've got the wrong pair of us."

"Well, we can't be seen together during the next day or two—"

"I know that. I'll be as careful as you are. Just don't bug me, all right?"

"And the ring?"

"I'll take care of the ring!" Glenda was shouting.

With an iciness in her voice Maggie replied, "You'd better. And what's more, I don't want to know about it. You understand?"

Glenda understood. She had messed up and now she was in trouble, and there was no one to help her out of it. She watched Maggie wrap herself up in the big, man-size mackintosh and pull a short wig over her hair and a bowler on top of that. Maggie scared easily, but she didn't. She was young and pretty, and she knew how to take care of herself. Once this was over, once they were in France with money in their pockets . . .

Maggie slammed the door behind her without even saying good-bye. Since Edinburgh they had not stayed in the same rooms, not even the same hotels. They'd pressed their luck, as it was. But the Terrier was greedy, and so were the others—Maggie's friends on the continent that Glenda knew nothing about, the brains behind the whole operation, as Maggie so often said. Glenda didn't care. She wanted it to end, to be over. Somewhere, deep down inside, she wished she could keep the ring. Heck, the old dame was already dead when she took it off her finger. How was Glenda to know that it would turn out to be a family heirloom three hundred years old, given to some precious ancestress by King William himself?

She looked about her. The room was cold and dismal. She didn't like it. She wanted a warm, bright room with a fire, she wanted to wear fancy clothes—spend some of the money she'd risked her hide for. But Maggie had decided back in Edinburgh that they'd have to play this stretch low-key. She didn't know how much more of it she could take.

She slipped the heavy emerald onto her finger. She

liked the feel, even the weight of it. She decided she would wear it to bed, sleep with it for good luck. In the morning—well, she had ideas for the morning. Right now she wouldn't think about that. Right now she'd have a stiff drink and finish off the last of the shortbread. Just a little treat—make it easier for her to settle down and sleep through the night.

———

Callum was encouraged. He had been on the telephone all morning to his contacts in Edinburgh and Stirling, and for the first time with promising results. An Edinburgh art dealer who ran a large gallery had supplied the inspector with names of two men, one in Paris, one in Prague, who he had reason to believe might be involved in black market dealings. He had only just returned from a buying trip abroad, and something he had heard there disturbed him, set off an alarm in his mind. It was a little thing, really, but he had heard two men in private conversation discussing a painting. By sheer accident he had overheard the name of the work, and thought it the same as the piece which had been filched in Stirling. Indeed, it was the very Constable, as he discovered when he arrived back home and checked it out.

"The men were in the library of a large estate house, shut off from the others," the inspector explained to Callum, "and thought themselves safe enough. But our friend Mr. Grant came in search of his glasses which he feared he had left in the room earlier that same day. 'Twas a large room, and at first he didn't notice them, all huddled down on divans in the corner of the place, as they were. By the time each had realized the presence of the other, well . . . some things had been said."

"I want a watch placed on Grant and his family," Callum instructed. "Have you got enough men for that?"

"You think he's in danger?"

"He very well may be."

"Right, then. You can depend upon us, sir. Consider it done."

Callum smiled at the man's flamboyance. While he was still ruminating on this new development, the inspector from Stirling rang up. One of his street contacts had given him a tip about Willie "the Terrier." Word was that he was heading up north, then to France. Could he be in Oban right now?

Callum took immediate measures, placing plainclothes police at every dock, every wharf; the smallest pier where a boat might slip through. He informed the other coastal towns of the situation and was pleased by the extent of their cooperation. Of course, the tip could be false, set to purposefully mislead them. But he didn't think so, not from this particular source. And it made sense. His ladies were here, and the game was nearing conclusion. London—all English ports would be too dangerous; controls had been set there for weeks. Particularly, if his ladies were not on to him, Callum conjectured—if they thought they had only locals to deal with. An idea was forming, slowly. He'd run it past Fraser before he made up his mind. And hopefully Fraser would have something to report to Callum himself before the day's close.

—————

Penelope awoke slowly. Before she even opened her eyes she was aware of the feel of the place; her foggy mind remembered the cavernous entry, the endless hall with rooms leading off on each side, statues in nooks in the walls and high glass chandeliers that had tinkled melodiously, as though a band of fairies, in passing, had stirred their sweet music.

She snuggled into the silk-covered eiderdown, wondering if the maid would appear again this morning with food and hot tea. She could hear the small sounds of someone moving about and knew it must be her mother, who shared a room that connected to hers by an inner door.

"Penelope, dear, it's a beautiful day, not a rain cloud in sight. Hurry now so we can take advantage of it."

Reluctantly Penelope opened her eyes. Chintz bed curtains of a soft rosy color framed a portion of the room: the fireplace and a section of a wall where a set of Worcester plates were displayed around a small mirror, and beside them a series of small paintings of seascapes, so exquisitely wrought that Penelope fancied she could taste the sea air in her mouth and nostrils and feel it sharp on her face.

She dressed quickly, while her mother fidgeted. "Lord Forbes is off on estate business," she informed her daughter, "but he has left word that he wishes us to dine with him tonight. We can hardly refuse."

"You're nervous, Mother." Penelope smiled. "Don't be. There's no reason. He's impressed with you; couldn't you see?"

"Penny!" Laura was outraged, anger struggling with embarrassment. Penelope gave her a kiss on the cheek. "All right, dear, I'll hurry. I know you want to check out the churchyards, and I want to go out to that castle ruin—Kerra-something. I hope we'll have time for both."

"We want the recorder's office, Penny, remember? Let's check that out first."

It was a wise decision. The records showed that Agnes Cameron and her infant were buried in the Presbyterian manseyard on the east side of the city. As they drove down by the waterfront Penelope cried excitedly, "There's a steamer leaving right now, Mother! Please can't we go on it and check out the graveyard when we get back?"

With a sigh Laura acquiesced, following Penelope's mad dash toward the little boat at a more sedate pace. The sea both frightened and fascinated her, and she was not prepared for the heady feeling the salt air gave her, the spray like a mist in her face, the harsh call of gulls, the mournful cry of the curlews, and the occasional low blare of a ship's horn sounding hollow and foggy and far away. When most of the passengers went inside she stood by the railing, listening to the hiss of the water, watching the progression of waves, ever changing and never ending.

Most of the folk on the boat, she surmised, were local people, not strangers like herself and Penny. Some eyed them with a sense of mistrust, saying clearly, *The tourists are supposed to be gone by this season. What are you still doing here? We've our own lives to get on with, you know.* It made her keenly aware that she had no life of her own to "get on with." That life was no more. When she went home she must create some sort of new life, woven of different fabric. Standing alone in the keen, biting air she felt at one with the wide, terrible loneliness around her. In some ways she did belong. Suffering brought her kinship and hallowed her otherwise tenuous ties.

There was still a thin, spread-out group of them who got off the ferry after the four-mile ride and walked up the steep slope to view the little L-shaped castle of Gylen. It stood roofless and forlorn beneath the white sky where gulls circled, but its keep was intact and rose four stories high, looking down over the narrow neck of rock it once guarded. With the sea on all sides, sighing and moaning, always in motion, one could sense the old need of haven, perhaps even more than the need for protection.

The trip back to the mainland was crowded. "Last run of the day," someone said to the question in Laura's eyes and raised brow. Laura leaned on the railing, and Penelope, warmed by the strong rays of sun that broke through the dull sky and slanted over the sea, shed her warm jacket and stood beside her mother, feeling the breeze lift her thin blouse and caress, if roughly, her up-turned face.

Neither of them noticed the young woman who walked sedately, almost purposefully, past them, pausing almost imperceptibly when she reached the deck chair where Penny's coat hung. Her hand moved, shot out quickly and returned again to the folds of her gown—and she passed on, running her fingers lightly through the short, snappy cut of her thick yellow hair.

"You missed the confounded steamer!" Callum wanted to laugh and swear at the same time, but he did neither; he merely pressed his fingers together and scowled at the unhappy young man.

"Well, she pulled over at the last minute. You haven't seen the way this girl drives! How did I know they'd make a run for the ferry?" He shrugged his shoulders, an un-successful attempt to appear casual and unconcerned. "'Twas innocent enough, as it turned out. They only went out to Kerrera and spent an hour walking round the old castle, and we've got one of our men on the ferry, as well as those posted harborside."

"And one on the island as well?" Callum was getting angry. He hadn't expected this laxity from Fraser. "They made no contacts? Hid nothing? Retrieved nothing? For heaven's sake, man!"

"I'm sorry, Inspector. I'll do better tomorrow, I promise you."

Callum growled something and let the lad go. His own day had been productive enough, thank heavens, that he felt he could afford this one frustration. But he had altogether forgotten to outline his plan for Fraser. Well, tomorrow would be time enough for that, too.

———•—•———

As it turned out, Laura and Penelope did not go to visit the kirkyard that night. Both were too tired, and Laura was yet nervous about spending more time with the earl.

She should not have been. Here, in his own surroundings, he was the model of graciousness, initiating interesting conversations and even asking questions about their lives. Laura's experience, though somewhat limited, had been that most men possess little genuine interest in ways of life that are alien to their own, especially where women are concerned. They want to be listened to, not talked at. But Thomas Forbes listened and appeared to be interested, even sympathetic at times. He had fine, penetrating eyes and a sensitive mouth, but other than that he was the kind of man Laura shied from: large in person, with boldly drawn features and a confident air—a "man's man," she would have called him. Yet, he had been so kind.

Later, up in their rooms, she thought it over. Perhaps it was merely good breeding with Lord Forbes after all. She shouldn't expect too much and then be disappointed. Once she let down her reserve, she could be hurt. She walked out onto the small iron-railed balcony on the east side of the room. The moon was invisible, a mere glowing presence below a low bank of clouds that hung like immense silver curtains across a soft velvet sky. Beautiful clouds, etched in shapes and shadows that tempted the imagination and made her heart sore with a longing she could put no name to. *I have lived so much of my life protecting myself from hurt,* she thought, and the thought was a revelation that seared through her mind like a light. The clouds, thick and almost leaden in some spots, were stretched thin in others and took on an almost airy lightness. How she wished she could break through those clouds that obscured more than the darkened heavens. With a tremulous sigh she turned her back on the scene and reentered the bright room from which Penelope called.

———•◆•———

After the quiet of Inverary, Oban provided immense release. Corker strolled the waterfront, trailed by his undersized shadow, and drew in the rich, almost rank smells of tar and oil, of pounds of packed herring lying silver and red-eyed in barrels of ice. The ships' masts, many of them lighted, rose like slender sentinels against a gray, troubled sky.

Corker and Eddie had taken too long in getting here, and Corker knew it. But what real hurry was there? The boss had other things on his mind besides this mess of fish. They'd settle it up soon enough.

He located a string of pubs, brightly lit and inviting. "We'll have a drink or two in each," he told Eddie, "and see what we can learn. Couple of dames as good-lookin' as those two, well, they don't go unnoticed, and that's a fact."

"'Specially up in these parts," Eddie muttered. "Ain't seen a woman yet under fifty."

Corker chuckled. "That's right. We'll find 'em, no doubt about it. Meantime, won't we have fun?" He pushed open the heavy, nail-studded door of the nearest pub and walked into the warmth, his mouth already watering for that first drink.

8

Agnes Cameron's grave was easy to find in the section of the graveyard where all the stones were worn and tired, some faded almost past reading. Mother and child lay in one spot. Penelope could picture it: the woman's arms wrapped round her baby. It would be a pitiful sight. Laura refused to imagine it. She had been denied the privilege of wrapping her arms round the son she had cuddled and fondled and delighted in. She could not picture him dead—like the war photos she had gazed on with such horror. She would not, she dare not do that!

"Let's go to the castle, Mother," Penelope urged her, disturbed at her mother's gloom.

"You think that will cheer me?" Laura retorted, laughing lightly.

Penelope reached for her hand. She wanted to say, "I love you so much," but she knew that would sound corny. Her mother's eyes were so lovely, as gentle and feminine as the rest of her, unshadowed by the ambitions of women of Penelope's age. *It's just the two of us. Alone.*

Together, she thought, and she squeezed the soft hand, not trusting herself to put words to the things in her heart.

Hugh followed them as they drove the road northeast from Oban and stopped at the ruins of the great castle, which stood out boldly on the promontory where the clear waters of Loch Linnhe enter Loch Etive. The magnificent castle was but a shell of its former self—a shell with nine-foot-thick walls and a breathtaking view westward over the sea.

He mingled with the group walking round the ruins, grateful for the noisy Englishmen who wisely planned their holidays for when the tourists were gone. Now was the perfect time. He strolled close to Penelope, who, sensing him there, looked up and smiled. He smiled back at her out of the bluest eyes she had ever seen. It took her breath away for a moment and she asked him, rather stupidly, "Do you know these parts?"

Hugh blinked back. She was making it easy for him.

"Not well," he answered, "but I can tell you that the blue peaks you see beyond that narrow stretch of ocean are the mountains of Morven and Mull. Islands," he added, seeing the question in her eyes. "Oban is the gateway to the Western Isles, a whole different world."

"Is that what I feel in the air here?"

Hugh nodded. She was really very disarming. He must not forget his purpose. "I'm Hugh Fraser," he said, thrusting his hand out in a friendly gesture.

"Penelope Poulson," she replied. "Over there is my mother, Laura. We're here together." Of course they were together, Penelope thought, mentally berating herself. Why did handsome men render her awkward and speechless—still? Even with a college degree beneath her hat.

Ridiculous name, that, Hugh Fraser thought. "So you're Americans. Isn't this a bit late in the year?" He looked around him to the rowans turning crimson, the chestnuts stained a deep gold.

"Yes, it's breathtaking," Penelope mused, her eyes following his gaze. "We're not really tourists," she continued. "We're here doing family research." She nearly added, "And we're getting away, running away from my father's death, you see." But she remembered just in time that this young man was a stranger to her, and the partial answer she had supplied him would have to do.

After that Hugh stuck close to them; he had no trouble with that sort of thing. He knew how to make himself agreeable to mothers, turn on just enough charm to lull, not alarm. It was an easy thing for him, this conscious pleasing of females, and all the more convincing because he enjoyed it so much. He was sincere, as far as sincerity can be couched in such actions and such motives as he concealed.

The group milling round the ruins was large enough that Corker felt he could mingle and not stand out. This was a wild, desolate spot, and if his ladies strayed enough, perhaps . . . He kicked at the russet clumps of dead bracken beneath his feet. He walked to the edge of the crags and looked down the steep rise he stood upon to where the sea spread out below him—far below.

That would be drop enough, he mused. *Maybe that's what I ought to do, push them two dames off the cliff. Make my job a lot easier. I don't think they'll sign what the boss has in mind anyway, so it may come down to this in the end.*

To tell the truth, he was tiring of Scotland despite the abundance of good whiskey. It was getting cold here and he'd seen enough lakes and hillsides and herds of sheep to last him a lifetime. Besides, fate had played them a trick. He didn't even believe the man at the pub when he first told him—his two women invited home by the earl. Maybe there was more behind their demure exteriors than he had guessed. Be that as it may, he'd have a deuce of a time getting close to them now!

He stepped right up to the edge of the cliff and, with the tip of his boot, kicked a stone over and watched it careen downward, now and again striking against a sharp outcropping of rock. He was thinking dark thoughts of a certain nature that pleased him, that caused a weird light to glow in his eyes and twitch along the lines of his face.

Laura had strayed close to the cliffside, drawn by the terrible and beautiful view of the blue sea below. When the solitary man turned and she saw his expression, she drew back in fear. A dread sensation came over her. She averted her eyes and hurried back to where Penelope stood with that handsome young stranger beside one of the round corner towers. She was trembling inside. Not once since she had been in Scotland had she felt this kind of fear. What was it—so different from the safe, almost cushioned feeling she and Penny had known?

She hazarded a glance behind and, to her horror, the strange man was watching her still. Quickly she slid in front of Penny to escape that dark gaze.

Corker, watching her, chuckled under his breath; a low, gutteral, unpleasant sound. "Too hoity-toity for the likes o' me, are you?" he muttered. "Well, run while you can. It may not be so easy the next time. I can promise you that."

———•◆•———

It was late in the day when Hugh reported to MacGregor, obviously pleased with his own progress.

"It's a poor alias they have and a lame story to explain their being here," Hugh observed. "I'd expected something a bit more from them."

"I thought so, too," Callum agreed. "But perhaps it's on purpose; pick some boring, out-of-the-way place, you know, hard to trace, nothing exciting enough to attract attention."

Hugh nodded. He wanted to tell MacGregor how darned attractive that younger one was, but, of course, he couldn't.

"We'll put my plan into operation tomorrow," MacGregor was saying. "One of the local men swore he saw the Terrier at a particular wharfside establishment last night. They must be sticking around for some reason; perhaps it's the ring. But if they're after one more big job before they call it a day, let's give it to them!" He leaned forward a bit and absently rubbed the jutting line of his chin with a long, tapered finger. "Everything's set up and ready, and we'll have the help of his lordship, of course."

"Right. Well, I'll be off then, sir."

"You stay close to them, Fraser—you yourself, understand?"

"Meaning?"

"Meaning you outside the house at night, at least 'til the lights all go out. If something were to happen, you'd have access, being an admired acquaintance now."

Hugh let MacGregor's slight stress on the word *admired* go unremarked. "Yes, sir."

There went his plans for a quiet evening in that little dark pub he'd discovered on Charles Street. And sleep! MacGregor must think he could get along without any. Oh well, it shouldn't be much longer now. And tomorrow ought to be quite an adventure. Hugh walked from the room whistling "Sleepy-Time Gal" softly under his breath.

———•—•———

"He looks like Byron, that's who he looks like, Mother, with his thick, curly black hair."

"Byron?" Laura looked up from the postcard she was writing. "Lord Byron, the poet?"

"That's right."

"Penny, really."

"Well, it's true. He has a high brow and large, mournful eyes."

"I thought they were spilling over with pleasure and admiration this afternoon."

Penelope laughed. "Don't worry, Mother. You worry too much about me."

"And Mark? After Donald and now this young man, what about him?"

"I'm not sure of Mark. I wasn't before I left Utah, and you know that."

Laura sighed. She knew by this time that Penelope would live her own life, but it was difficult at times to have to sit back and merely watch, with no power at all. How lovely it had been when she was small and had looked to Laura for everything, trusting her care and her wisdom.

"Please, Mother, don't." Penny came up and kissed her mother on the cheek. "Do you still have your headache?"

Laura admitted that she had.

"I'll run down to the little chemist's shop across the street from Bess Brodie's and get you something for it."

"But isn't it too late?" Laura fretted.

"I don't think so. It's worth a try. I know my way, and it's not yet dark, Mother, so I'll be fine."

Penelope skipped out, and Laura lay back against the soft pillows that were piled on the bed. *What would it be like to live this way,* she wondered, *surrounded by luxury and beauty? Would it grow old in time? Or would the mind always be softened, the heart scented by such loveliness?* She closed her eyes and relaxed against the softness and thought of nothing at all.

———•••———

The chemist's shop was closed. As Penelope walked back to her car she felt someone behind her, and although her first impulse was to turn around, she put her head down and walked all the faster. She could hear footsteps now, marking her own. What could this mean? The narrow, brick-paved road whispered with shadows, shadows that seemed to tremble, to move with her, like the shadow that was following behind.

Ought she to cry out? All the store fronts were darkened, with shades pulled over most of the doors. A few more feet and she would reach her car. Could she get inside in time?

Suddenly a hand closed round her throat, another round her chest, pinning her arms at both sides. She cried out then, not knowing what she was saying, aware that she was struggling and writhing against the strong arms that held her from behind. The hand closed over her mouth and nose, and, with a sense of panic, she began to gasp for air.

"Shut up if you know what's good for you," a voice hissed in her ear. "I just want a little talk, miss, that's all." He tightened the press of his fingers over her mouth until they felt as though they were bruising her flesh. "I can end it all right now, if that's what you want, you little fool—real easy, I can."

The voice ate at her skin like an acid; it made her insides feel sick. With all the strength she could manage

Penelope lifted her foot and struck back at his leg with her heel. He reeled and swore under his breath—and lightened the press of his fingers, and Penelope cried out once more, though the sound was muffled and hoarse.

With a rough pull he began to drag her backwards, back to the dark, silent shadows where no one would see. She had not yet caught a glimpse of his face, and she thought, with a sick dread, *I am going to die. This stranger is going to kill me.*

Suddenly the cruel hold slackened, so suddenly that Penelope fell forward, scraping her knees on the pavement, then collapsing, limp and trembling and gasping for breath.

At first she was unaware of the arms that lifted her and the voice, kind but insistent, that kept repeating her name. As awareness seeped back she became conscious of the rough brush of a tweed coat against her face and a mild, woody fragrance that was subtle and pleasant.

"Penelope!"

She lifted her head. Hugh Fraser's lean, sensitive face was so close to hers that she could feel his breath on her cheek. His mouth, always lifted at one corner, looking as if it might laugh, was drawn now in a line of worry, which softened a little when he looked into her eyes.

"You're all right." The words were a statement expressing his own relief. "Did that bloke hurt you much?"

"I don't think so." Penelope touched her bruised mouth and was suddenly aware of the stinging pain in her knees.

"Who was he?"

"I have no idea."

"No idea?" Hugh tried to keep the disbelief he felt out of his voice. "I ran after him for a spell, but he had too much of a head start—saw me when I started across the street to you. That's when he let go."

Penelope was trembling again. Hugh wrapped his arms around her and held her again, stroking her hair that was damp with the night fog. "We've got to get you home, get those cuts taken care of."

She pushed away from him. "I don't want my mother to know of this. It will scare her to death. She'll probably book a passage on the next boat to New York, and I don't want that."

"I don't either," Hugh said, his voice as soft, as caressing as the hand on her cheek. "All right, for right now let's take you round to my place and call the castle from there. You can talk to your mother and tell her—what? That we ran into each other and I talked you into spending an hour with me at the local pub, and that you tripped over a break in the sidewalk and skinned your knees. Does that sound all right?"

Penelope was trembling, but she nodded. "You're very good at this," she accused, laughing shakily.

"More's the pity," he agreed. "I fear I've enjoyed a spoiled and desolate youth."

He guided her gently toward his own car and saw her safely inside before he went back to lock hers. The cottage he had rented stood a bit out of town; on the same road, in fact, that led to the earl's house. Once he got her safely inside and dialing her mother, he dashed back out to his car and drove the quarter mile to where one of the locals was posted, giving him a hasty recounting of what he had seen, wishing he could describe the attacker with more accuracy. But the narrow street had been dark and the man had worn a wide-brimmed hat pulled low on his face.

"Get word to MacGregor," he instructed. "Tell him I have the girl with me."

He was back before Penelope noticed his absence enough to take alarm from it. When he sauntered back in he walked through to the kitchen and put the kettle on to boil. "I'm going to feed you some chamomile tea," he insisted, "my mother's trusted remedy for every ill when I was a lad."

This was awkward. A normal pair of young people in such circumstances would enjoy the opportunity of getting to know one another a little—perhaps even a little more intimately, but he had to be careful with her; he dare not go too far beyond the delicate balance that his guise demanded. And yet, how pleasant it would be. . . .

"I can only stay a few moments," Penelope Poulson was saying. "But I would like to try that tea."

The few moments stretched out with such gentle ease that neither one was aware, until the little cuckoo clock on the wall chimed the hour of ten.

"Oh, dear." Penelope set aside her empty cup. "You'd better take me back now."

"All right." Hugh made no token protest, something this girl would be sure to see through. She was sharper, much sharper, than he had been led to believe. When she told him of her university studies and the plans she had for the future, they had the ring of truth to them. She knew what she was talking about. Poetry. She could quote Burns better than he could, and Byron and Keats. He had read some of his own favorites to her, and she had recited for him—recited by memory poems that she especially loved. He had told her, not unfalsely, that his father was titled and he was a younger son, doomed to make his own way in society, nearly through Cambridge himself. What after that? A chair at one of the colleges, he lied, and that had impressed her. Would a dame like the lovely ladies even know what he was talking about? Or care?

He walked her to the door and left her when the

earl's man opened it. *She must be good at what she does,* he reminded himself. *How many lines has she strung? How many roles has she played so convincingly that she could gain people's trust?*

He tried to whistle as he drove back to the cottage, but he had no heart for it now. The girl had been frightened; he had seen the terrible darkness of that fear in her eyes, he had held the warmth of her near to him. He had comforted her, helped her—and it was obvious how completely she trusted him. MacGregor would say only "good" to that: "Good work, lad." But it distressed Hugh to know that she thought him her friend, yet he was really the enemy, the betrayer—the hunter—and she went unawares, with trust more tender and helpless in her dark eyes than even her fear.

———•◦•———

"Don't go off without me no more, ya jerk!" That was Eddie's reaction when Corker limped back to him, bruised and angry as a bulldog, with the same black stubbornness twisting the lines of his face.

"Shut up," Corker countered. "Two of us and we wouldn't have got near her, 'specially as clumsy as you are—"

"Two of us and she wouldn't have gotten away."

Corker snarled in reply and opened another bottle of whiskey.

"What did you want, anyhow? To frighten her? Geez, Corker, that's all we need is the cops breathin' down our necks."

"Yeah, stupid, if I frighten her she'll get the heck outta here—we can't do nothing while that lord has his hands on 'em."

Eddie swore emphatically, leaving Corker with no

doubts as to his opinion of him, and poured himself a stiff glass. *Pretty soon,* he thought. *Somethin' better happen pretty soon now. I can't take much more o' this guy.*

———•◦•———

"If it's off, all the better," Glenda pleaded. "Let's get outta here, Willie."

There was a whine to the girl's voice that irritated the Terrier. "Shut up," he shouted. "You do what you're told and nothin' else, understand? You've messed up enough as it is, Glennie. You got to be careful. The boss wants one more good one, a plum, Glenda, and then it's over the water for you and Maggie."

"I want to go now."

The Terrier ignored her. He sat with his elbows on his knees and opened his hands. "The ring, Glennie. Give me the ring."

"What do you want with it?" Fear trickled along her backbone. "Maggie told me to get rid of—she said nobody would touch it!"

"Well, Maggie was wrong." Willie leaned close, his thick lips tightened into a hard line. "Get it, Glenda. Right now!"

She backed away from him, upsetting a table lamp, which clattered to the floor and broke into pieces. She put her hand to her throat. "I don't have it!" she gulped. "I did what Maggie told me—"

Willie rose and swung at her in one tight motion, his outstretched palm hitting her alongside her head. She staggered, but did not fall. He called her half a dozen names that were all little and ugly; she cowered beneath them as much as if he had struck her again.

"I know where it is—I can get it," she stammered.

That calmed Willie a bit. He swore again, reminding her of her utter worthlessness, and delivered a kick to her shins. "This time tomorrow," he said, "and you'd better have it, Glennie." His face relaxed into a terrible softness, but his small eyes went hard, hard as two gleaming black rocks under the ledge of his forehead. "You get me that emerald—or else."

There was no need to explain the "or else," to say a word more. The Terrier walked from the room, slamming the door behind him. Glenda remained where he had left her, trembling from the force of his cruelty and the threat that left her no loopholes, no place to run or to hide. Then she wiped her mouth with the back of her hand and swore under her breath. It made her feel better, so the next time she swore louder, calling Willie a few choice names in return. That he wasn't there to hear her didn't really matter. She walked past the pieces of glass and locked the door Willie had slammed.

"Just let him try," she muttered through clenched teeth. "I'm sick o' the two of them, both Maggie and him." She sat down on the sofa and tucked her legs up under her. "Maybe I'll take that old ring and light out myself. Serve 'em right if I did."

She was afraid, more afraid than she'd ever been. It was a dumb thing to do—plant that ring in the American girl's jacket. She had thought at the time that it was clever. If the police were after the girl and her mother and they found the evidence right on them, they'd be nailed nice and tidy now, wouldn't they, and Glenda'd be free—free to walk away, free to go wherever she wanted. The ring had to be there! At the time she hadn't cared much if the girl had discovered it. All the better for her. Who would have believed her if she'd taken it in to the authorities playing innocent, pretending she didn't know what it was doing there? Where was it now? Safe in the corner of the pocket where Glenda had stuffed it? It had to be!

A coldness crept through Glenda, a coldness that set her shivering and swearing softly again. She rocked back and forth, crooning in her fear: "Let it be there, safe where I put it—merciful heavens, please!"

9

It would be my pleasure; please, ma'am, indulge me."

The earl stood in his tweeds and riding boots looking every inch the fairy-tale image of the tall, handsome lord.

"But you must have a dozen better things to do with your time," Laura protested.

"On the contrary. I love nosing about auctions and would like nothing better than to show up with a beautiful lady on either arm and startle the countryside."

Penelope laughed, and the whole matter was decided, the way such matters are.

They rode out in the earl's chauffeured car, Laura sitting awkwardly beside Penelope, Penelope leaning and straining to see spots of interest the earl pointed out for them. "This is smashing," she cried. "I'm always in the driver's seat and don't see half this well."

It was a clear, crisp morning, and the auction was crowded with people, all looking purposeful, as if they knew just what they were about. Laura disliked crowds, particularly crowds of strangers, and would have hung

back. But the earl strode determinedly forward, his confidence so absolute, his manners so flawless that her admiration for him soared. Penelope leaned close to her
mother and whispered, "Too bad His Lordship isn't
twenty years younger!" Then Laura was able to smile and
to relax just a little.

It seemed a tedious and perplexing business, this bidding on the various lots as they came up. Laura couldn't
keep track, though the earl every now and again, in his
kindly manner, would lean close and explain some point
to her.

"Watch that old gentleman in the third row to your
left. See how he has laid the tip of his index finger
against his nostril? He has raised the bid with that signal—the Raphael has just been climbed above fifty-five
thousand pounds."

It seemed frightful to Laura. She could not understand how one would justify spending such large sums of
money on one solitary item, despite its beauty and the
value so-called experts placed on it.

"Do most people purchase art because they appreciate it?" she asked the earl. "Because they have fallen in
love with some artist or some particular piece?"

"Investment," he answered, "largely for investment.
Sometimes for pride. Pride of possession's a terrible and
powerful thing, lass, and lies deeply embedded in most of
these folk by now."

He rested his arm on the back of her chair and
leaned a bit closer. Laura was aware of the subtle mixed
aroma of cloth and leather that clung to him and the almost bitter citrus scent of the aftershave that fragranced
his cheeks.

"There is a little Rembrandt I want that's of particular
value," he confided. "It should be coming up the lot or
two after this."

While her mother and the earl chatted Penelope entertained herself by watching the people around her. So many lovely, slender legs she had never seen before in one place. High-heeled shoes with delicate straps around the ankles, skirts made of cashmere and fine, soft wools—and every variety of the cloche hat one could imagine, pulled down low on the brow: peaked and rounded, feathered or festooned with large silk flowers clustered over one ear. Hats were worn everywhere, all year round, no matter what the occasion. Penelope was secretly proud of the fact that her face and features lent themselves so well to this fashion. Besides, hats were such fun to wear. She noticed several women with bobbed hair like her own, and one girl whose black bob was more dramatically chopped, especially at the neckline, into the latest "shingled" style. It made her itch to go out and buy a new outfit, right down to the hat and shoes, to show off back home. Home. It wouldn't be long now. Her mother had found her lost relatives, something she had hardly dared hope for, and as the autumn days grew shorter and colder, she longed to return to what was familiar and known to her. Not so Penelope. She wished she could talk her mother into spending the winter in Italy, or even the south of France. She could travel like this for a long time, she knew, before she would tire of it, would long for the old securities. But then, she was young; she was not bound with such strong ties as her mother was to one place and one house, one pattern, one way of doing things. How grand to be young! She felt the thrill of it play along her skin. She sat up, perky and straight. She knew she looked as smart as most of the women around her—and besides, she sat by the earl. She had seen many eyes discreetly notice that. And such a handsome earl, too. Such a bright, bonny day to be alive and in Scotland. So Penelope concluded as the auction went on around her, and the web of circumstance tightened before her eyes.

———◆——

The earl did not get the costly Rembrandt; another titled gentleman outbid him. But during a gap in the bidding he managed to pick up a sleeper, a Whistler landscape he had noticed Laura admiring. Not everyone knew that Whistler, while an American, had done much of his work in England, where he was influenced by the Impressionist movement. When the soft little landscape made Laura draw in her breath and, unconscious of herself, lay her hand on the earl's arm, the earl proceeded to buy it in the confusion following a facedown by two major dealers who had driven their bids sky-high. While the crowd buzzed about it he got his piece for fifty pounds less than the presale estimate, and he was well satisfied.

"The Rembrandt was too dear for me," Thomas Forbes lamented. "If I'd have known Hailes would be here to bid against me I would not have even attempted it."

Dr. Robert Hailes, also ninth baronet of that name, had a great house in Fort William, as well as a thriving practice. Family money as well as a substantial income. And he was leaving the following morning to spend the next six months on the continent—wouldn't even be around to enjoy his acquisition.

"Too bad," the earl lamented, trying bravely to make light of his loss. "Rembrandts seldom come up in these parts. I may not get such a chance again for—" He raised a curved eyebrow at Laura and shook his head slightly. "Well, perhaps not again in my lifetime." He rubbed his hands together, dismissing the matter. "But be that as it may, what's done is done. Nothing a fine meal and a dram of good Scotch whiskey can't ease."

The Bentley was waiting. They slid into their seats, and the long car pulled noiselessly away. At once the commotion and confusion dropped behind them. All three were hungry after the tedious, confined hours. Laura had to admit that it was soothing after being alone with Penelope all these weeks to have a man, a gentle yet forceful man, to take charge.

———•◆•———

Corker had followed the Bentley that morning when it pulled out of the long drive heading west through town. He made Eddie drive while he sat hunched up in the passenger's seat cleaning his nails with his pocket-knife and swearing a blue streak. He was right, of course; there was nothing he and Eddie could do while the big earl was there. When he saw the crowd of affluent people packed elbow to elbow, he made Eddie turn around.

"Drive up in those mountains," he said. "We've got to have somewhere to take 'em once we nab 'em."

Eddie stared back at him blankly.

"We will nab 'em, dolthead!" he blared. Then he cuffed Eddie alongside the head, because the insolent set of his face had not altered, and Corker didn't like the look of him, especially the expression in his close-set pig's eyes.

"You got 'til the end of the week, Corker," Eddie said, obeying directions in spite of his defiant tone. "Your methods better work by then, or I'm trying my own."

Corker knew what Eddie's methods were, and that's why the boss had sent him tagging along. He was far more trigger-happy than Corker. He had a good aim and no heart, nothing to trouble him when he put a clean hole in somebody's skull and then walked away.

But these are such pretty skulls, Corker thought. *It would be a pity.* If he could just get their ears, get close to these gals for long enough to explain, he felt sure they'd be scared enough to do whatever he asked them. But he knew Eddie meant what he'd said; he knew the time that had seemed so long in the beginning had nearly run out.

———•◆•———

The front door was not locked. Glenda whistled under her breath at the luck of it. Most rich folk were dolts when it came to such stuff. She drew a deep breath and started up the long stairs at a brisk, jaunty pace; half skip, half run. That's the way that cute little American girl always did it wherever she went. Glenda had the voice down well enough, she thought, if she were to have to use it. That was a natural gift of hers, to be able to mimic others, imitate anything at all once she had heard it. It had served her well, as well as her beauty and what the Terrier called her "brass."

The trick would be in finding the girl's room quickly. No one appeared in the long stretch of the upstairs hall. She tried the door of one room, then a second—then another and, carefully, yet another. By now her fingers were trembling and moist. She switched to the other side, and the second door she tried revealed a lady's boudoir. She slipped gratefully inside.

This was the place, all right. With practiced efficiency she began to search, first the closet, then the standing wardrobe, then large drawers, the clothes box in the corner, the suit bags and trunks stacked neatly behind a silk screen. She could feel a thin layer of sweat at the back of her hairline. *Where could it be?* Hardly able to contain herself, she sprang for the inner door connecting this room to another, which was obviously used by the mother. Glenda repeated the same process here. She became a little more careless, a little more frightened as again she found nothing. For goodness sake, it had just been a simple tweed coat! Just her luck if the girl was wearing it again. Or had she found the ring and turned the whole thing in as evidence?

An unpleasant shiver ran through Glenda's body. She tried the less likely spots now. Nothing—nothing! She stood alone in the center of the room, trembling all over, aware suddenly of muffled sounds from the hall. It would do no good to be caught here, especially with the mess around her. She held her breath, pent-up and beating painfully in her chest. At last all was silent again. She slipped out, feeling heavy and awkward this time, trying hard to resume the carefree girlish gait she had come in with.

She had nearly reached the front door when a voice behind her said, "Miss Penelope, is that you, ma'am?"

She swallowed a moist, bitter taste in her throat and responded as her fingers closed over the doorknob, "I just forgot something. The others are waiting—" She turned slightly, half out of the door. "Bye for now."

That sounded American. She didn't wait to see if her accent and performance had been convincing. She headed across the lawn to a line of hedge tall enough to swallow her. In a few minutes more the chambermaid, standing wondering and perplexed, saw absolutely nothing at all.

Glenda didn't stop at the privet hedge. She didn't stop 'til she reached her own narrow, dark room and threw herself down on the bed. She was half-sick with fear, and her body was coated with sweat. "I'm done for," she kept mumbling over and over again. "I'm done for, that's sure."

She huddled there piteously, having nowhere to go and not knowing what she might do to avoid the inevitable reckoning that hung, black and ugly, above her head.

When they came back to the house, Laura's feet hurt and Penelope was sleepy with the food she had eaten.

"A nap is in order," the earl assured them. "I have business to attend to, but you ladies pamper yourselves." He winked at Penelope, whose return smile was grateful. That sounded luscious to her.

"I'll leave you here," he said as the car pulled up before the front entrance. "You instruct Janet, Penelope, as soon as you find her." He arched his fine brow. "And see to it your mother complies."

His voice was heavenly; it was his voice that charmed Penelope as much as anything else. It had a resonant timbre, yet it was not harsh. And the accent, the soft, rolling Scots accent, left her feeling silly and weak.

Once inside they headed up the hall to their own rooms and ran into Janet right there on the stairs.

"I've polished your shoes, miss," she smiled. "Left 'em outside your doorway. And you two going to have a wee rest?"

"Earl's orders," Penelope answered.

"Very good." Janet smiled with the almost conspiratorial kindness of another young girl. At the bottom of the stairs she turned sharply round again and called after them. "And oh, miss, I've taken your tweed jacket—the one that had the mud on the sleeve—and your knit coat, the rose one, out to be cleaned."

"Thank you, Janet." Penelope could get used to such cosseting, she feared, with alarming ease. She stooped to pick up the shoes that were lined up in front of her and opened the door.

"Your plan is in action, sir. First phase successfully completed." Hugh smiled.

"Yes. Thanks to the earl's cooperation."

"Thanks to the earl's brilliance," Hugh amended. "He seems an old hand with the ladies, and he handled our two splendidly, don't you think?" He grinned, trying to get MacGregor to grin back at him, but the inspector was solemn tonight.

"Do you think they'll take the bait? They've just got to, lad. We haven't much more time to play with, and that's the truth of it."

Hugh nodded. "Any more on the Terrier?"

"Not really."

"What about the Paris and Prague connections?"

MacGregor's face lightened a little. "We may just be closing in on our two suspects. I spoke with Thomas Howe this morning. He's sent a couple of his best detectives over there, speak French and Czech like natives."

"Do you think these two are our men?"

MacGregor pressed his fingertips against his broad temples. "I've got a hunch that they are, Fraser. And while the one may be French, I think the other is very probably German, or maybe even an Englishman working out of that country, perhaps under an alias. We have a few leads, a few ideas. If we could tie these two to our ladies . . ."

MacGregor attempted a smile, but it came out more of a grimace.

"You look tired, sir," Hugh said.

"Yes. Well, right. I believe that I am."

"A strong cup of tea and to bed. How does that sound, sir?"

Callum grimaced again. "See you bright and early, m'lad," he replied, dismissing Fraser. "It's a day on the pavement for you, entertaining our two pretties."

Hugh sighed. "This is a rough assignment, chief inspector, one of the roughest I've had."

"Off with you!" Callum waved him away, finally smiling, even chuckling a little as he heard the younger man whistle, the sound growing dimmer and dimmer as he disappeared down the long office hall.

———·•·———

Laura ran right into her daughter, for Penelope stopped cold after taking one step into the room. She had her hand to her mouth, looking wildly around her from side to side.

"What in the world?" Laura pushed past Penelope, then shrank close again, overwhelmed by the brazen disorder before her. "Who—what—" she stammered. "Penny, what can this mean?"

"I have no idea, Mother." Penelope moved woodenly, like one in a daze, and sat down on a nearby chair. "Someone terrible has done this thing. I can sense it. But who would search our rooms, Mother?"

"And for heaven's sake, why?"

A silence swallowed their words. Penelope felt bruised, as though someone had delivered an unexpected blow to stun her. Her mother was methodically checking closets, drawers and cupboards, the tall oak wardrobe, even the cabinets in the tiny bathroom they shared.

"I find nothing missing, Penny, no jewelry, nothing of value. Not even a tube of that gruesome lipstick you wear."

Poor Mother, Penelope thought. *She's trying to make light of it all.*

"Sit down, Mother," she said with some concern, "and try to relax." Deep inside something was beginning to gnaw at Penelope, a vague memory buried beneath days of travel and discovery, a myriad of impressions.

"I'm perfectly fine, dear. Don't worry. I just can't understand . . ."

With a cold tightness at her heart Penelope thought of the night before when she had gone out to the chemist's, when the stranger had accosted her. It could have been no one but a stranger, surely. It could not be connected to what had happened in here!

"Do you think Lord Forbes is in the house? We must tell someone, Mother."

"I don't know. Oh, he'll be shocked, Penny, really. He'll think we're—"

"He won't blame us!" Penelope knew well her mother's reactions by this time.

"I'll start to clean up the mess. You go and see who you can find."

<hr />

The earl was not at home. With Janet's indignant help they put the rooms to rights and then lay down to rest awhile. But neither could sleep. Laura's mind was cluttered with confusion. She had felt so safe here. She did not want that to change. Penelope wished to get to the earl first, without her mother, and tell him all. Then there was Hugh. Perhaps she ought to have Hugh speak to Lord Forbes as well.

They ate alone, in the small, usually sunny nook off the monstrous dining room. But the room was not sunny now. Just as it trapped the evening shadows, it seemed to trap their misery into a little hollow of grief. Neither ate much. Laura excused herself with a headache and went back to her room.

Penelope was restless. She walked out into the small, walled garden. Though darkness was draining the colors from the blossoms, the fragrances still were there. She was surprised at how many flowers still bloomed this late in the year. Gentians of several varieties bordered the paths at her feet: daisies, of all things, and tardy roses, and some white, delicate blossoms that hugged the tall hedge. In this gentle grayness the sky had not yet lost its glow, and a sifting peace settled over her troubled spirits.

She found the earl there, came upon him sitting in a shady corner, nearly screened from view by the slender, bowed branches of a willow.

"Please, sir. I am so glad to have found you! Something terrible has happened to us."

Penelope slid onto the seat beside him and told him her tale. He listened intently, his eyes clouding with concern. Gently he began to question her, taking her back to the beginning when they came across on the boat.

"We came across on the *Maureania*," she told him proudly. "It's a British liner launched in 1907 and holds the blue ribbon for crossing the Atlantic at a record breaking speed—twenty-seven knots, I believe."

The earl was watching her closely. "How do you know all this?"

"I read the brochure several times during the crossing, and I paid attention, since I had to continually reassure Mother that we were all right."

He made her go over her London days: where they had stayed and what they had done there. He knew the dealer from whom she had purchased the Morris Oxford.

"It was a wise purchase, wasn't it?" she urged, wishing him to admire her powers of reasoning and discernment. "It's a tight, dependable little car," she explained, "and I paid only 125 pounds, plus two pounds extra for a windscreen made of safety glass. We spend only shillings for gasoline. It's a wonder."

The earl knew that it was. He continued his questioning, but they seemed to be getting nowhere. Then she told him of the first dim impression she had buried away, of that day on Loch Lomond when they came back to their room and she had been aware of certain little differences—so small, she admitted, that she had thought she must be imagining them. But now this—and that night when Hugh Fraser saved her.

"Obviously someone thinks you have something," said the earl. "And it must be something very important, or they would not go to such pains."

Penelope agreed. But they still had no place to go from there.

"Go up to your room now," the earl advised, "and try to sleep. Put this out of your mind. Tomorrow I'll make inquiries. And meanwhile, this lad of yours—perhaps he could be persuaded to fill in as protector again." He winked at her and placed his large, warm hand on her head. "Not an unpleasant role, that, I'd say."

She felt much better as she walked back to the house, which sprawled before her like a long monster, scaled and gnarled, in the unsure light.

———•———

Maggie was decent. Maggie stood beside Glennie while the Terrier vented his anger, and kept her from harm.

"You'd be dead right now, 'cause you're worthless," Willie snarled at her. "But the boss wants one more job done, and we've found the perfect setup. A fella bought a very nice Rembrandt at auction today. Nice fella, taking his family to Europe tomorrow, be away for six months."

"Tonight then?" Glenda's voice was dry in her throat.

"Naw, we'll give 'em one more night just to be sure they're out of there, in case the place might be watched"—he ran his moist tongue over his pale lips—

"and to make our own plans." He looked straight at Glenda, his whole face a snarl. He made a fist and held it out to her. She could see, scratched into his arm, the wiry black terrier, all lines and squiggles, and the limp body of a rat dangling from his jaws. "You get the picture, don't you, sweetheart? No more room for mess-ups from you. You do your job and you do it fast, and you get outta there. Right?"

"Then we're out of this place so fast," Maggie crooned, "they'll be chasin' their tails round in circles wonderin' where we've gone."

She laughed out loud. Willie laughed with her and licked his moist lips. But neither would look directly at Glenda, and it made her insides go cold.

"Who's got the tickets?" she asked pointedly.

"All in good time. What is it to you? You got no brains—you got no rights." The Terrier spoke from far back in his throat, and his voice was low and silken. That was worse than if he had shouted at her and called her bad names.

After a few minutes more the two of them left her, going out arm in arm. It wasn't hard to imagine what they'd be doing for the rest of the evening. But Glenda had nowhere to go. She had her orders, and she'd better do those things precisely, and nothing else. She had wanted to try again for the ring, but they wouldn't let her. She wondered if they'd even believed what she said she had done with it. Did they think she was holding out on them? Even she wasn't stupid enough to try that.

She pulled her knees up and sat rocking back and forth, back and forth on the divan, her fingers playing with the thin gold chain at her throat.

10

MACGREGOR MET WITH HUGH FRASER EARLY IN THE MORNING, before the sun had burned the thick mists away. The cold was moist and therefore chilling, but it invigorated Callum. The tangles of police work at times wove cobwebs inside his head. The mist, like those cobwebs, curled in gray swirls around his feet. But the far mountain peaks rose clear and free, and the mere sight of them was a balm to his mind.

He almost envied Fraser his freedom of movement, his youth, his openness. He had been caught up these past days coordinating men and movements, receiving reports that were most often meaningless, trying to piece together the bits and snatches of information that came to him, discard the superfluous and find a place for the rest—to peg each into its little slot like a piece in a puzzle. But this latest—this latest that had come from Lord Forbes had him completely stumped.

He laid it all out for Fraser, who kept shaking his head as he listened.

"It makes no sense at all. In the first place, if it's Willie or other members of the group they've been working with, they'd use rougher means and they'd find what they were looking for, or that would be that."

"That first time by the lochside," Callum reminded him, "it was I, you recall, who went through their rooms. I found nothing, and if the girl's telling the truth"—he snorted at his own words—"whoever got into the castle to search was unsuccessful as well."

"But why would they tell the earl? Do they believe they might solicit his protection in some real way? Do they need it?"

"Perhaps they do." Callum was thoughtful. "Perhaps they are in no way onto us, have no idea at all that they're being watched or monitored or suspected."

Hugh shook his head once, emphatically. "I find that hard to believe."

"So do I. But let's just say that's the way of it."

"All right, let's. Even then, they would not wish us to know something as unnatural and disturbing as an intruder searching their rooms."

"Could they really believe they have the poor earl fooled hook, line, and sinker? He doesn't appear that gullible to me, Fraser. Does he to you?"

"Not hardly, sir." Hugh smiled apologetically. "Perhaps they have some vendetta of their own against their fellow conspirators. Maybe it has something to do with that ring."

"But if they exposed any link of the chain, they'd expose themselves, too."

"Maybe they don't care. Maybe they want to see these guys snuffed out and they'll take their own comeuppance and hope for clemency."

"True." Callum ruminated a moment. "I'd like to

know where that ring is right now. I wish it would turn up somewhere!"

"If that's what they're searching their rooms for, if that's why the young one got bullied in the street, why in the world would our ladies hang on to it?"

"Perhaps that's the crux of it." Callum stood and began to pace the room in long strides. "Perhaps they did double-cross their friends and fence the gem elsewhere."

"That would explain a few things. They can't give it up to the toughs, and they can't explain what they've done with it."

Callum paused, deep in thought. "Blast it, lad, that doesn't explain how they do it. How they appear so innocent, so—"

"You're telling me! And I've a whole day of it in front of me, Inspector. That Penelope! In truth, sir, sometimes I wonder . . ."

"We're not paid to wonder, lad." MacGregor's big voice was laced with an understanding that pleased Hugh. "Just keep doing your job. Especially now. Will you be with the young one all day?"

"Aye, that I will. And I'm to meet you tonight at Fort William?"

"No, there'll be a guard on the house. I think they'll be cautious and not strike this first night. Don't worry."

"In other words, have a good time with the lovely Penelope."

MacGregor grinned finally. "That's right."

———————

Hugh did have a good time. He enjoyed every moment of the long, agreeable day. It was easy to pretend they were off on a lark together, exploring ruins, riding round the islands on a ferryboat with the cold spray numbing their faces and wetting their hair. At first he tried to draw her out, and she wasn't unwilling. It was simply that she was—what? Too curious? Too interested in the things around her to keep the attention tuned to herself? They laughed together. He taught her Scottish songs. And they were silent together, something he didn't believe he could be with a little snippet of an art thief. The wind in her hair, the scent of her skin, the sound of her laughter—this was breaking his heart! He tried to steel himself, but she was so open and artless, so—the word *naive* came to him. But how could she be? He struggled to remind himself of all of which this young woman was capable; he tried to think solemn thoughts. His efforts wore him out, but they were not successful. She was a professional; he had to admit that much, at least to himself.

———————

Laura had been happy to let Penny go. She spent the day in quiet comfort by the earl's fireside, listening to the chatter of the household servants, washing and mending, and reading a little on and off, to spell her more mundane tasks. It would have been nice to write postcards home, but she could not quite pretend, not quite side-step yesterday's horror and pen the usual things. It had distressed her when Penny reported her conversation with Lord Forbes the evening before. Somehow she had expected him to know how to take care of it, to have all the answers for her. With a sense of unease she recognized the pattern: That's how she had been all her life. She had never questioned Gerald concerning his responsibilities nor thought of them as burdens; he did what was expected of him, just as she did what was expected of her. How terribly isolated. How lonely. Had he felt the same way, locked in his own vacuum? Had he died feeling lonely? The question troubled her mind and laid a depression upon her spirit.

At teatime, midday, she found her way down to the kitchens, where the housemaids welcomed her and cleared a place for her to sit down. After a few moments of sipping her hot Postum she noticed for the first time an old lady seated in a chair by the fire. She rocked back and forth, steadily, rhythmically, looking at no one and nothing at all.

"That's me grandmither," Janet said. "She bides with me and does a little needlework for his lordship."

The old lady turned at the sound of the young voice, and her eyes sought its source.

Janet smiled. "Shall I warm up yer tea, Granny?" She scampered over and poured fresh, hot brew into the half-empty cup.

Laura moved her chair close and began to speak to the woman, who responded in a low, musical voice, so thickly accented that Laura had to listen carefully, and even then she was lucky to catch two words in three. As she began to tell Laura about herself, Laura forgot the language barrier and moved close enough that their skirts brushed, that she might be able to hear every word. *So similar the stories of these simple people,* she thought as she listened. *Suffering and patience, sorrow and fortitude repeated time after time.*

". . . So when my father was lost at sea my mither went into service, became cook's assistant at first, but she was a rare one, me mither, and did not stay there for long. At length the great lady herself requested my mither for her personal handmaid, and that's when our fortunes rose."

Laura smiled. "What was the great lady's name?" she asked.

"Sarah MacGregor, lived near here, above Fort William. Lost her husband, too, in the king's service."

"I have a Sarah MacGregor in my line," Laura replied. "She had three daughters: one named Sarah, after herself, one named Anne, and one named Laura." She smiled at the birdlike intensity of the frail woman's gaze. "The one named Laura became my grandmother."

"They sound like one and the same. Did your grandmother leave Scotland as a young lass?"

"Yes, she took a ship to America with her new husband."

The old woman nodded sharply and clapped her hands together. "They must be one and the same! My mither knew her, said she was her favorite of the girls, and it was a black day for everyone when she went away."

Laura leaned back against her chair for support. How could this be? A stranger in a great man's kitchen in Scotland revealing treasures to her? She lowered her head. "It is too good to be true," she whispered. But she lifted her gaze and went on. "My grandmother spoke seldom about her family," she explained, "and she kept no records at all."

"That was the way of it," the old lady replied, nodding slowly. "Too painful to think back to an unhappy family who had forbidden their leaving, as Laura's mother did hers."

"Yes, that was it, I'm sure." The melancholy that had been with Laura all day threatened to suffocate her. She attempted to smile. "But she did tell the stories and legends of Scotland," she said softly. "You see, I grew up on her stories of ghaisties and silkies, of lost armies and princes." She could no longer keep the tears from her eyes. "It was really my grandmother's stories that brought me here."

The old lady lifted her hand and placed it gently over Laura's, and no word passed between them for a long, quiet time. "Do you know anything about the family?" Laura asked at length. "Anything about my grand-mother's people?"

"Aye, dearie, some. I know who the other girls married and a little of what happened to them. I know that Sarah, with her husband dead those many long years, went back to live with her own people, the MacDonalds, spending her last days with a maiden sister, I believe, rather than one of her daughters."

"MacDonald?" An instant warmth spread through Laura's body, and she could feel her pulse quicken.

"Aye, that's right. She was a MacDonald by birth."

"Then I have MacDonald blood in me," Laura mused, "though it is from far back."

"That matters not," her new friend countered. "For the blood may run strong in one person and weak in the next. And what the blood dictates determines the will, sometimes the course, of one's life."

Laura knew now, with a sudden quickening inside her, why it had been that her heart had responded with such anguish to the ordeal the MacDonalds suffered in the Pass of Glencoe. So long ago, and yet her spirit had felt it, and understood.

She realized suddenly that the kitchen was silent; all the servants had gone. The fire burned cozily, and dear little Janet, before slipping away, had filled both their cups to the brim.

The grandmother, watching her, grinned. "Aye, we two can sit awhile longer, lass, if ye like."

Laura wished to; she was gladdened at the prospect. She pulled her chair a bit closer to the fire and picked up her cup.

Laura had hoped Penelope would be home in time for supper, and was not altogether pleased when she called to say that she would be dining in town with this young Fraser and then going to the pictures afterward. *I have enjoyed a good day,* Laura reminded herself. But after eating her solitary meal a restlessness came over her; she could not settle down to any quiet activity. She tried to sew, write letters, look through the latest magazines—she even attempted a book—not the D. H. Lawrence novel Penny had left on her bed, cover down, knowing her mother did not approve. But neither Jane Austen nor Mrs. Gaskell, nor certainly Charles Dickens, could hold her interest tonight. She decided to walk down to the library in search of something different that might tempt her mind.

As she reached the bottom of the stairs she heard the first faint strains of music, which grew loud and full-voiced as she approached the room. She hesitated for a moment on the threshold. It sounded like a Chopin étude, but she couldn't be sure.

"Come in," a voice said. "How may I assist you?" The earl sat with his feet to the fire and a book in his lap.

"Oh, no—I had no idea you were here," Laura stammered. "I don't wish to disturb you."

"You shan't disturb me," Lord Forbes replied softly. "My thoughts are gloomy tonight." He turned and smiled at her. "So, you see, you interrupt nothing of any moment. Please, do come inside."

Laura came slowly, gliding like a bashful young girl, and the demure manner which was natural to her suited her well. In the dim light cast by the fire and one small tableside lamp, she appeared wraithlike and vulnerable, and younger than her years. Lord Forbes felt it, and shuddered at the sensations it drew from him. He indicated a chair close to his and said, "Come, sit down."

She sat on the edge, tucking her legs beneath her, and together they listened to the music as it welled from the gramophone. Then he asked quite suddenly, "Tell me about your day."

Laura began hesitantly but after a few moments forgot to be tense and shy as she was caught up in the excitement of her discovery, of the gentle wisdom of Janet's old grandmother, of the wonder at strands which connect people to each other, no matter how great the separations of distance and time.

"Do you believe in that?" she asked the earl. "Do you believe that the ties of blood can speak loudly to the spirit and influence one's heart?"

He was silent for a moment. When he answered, his voice was hesitant and low. "It is too strong to deny, though it is past our finite ability to understand or explain. We Scots have always expressed it this way." He quoted the lines. "'From the lone shieling of the misty island, mountains divide us, and the waste of seas; yet still the blood is strong, the heart is Highland, and we in dreams behold the Hebrides.'"

There were tears in her eyes. She brushed them quickly away with the back of her hand.

"You've come for a book, have you?" he asked, kindly providing an escape route. "Let me show you what we have here."

Together they walked the length of the room and back again, pausing now and again as they perused the seemingly endless volumes stacked inside the tall shelves. As well as novels past and current there was history—English, European, and Asian. There was an entire shelf of science books, with pages closely written and technical in nature. There were books on world religions and social customs, volumes on art and art history, and books of philosophy. Laura pointed out several of Emerson's proudly set out next to Carlyle.

"Did you know they were great friends, the two of them?" the earl asked her.

She had not known. She knew so little. Not until Penny began taking classes at the university did her own mind seem to wake up. Perhaps that was Penny's doing more directly than she had realized. But slowly she became interested, then intensely curious about a variety of things. It began to horrify her that she had been so many years content with cookbooks and the latest women's magazines. The depth of her ignorance frightened her more than she let on, even to Penny. When her daughter came home rattling off her excitement about the things she was learning, Laura took mental notes. She began to read the books Penny recommended; she began to get books on her own. But all that had ended with Gerald's death; Gerald's death froze something within her and seemed to put her whole life on hold.

What life? she thought. *Remember, Laura, you must make a new and different life now.*

"You are thinking about something very deep and very distressing." The gentle voice seemed to come from a distance. "What is it?" The earl placed his large, firm hand on her arm.

"Only what a different person I am now that my husband is dead."

The earl said nothing. He was studying her carefully. Beneath his penetrating gaze she felt strangely warm and strangely alive.

"He died very recently?"

"Yes."

"My wife died not long ago."

"Did you love her terribly?" It sounded a naive question, or else a cold, unthinking one.

"Yes, I did. And since she died young, well, there is nothing to destroy the perfection of that love and that joy."

"Too much reality," Laura said softly. "Too much of the everyday kind of reality, that's what you escaped."

"Yes. I've known that for a long time. It is the only advantage, the one blessing in death I can find."

"There are compensations, if not blessings, in other stages," she responded. "Opportunities for growth, I suppose one might call them." She attempted to smile, but her mouth formed into a sad, misshapen little thing that trembled as she continued to speak. "Painful, though. Such things are so painful, I find."

Lord Forbes sighed and removed his hand from her arm, and she sensed his frustration at her sorrow. "Do you have children?" she asked.

He told her of his son who lived in London, another who was stationed in Africa, and another who was an accountant in Aberdeen. Then, to her own surprise, she told him about Peter. It was only a brief, terse telling, but since his death she had spoken of her son to no one. Those who knew Peter knew he had died, and did not need to be talked to. These friends respected her privacy and her grief. If at times her pain had reached out for expression, she pushed those feelings aside, reburied them beneath new layers of suffering.

Lord Forbes listened, the tips of his fingers pressed against one another, his gentle eyes dark. "Hundreds, thousands—" His voice was rough with emotion. "Why, hundreds of thousands of boys died in that war. But each was precious! Each the *only one* to someone! I'm so sorry," he sighed. "So terribly sorry." He reached for her hand and sat stroking it, silently comforting her.

Penelope found them that way. She froze at the sight before they looked up and saw her, and the magic crumbled, and they were merely two people again, asking with forced brightness about her evening, and had the movie been good? *Orphans of the Storm*—yes, it had been smashing. And he had bought her ice cream and—she wanted to add, he had kissed her as they stood at the door, a little kiss, really, merely a gentle pressing of his lips over hers. But it had made her heart flutter like a small bird inside her and her head had felt light, and she had thought it the most breathless, romantic moment she had ever had . . . until she came here and stumbled upon their silence and upset a spell she could only sense, but was wise enough to know she could not understand.

11

LAURA WAS ADAMANT. SHE WANTED TO SEE FORT WILLIAM AND the area around it—land where her fathers and mothers had lived. The stories of Janet's old grandmother, Mary, had bit deep into her heart, exposing an emptiness, a hollow that she must fill with her own experience—the touch of her own senses, and nothing less. The morning was raw, and a chill wind blew the mist into swirls and weird shapes that were never still. They left early, without telling a soul; they crept out of the house, despite Penelope's protestations.

"Please, let's take Hugh Fraser along. He's a good, quiet lad, Mother, and could help me with the driving. The day's so gloomy and dark!"

"No." Laura was unusually quiet. "This must be just the two of us. We can manage quite well." Her words were terse, but in her voice was a confidence, a note of authority Penelope could not remember ever hearing before.

They took the road from Oban to Ballachulish. "There will be a ferry there," Laura explained, "which will take us over Loch Leven to Fort William and save us oodles of time."

Penelope said nothing but did as her mother instructed. After a few miles she asked tentatively, "What shall we do once we reach Fort William?"

Laura was ready with a quick, succinct answer. "Go a few miles further on the A831 to a place called Glenfinnan."

"And what in the world might that be?"

"The spot where Charles Stuart landed—the Young Pretender, they called him. He gathered the clans there, those Highlanders who were willing to help him regain his crown."

"What was the year?"

"1745."

"Where did you learn all this?"

A bit of a smile crept into Laura's voice. "It's only in every guidebook you lay your hands on, Penny. But actually, it was Mary who told me. And did you know that the monument there was erected by a MacDonald in 1815—grandson of a MacDonald who was one of the Prince's first supporters when he set foot on this soil?"

"And you must see it?"

"That's right."

They drove in silence under a lowering sky. A quarter of a mile behind them a gray car followed, a long, sporty model. And a scant few yards behind him another car, dingy in color and nondescript. But it stayed on the tail of the sports car with unerring accuracy.

Hugh phoned Callum from a booth outside the office where tickets for the ferry were purchased. First he made sure that the little green Morris was safely over the gangway and onto the boat.

"You're tailing them!" MacGregor growled. "Why aren't you with them?"

"They didn't invite me along." Hugh laughed to cover an awkward sense of embarrassment or failure, or something he could not quite define. "Left the earl's house before the sun had fair risen."

"Was their purpose to lose you?" Callum had grown thoughtful.

"I don't rightly know. What would you like me to do? I could always happily run into them and—"

"No, that would be too obvious. They have reasons for what they're doing. Perhaps it would be wisest to keep to your present course; perhaps you could learn more that way now."

"Right, sir."

"Can you check back in a few hours?"

"I'll certainly try. Depends where these two loony ladies are heading, and just what they happen to be up to."

"Well, do what you can, Fraser, and look sharp."

"Right, sir."

Hugh hung up the receiver and walked back to his car, which he had parked discreetly in the bushes several yards from the roadside. It was going to be tricky trying to take the same ferry as the ladies. Perhaps he ought to risk it and take the next. Only a few minutes would separate them; he ought to be able to pick up their trail. No, perhaps it would be best to simply inform the pilot and take measures to obscure his car, cover it with a tarp or something, and keep out of sight during the crossing. He felt good about that.

He walked slowly, deliberating on his plan of action. He heard nothing at all. The blow Eddie delivered to his skull cracked with a sickening sound, and he slumped to the ground. The two men dragged him the few remaining feet to his automobile and sat him inside, tying his feet together and his hands securely behind his back.

"That oughta keep him for a while," Corker grunted. "What say we get a move on it so that ferry don't leave us behind?"

———•••———

The sense of eeriness only grew stronger as they crossed the gray loch. The flat, beetle-like boat was worked by two men who spoke back and forth to one another in the soft Gaelic tongue, more foreign-sounding than German or Italian but strangely sweet, harboring a vague sense of rhythm and melody; the sensation of song.

They stood alone, looking down at the water, slipping black and oily away from them. Suddenly to their senses came the awareness of slender black shapes moving just below the surface of the water.

"Seals," Laura said. She reached her hand out, and just then one surfaced and arched his handsome head close to the boat. His eyes, black and unfathomable, gazed at them for long, quiet seconds; in their gaze Laura could feel the loneliness of all men who had ever lived—and the dark, voiceless loneliness of ancient and unmarked times.

Then, soundlessly, he slid under the water and disappeared from their sight. To speak would have been irreverent. They stood clasping hands, waiting and watching, but the graceful seal did not resurface again.

"Perhaps he was a silkie," Laura said in all seriousness, "sent to greet us, to guide us, even. Some people hold such things to be true."

"A sealman, like in the old legends?" Penelope spoke softly and carefully.

"Yes, a sealman, like in the stories my grandmother told."

———◆———

There was quite a queue of cars maneuvering their way off the ferry. Penelope was glad to feel the sensation of solid ground beneath her tires again. As they approached Fort William she asked, "Shall we stop here for something to eat, Mother?"

"No, it's a bit too early, and I want to get on to Loch Shiel. The sky looks terribly threatening, and I'd like to see the monument before a storm hides our view."

They drove the seventeen miles past Fort William wrapped in that same strange silence they had felt on the boat. The pine trees were a green gloom in the distance, and strange rocks rose up from the colorless moors like enchanted men. The autumn colors were deep, moist stains in the landscape of mottled browns and grays.

Penelope pulled off the road at the head of the loch and parked the green car in the visitor's section, graveled and marked off for vehicles. Then together they began the long walk across a boggy morass to the head of the loch and the lighthouse-like tower that rose, pencil thin, into the still mountain air. There was no other sign of man in this bleak and beautiful landscape. The monument was surrounded by a low stone wall. They sat on its uneven surface and looked out across the broad silver water and the black mountains that flanked it, layer upon layer on either side, pressing the water into a narrow pathway that led out to the sea. The sense of what lay beyond was a mystery that hummed in the air.

As they looked, a ray of light broke through the thick clouds and fractured in golden-white splendor across the sky, lighting a pathway along the water that sparkled like gems. Soft and yet startling, the pale light trembled, then disappeared, and shadows reclaimed the water and the low, stretching hills. The air was still. There was no sound but the high whisper of leaves in the wind. The peace of the place was hypnotic, and ancient, and deep.

———•·•———

Corker and Eddie pulled their car to a stop just beyond the little green car and set to work. It would be easy to immobilize the engine by pulling a wire or two. But they wanted more than that, they wanted the car to be seriously out of commission. A hole in the radiator and two slashed tires were a good beginning. But that was the furthest they got. Several cars and a bus pulled up in quick succession, and they were suddenly surrounded with people. They slunk back quickly to their own vehicle and pretended to be busy with maps and camera inside.

"It's a bunch o' school kids," Corker observed. "They shouldn't stay long. We'll wait 'til our ladies are done and these dopes have cleared out." He grinned, and his long nose narrowed and looked sharp as a stick. "Then we'll offer them help with their car, won't we, Eddie? And a ride into town."

Eddie said nothing. This work was driving him crazy. There was no action at all. Corker was too soft. If he'd been in charge, this all would have been over and done with days ago and they'd be heading back home.

"It's gonna rain," he griped. "First thing I get back to the States I'm gonna buy me a ticket to Florida and spend a whole week doin' nothin' but sittin' on the beach in the sun."

———•·•———

Andrew Ross was a tall, spare man with a low, pleasant voice. He had been teaching school for nearly thirty years, and parents fought to get their boys in his class. He stood now outside the Prince's monument, with a ring of bright-faced, attentive students who knew what was expected of them and were glad to comply. He was fairly into his little talk about Charlie and the Rebellion before he noticed the two women huddled close on the wall, watching him with large eyes and taking in his words with rapt attention. He paused and smiled.

"Come closer, please, ladies, and welcome. That is, if you are interested." Mr. Ross knew they were interested; he'd been a teacher too long.

Laura moved with a swiftness that surprised Penelope. "Thank you," she said.

Andrew Ross nodded graciously, and the well-trained boys did their best to refrain from staring at the ladies, especially the young pretty one.

"Picture Charlie rowing a small boat across the loch with only two quiet, rather unsure companions. In his prince's heart he had expected to find the low shore crowded with men. But there were none save a few MacDonalds, patient and silent, awaiting him."

Laura smiled at Penny, a candid, childlike smile that went straight to her heart.

"The gulls wheeled overhead, breaking the silence as Charlie paced the watery shore. Two long hours he waited in the stillness—then came the sound of pipes, and from the sides of the hills ran the gentle Lochiel and his Camerons."

Penelope whispered to Laura. "You mean there were Camerons, too? Your people certainly came out strong for the Stuarts."

As the eloquent schoolteacher went on to describe the men and their banners and the brave, noble words they uttered, Laura's thoughts turned away . . . to the women who waited in the high mountain shielings, who would bear the price of Charlie's dreams and Charlie's battles in their own bitter ways. All the glory . . . and all the heartache.

"Would you like to go with us to the top of the tower?" Mr. Ross was standing over her.

"Is it far?" Laura asked.

"Not far, and not difficult. And I'll be right there to assist you."

So they climbed the steep, winding stair inside the column, eighty feet to the top. Andrew Ross went before and helped her through the small opening. She found herself on the top, standing beside the kilted figure of Charlie, looking out to the sea. Just then a thin rain began falling, really little more than a mist which wet their faces with the soft impression of tears.

"He was like a boy playing a romantic game," she sighed.

"Yes, he was, and he forced or cajoled many to play with him, despite the high odds."

Laura shuddered as a gust of wind tore at her scarf and found its way inside her wrappings. She didn't like to think of that time, despite all the grand sentiment. The fate of those men and their families—the wretched fate of Scotland after that day.

Mr. Ross stood watching her with sad, gentle eyes. "Aye, they suffered more than their prince did." He sighed. "They're suffering still."

12

THEY WALKED BACK THROUGH THE MARSHLAND, NOW PUDDLED and sodden, with the teacher, talking quietly together, his boys trailing behind. When Eddie saw them he swore roundly and was all for bolting out of the stuffy, steamy car, making his way to the bushes, taking a couple of long shots, and ending the whole thing right there.

"We can't get close to these dames! It's freaky, Corker, ain't it?"

Corker, his eyes on the figures, hazy through the rain and fog, nodded shortly. "We'll have our chance." He punched Eddie's arm, half in jest, half in anger. "Ya got no patience, that's your trouble, Eddie."

Because the conversation was too good to let go of, Mr. Ross walked his new friends to their car, and while Penelope set about starting the Morris the boys piled into their bus. After several attempts all three realized suddenly that something was wrong. Andrew Ross lifted the bonnet, rain pouring from his hat brim, and peered inside. It took him a while to notice the hole in the radiator.

Meanwhile, Penelope, prowling from side to side, discovered the flaccid, useless tires.

"What has happened?" she cried, a sudden constriction making her throat ache and her nerves tremble.

"This is most strange." Mr. Ross muttered the words, his hands in his pockets. "If I didn't know better I'd say this looks like foul play."

"Yes, it does," Penelope admitted, fighting a sudden longing to cry.

"Then we are well met," he cried, "and I was right to hazard Glenfinnan on such a threatening day."

That was the end of it. He hustled them onto the bus, taking no excuses. "I must get the boys back to school," he apologized, easing the unwieldy machine over the wet, crackling gravel. "But if you can bear to wait there a short while with me, I'll take you back to my place, where you can warm your bones by the fire." He looked at them sharply. "Have you had tea?"

They were forced to admit that they had not, and Penelope, with true loyalty, demurred placing the blame on her mother, where it surely should be.

"We will be fine," Laura insisted. "You may drop us off in Fort William and we can find a place to stay for the night."

He would not hear of it. "I know a respectable garage where they'll drive out and tow your Morris, though I'm sure it can't be repaired 'til tomorrow."

Despite herself, Penelope sighed. If only her mother had let her bring Hugh Fraser along for help and protection, they wouldn't be in such a stew now. She missed him. Up there on the top of that statue, looking out over the whole world spread under her feet, she had wanted to see the way his eyes looked at her, see the lift of his mouth that made him look as if he might break any moment into faint, gentle laughter. His voice was low and he spoke his words slowly, but that same hint, that same murmur of laughter ran through them, too.

"Mr. Ross, please," her mother was saying. "We dare not impose on you further."

"But you are not imposing at all. I'm a simple old bachelor. I rattle around in a house that has room for a dozen children. Please allow me to share it with you for one night."

What could Laura say further? His sincerity was transparent, his motives the kindest, and his Scottish accent disarming in the extreme. Both women relaxed and allowed him to carry them whithersoever he deemed wisest, in perfect trust.

Hugh was uncertain how he arrived there, but the familiar pillow beneath his head felt good. He remembered awakening, his muscles cramped and in agony, his head bursting with a pain that was nearly unbearable. He must have fainted again and was only dimly aware of gentle hands lifting and moving him, of the long, uncomfortable ride, of the bright lights in the hospital that seemed to pierce right through his head. He winced now as he attempted to ease his position.

"You should have stayed in that hospital room," a voice growled at him, "with the concussion you had. But you gave everyone fits, like a spoiled child, until I promised to bring you back here." Callum jerked his head to indicate the back of the room. "There's a nurse standing by. For the next twenty-four hours at least." He placed a big hand on Hugh's arm. "Can you tell me, lad, what happened at all?"

"I have no idea. I walked back to my car after calling

you—I think I must have been walking still when I got hit from behind."

Callum nodded. "There were no signs of a struggle. But someone had obviously dragged you through the dirt and bushes to your car." He raised an arched eyebrow. "What of our ladies?"

"They were safely on board the ferry. I watched them myself."

"I don't mean to indicate that they did this to you. 'Twas too heavy a blow. But might they have been implicated? Might they have been traveling in consort, or met someone at the ferry?"

"I saw nothing suspicious at all—nothing, I tell you! And I watched carefully, MacGregor."

"Easy, lad," Callum soothed, patting the fevered arm. "You get some rest now, you hear? We've got the Hailes's place ringed with men, both inside and out. We can only assume—and hope—that that's where they're headed tonight. We're not going to let that Rembrandt get away."

He rose from the chair where he had been seated, while Hugh struggled to reply. "I want to be there!" he said through clenched teeth.

"I know, lad." MacGregor sounded gentle, almost fatherly. " 'Tis a tough break indeed. But I'll cover you. That's where I'm headed right now."

Hugh watched the older man walk from the room, leaving only a dull, ringing emptiness behind. Could it be true? Could his seemingly guileless Penelope have betrayed him this way? Beguiled him into . . . With cruel honesty he forced himself to laugh at his own ignorance and blindness. *I saw what I wanted to see. I saw something more, so much more than was there.*

He let his head sink into the pillow and closed his eyes. He had to convince himself that Penelope was noth-

ing more than a thief and a liar, a coarse and vulgar
woman who deceived him—or else he would go mad.

———•◆•———

Some cities may nestle up against gentle mountains,
but Fort William crouches at the foot of rugged Ben
Nevis, the highest peak in the British Isles. This landscape appealed to the restlessness in Laura. The rain had
continued to fall for the rest of the day. The earth gushed
water; new crevices and gullies scored the sides of the
hills, and the bare boulders wore a sheen on them like
brown glass.

Laura stood in the schoolteacher's garden and
watched the sun set. There would come such an un-
earthly glow in Scotland at the ending of day: a blue
light, deep and warming, lit from behind with the gold
that would soon burnish its hue and claim the whole expanse of the sky. The sun burned itself out in an intense
fire of red and amber above Ben Nevis. And in the stillness that followed, Laura felt an uneasy fear, a thrill of
fear, almost of expectation. She thought of the cold,
sleek silkie with the great, sad eyes. She thought of the
strange things that were happening to them, the unknown dangers her mind could sense. All seemed
clouded. She had no understanding, no answers, only
these feelings that were nearly too strong to bear.

She walked back into the house. "Did you phone the
earl, Penny?"

"I couldn't get ahold of him. Janet answered the
phone and apparently he's gone off for the duration; she
doesn't know when he'll be back."

"Well, at least they know where we are, so they won't
worry."

"Yes, Mother. Are you all right?"

Laura smiled. She was, strangely, all right. She had never felt more alive. The stirrings within her, though mysterious, even painful, had an exhilarating effect on her mind, on her entire system.

Andrew Ross came through the doorway.

"We're dining at my favorite restaurant tonight," he announced. "My treat."

Laura was glowing and gracious, but Penelope was despondent. She felt the change in her mother, as well as her own uncertainties and fears. What in the world were they doing? And was there really someone after them? When the Morris got fixed tomorrow and they drove back to the earl's house, then what?

Perhaps her mother had been right. They had gleaned all they possibly could from their sojourn in Scotland. Perhaps they ought to go home. Right away. But if they did that, what about Hugh Fraser? What if she never saw him again?

Oh, why does it matter? she asked herself angrily. *Nothing in Scotland is real. It is all like a sad, sweet dream that we must turn our backs on and leave behind.*

———◆———

Part of the Terrier's plans had been to send Maggie ahead to more or less case out the joint. She was an old hand at such matters and, through a series of leading questions and false starts of her own, was able to draw out an amazing amount of information. Servants are usually bored—and they usually welcome a good excuse to talk.

The baronet's house stood, somewhat isolated, on a wooded rise outside Fort William. Maggie had gone there alone, driven several times round the area and then the estate, after which she proceeded to explore the grounds more closely on foot. She had a long history behind her and she knew well what to look for by now. Not far from the main house stood a small stone cottage with a long screened veranda which, she guessed, was used for summer parties and, therefore, would have a large kitchen and basement cellar as well. Following that hunch, it was easy to contrive a story; one of several varieties she'd already used before.

Dressed as a middle-class woman hoping for better things, she went round to the service entrance and knocked at the door. It took her no time at all to engage the upstairs maid in conversation, for Maggie had gauged the time of day when the girl's tasks would be lightest, having done service in over a dozen households herself. In fact, she asked for the upstairs maid particularly, grateful to find the girl young and inexperienced.

"You see, my mither worked at this house when she was a young lass herself," Maggie explained. "She spoke fondly of it. But, of course, that was before I was born."

She went on to speak of her mother's sad death from tuberculosis and of her own struggles alone in the world. After a while the girl poured tea for both of them, and they sat in the cook's warm kitchen and grew quite chummy.

"Is there still a secret passageway of sorts from here to that summerhouse in back?" she asked, acting on her hunch.

"Aye, 'tis," the upstairs maid readily responded.

Maggie smiled in a conspiratorial manner. "The tales my old mum used to tell!" She leaned closer. "There was a kitchen maid in her time who would entertain lovers there. Bold as brass, she was!"

The girl nodded, her eyes sparkling with her own untold tales.

Maggie lowered her voice even further. "And then there was the time when the lady of the house . . ."

Twenty minutes and half a dozen scandals later Maggie had been shown the entrance, then escorted through the famous passage to the infamous tryst setting itself. She had learned all she needed to, and more. This last heist would be a breeze.

She eased herself away from the young maid's attentions, profuse in her thanks, falling back on her confusion and humility, and leaving the girl feeling good about herself and her kindness to the poor, strange woman who had wandered into her life.

Aye, Maggie was a clever lass if there ever was one. All things were in readiness now. And the black, murky night made their job even easier. This job should go smooth as icing, and then they were through. That thought hung in the back of their minds like a bright prize drawing them onward, but a prize they dare not gaze at too closely—not yet.

13

CALLUM WAITED UNTIL DARK TO POSITION HIS MEN AROUND the house, in case the thieves or any of their conspirators happened to be keeping their own watch. He was generous in his assessment of how many men might be needed; he situated them at all strategic points, inside and out: doors and openings of any kind, accessible windows, beside trees and bushes that stood in shadows and might be used to conceal.

He himself sat in his car beneath the black shade of the tall trees that lined the front drive. Here he had scope of vision and freedom of movement; he preferred that to being confined to one spot, either inside or out. To sit and wait; every muscle, every sense taut in expectation; that was the difficult part. But never more difficult than now, picturing Laura and Penelope sneaking toward the dark house disguised in masks and gloves and black clothing. The image made him shiver inside. *Not possible,* some voice within him taunted. He pushed the cruel voice aside and prepared to carry out, and to carry out well, the job he had been sent here to do.

— • • • —

Maggie and Glenda took a long, circuitous route that led to the back of the summerhouse. They were in place before the sunset had burned itself out of the sky. Maggie had a pretty good idea of how many servants slept in the place; luckily their quarters were in a back wing, far distant from where the painting was hung. As a matter of fact, she was not quite certain herself of just where that might be. But she had walked through enough of the house to know where the library, the formal sitting room, and the morning room were located. They would try these three first. Nine times out of ten—maybe ten out of ten—a valuable acquisition like the new Rembrandt would be in one of those rooms.

The two women moved through the cold stone passage with their usual speed and efficiency. The darkness was thick, and as cold as the stone walls that pressed in on them. Maggie picked the lock to the door that admitted them into the great house. It was low—they had to stoop to get through it—and well obscured behind a tall clothespress in the laundry room off the kitchen.

They made their way up the stairs to the main level of the house; all was still silent and dark as midnight. It was Glenda who heard the sound; a slight, scratchy noise like mice in the wainscoting. Both women froze. The sound was, in fact, one of Callum's inspectors attempting to stifle a cough. Glenda took a step forward, but Maggie placed her hand on her arm. Beside them, on a long commode, stood a small painted statue of a woman carrying a basket of flowers. Maggie picked it up in both hands and tossed it as far as she could into the cavernous opening of the morning room.

The response was immediate: a thin beam of light darting round the room and a shuffle of feet. In the same breath of space that this happened, Maggie and Glenda turned and fled back down the hall. Like two shadows, blending with the various shades, the thinnesses and thicknesses of the unlighted house, they glimmered for an instant here and there along the corridors, approaching the stone-flagged laundry room, and then were gone.

There were several torches now, sending their lights in crazy patterns through the deserted rooms. Muffled voices as well as muffled feet broke the silence. The men guarding the exits to the house had been alerted by the first signs of commotion inside. The usual scramble and controlled confusion accomplished nothing; there were no thieves to be caught. Men at their posts redoubled their efforts: the burglars must be somewhere! Every window was checked, the perimeters of every bush, every tree, every outbuilding. Men crawled like dozens of frenzied pygmies through the immense blackness of earth and sky, with no friendly stars overhead, nothing to assist them but the thick, wavering glow of their torches. The longer they searched, finding nothing, the more frenzied their efforts became, churning up the still night with their insufficient torches and their impotent cries.

Callum, scanning the house with his binoculars, caught the first throb of light from the morning room. He knew he had enough men inside to nab the thieves if they were caught in the midst of the thievery. If, somehow, the light had forewarned them, they would be long gone by now. With aid of the glasses, he surveyed the expanse of the building—windows, doors and balconies— once more, quickly. Then he started his car and, following his hunch, drove at full speed down the narrow, unpaved road that bordered Robert Hailes's property on the north. He drove with no lights, bumping over rocks and potholes he couldn't see. At the back of the property he swerved to the left, and the road now became little more than a lane.

The women heard him coming. They were yards away from the roadway. They dropped down flat and lay on their bellies in the profusion of weeds and meadow flowers, forcing themselves to remain there long minutes after the black car had passed. Then they crawled, still low to the ground, through the meadow, kitty-corner to where another path intercepted the road Callum had chosen. There were other cars about now, and lights flickering through the manicured gardens and approaching the tall meadow grasses that skirted the baronet's estate.

But Maggie and Glenda had crossed the intersection of roads and walked through yet more farmlands before they retrieved two bicycles from a ditch and headed at full speed up a dirt path into the low hills. Here at last a car and driver waited.

The driver was not well pleased. He had expected the women to show up with the Rembrandt. When they told him how extensive was the police trap waiting them, he knew the ugly suspicions he had harbored were accurate. Curtly, he told Maggie to get into the front seat beside him. He pushed Glenda into the back, face down, with her hands tied behind her and a gag stuck in her mouth.

Maggie said nothing as the Terrier drove at breakneck speed across the dark, unmarked hillside. He gave the police and the scene of the crime a wide berth and came down on the opposite flank of the town. Maggie knew what he was going to do. She gritted her teeth and prayed that he wouldn't ask her to help him. She didn't know if she could. She didn't even know if she'd have the stomach to watch.

He'd lost them! Callum ground his teeth in pure rage. He didn't see how they could have slipped through his network—he had men posted on every roadway, at every farmhouse and deserted byre or granary for a radius of miles. Two little mice, sleek and canny, had found an opening somewhere in the maze. A grudging admiration rose up to mingle with the bile of defeat that choked in this throat.

———◦◦———

Hugh was wide awake by the second ring of the phone and struggling to sit up in bed. It was MacGregor himself on the other end of the line, and the news was far worse than he had expected.

How could you have lost them altogether? he wanted to shout. But he bit back the words. He well knew how bitter the inspector's feelings must be right now.

"The moment they come back we'll confront them for certain, maybe even charge them," Callum said.

"You think they'll come back?"

"They have all their things at the earl's house still. I believe they'll at least try to return, perhaps act as though nothing happened."

"Have you set up roadblocks?"

"A maze of them, Fraser." MacGregor's voice sounded tired. "But I don't know whether to stop them if they come through or to merely follow them back to Lord Forbes. A surprise confrontation there might produce better results than a routine police interrogation."

Hugh agreed. "Keep to that, sir," he encouraged, guessing those were the orders MacGregor had already given. "If you find them—anytime—will you please—"

"Yes, I shall. Most definitely. I want you there, Fraser, if anything starts to happen. I couldn't go this one alone."

Hugh grinned into the dark room as the warmth of those words spread through him. "Thank you, sir. Good luck then."

The receiver went dead in his hand. He knew without thinking about it why the chief inspector wanted him. The tough, surly, experienced London specialist, with years of experience and an impressive record behind him, was feeling the same way Hugh felt. He couldn't conceive of facing those two women and accusing them of crimes terrible and heinous. It seemed a ludicrous thing; a pitiable, unpardonable thing.

Hugh tossed and turned in his fevered bed and tried to sleep. The nurse came in with a potion that would help to relax him, but he refused it with energy. He did not want to be inaccessible, even worthless, when MacGregor's call came. And something told him that, whatever his qualms and misgivings, the call would come.

———•◦•———

For Callum night would run into day, both would merge together into several black nightmares, before his work would be done. In the damp, awful hours of the predawn stillness he paced his temporary headquarters, monitoring calls and reports constantly coming in from half a dozen sources and locations at the same time. His was the precarious task of weighing them and assigning each its proper importance, its credence in view of the whole picture. Which leads did he follow up—which discard? All he could do was rely on his years of experience and his own hunches, those flashes of inspiration or impulse which all natural-born policemen seem to possess.

Around 5 A.M. a call came through from one of the foresters who had been induced into temporary service. It seemed he had found a body in a ravine about a dozen yards from the roadside. It was the body of a young woman. Though the face was badly mutilated, the girl's hair was reddish blonde and worn in a short bob. Would the chief inspector like to come out and investigate?

Callum appointed a temporary replacement and left instructions to be followed carefully during his absence. He picked two local inspectors to accompany him, one an outstanding forensics man. Then he placed one call—to Hugh Fraser in his room in Oban. Grimly he set out for the low ridge of forest land where a blonde haired woman lay dead with her face buried in the damp, still earth.

14

Corker sent Eddie back to Oban. "Watch the earl's house," he ordered, "and keep your eye on that young upstart we took care of back at the ferry. I'm sure someone's found him by now. I'll stay here and look after the ladies." He touched the brim of his hat in mock deference. Eddie said nothing by way of reply. He was tired of Corker and this whole fishy business. The boss had gotten himself into a rare one this time. If it had been up to Eddie he would have handled it differently. He shrugged his shoulders and left.

At 5:17 the next morning, when Hugh backed his sports car onto the black ribbon of road, Eddie was right behind. He'd lifted an old rattletrap Austin truck from a farmhouse outside Fort William, and it chugged along so noisily that he was sure the young man would suspect him; what foolhardy farmer would be on the road at this hour? What fool of any sort, for that matter? But the boy drove steadily, with increasing speed, 'til he had cleared the town limits and was approaching the low brown foothills that stretched away from the sea. Eddie fell back as far as he dared, trying to figure out what might be going on here. Just then a police car and an ambulance turned the corner from the west side of the road and fell in behind the low sports car. Eddie cut his lights and shifted gears. He could follow this way for a while, but if they climbed too far up the mountain he would have to turn back.

———•◆•———

It was cold. Callum blew on his fingers, and his breath was as frosty as the swirling ground mists that hung like gray witch's tatters along the stark, bare-limbed trees. He followed the path of fear and death, the light from his torch thick and yellow in the mist, showing the tire tracks that had bit deeply into the wet earth and the crushed and bruised leaves where feet had trampled and a limp, lifeless body had been dragged. He cleared the area and walked it himself, examining each inch of ground, trying to recreate what had happened here just hours ago. He did not go near the body nor allow anyone else to, not until his careful searching led him step by step to the spot.

He made himself concentrate on what he saw before him. There were three sets of footprints; two clearly made by women's shoes. He had one of his men measure the prints and make impressions. He followed the path the three had walked to where it ended in a small copse of trees. Here the matted ground growth would have obscured their passing, but the man and women had stopped short, just off the path. The larger of the women's prints ended several feet behind in a morass, as though she had walked back and forth, round in a little circle of frustration, before moving on. The other two, for the last few yards, were closely mingled, the man's steps firmly planted and sure. But it appeared as though the girl had been partly dragged across the soft ground, from the way the prints told their tale.

The forester, coming up behind, said matter-of-factly, "She came a bit unwillingly, didn't she, sir? See the marks of him half dragging, half pushing her?"

Callum smiled back at the man. He had good intentions and, in truth, Callum did not mind the company. He knew where this journey was taking him, and he dreaded facing the end all alone.

It appeared the man had pushed the woman, whose hands had been tied behind her, into the trees before he had shot her. But, why in the face? Why such a gruesome, unnecessary act?

Callum rocked back on his heels, his hands in his pockets. The forester stood respectfully a few steps behind. From here the body had been dragged to the edge of the gully and then rolled in and covered hastily with ground mulch and dead leaves. Only the man's steps had taken that journey. The second woman, the one who had survived the violence, remained behind.

Callum walked back to the beginning and began the circuit again. By this time the Fort William police had arrived with an ambulance in tow, but he paid that no mind. He scrutinized the area inch by inch, forcefully clearing his mind of the activity around him. What had it been like? What had the three people done and said during those last dreadful moments?

"I believe it was the Terrier did her in, sir." Hugh Fraser had come up behind him. His face looked pale in the lurid light of the lanterns. "Two more sightings of him have come in from reliable sources."

"I agree." Callum's voice was terse, the muscles of his

face working to conceal his thoughts and reactions. Now that Fraser was here an unexpected weakness attacked his whole system. One glance at the lad's eyes and he knew Fraser was suffering the same torment, too.

"Is it true, sir?" Hugh lowered his voice. "Did he shoot her in the face—" He couldn't continue.

"Yes. Apparently the girl's face is destroyed past recognition. I haven't—" He paused and swallowed painfully. "I haven't examined the body myself." He nodded in the direction of the gully. "Haven't got that far yet."

Fraser's face went a shade whiter, if possible, and he swayed on his feet. "Why ever? Why in the name of heaven—"

"I b'lieve I know what happened."

Hugh leaned closer, prepared to listen carefully; steeling himself to listen and put all else from his mind. The forester, quiet and intent, stood at his shoulder. The other men, well trained, kept their distance and waited, just outside the dim, wavering circle of light.

Callum picked up a stick and traced the path of the footsteps leading down through the woods. "Up to this point, you see, the three were walking together, the one woman following a bit behind, the other held in front of the man and at times forced along—you see—here—and here—" They moved a few paces forward together. Then Callum pointed with his stick to the disturbed spot of earth where the last woman lingered, pacing back and forth in her agitation.

"Perhaps neither believed, up to the last moment, that—shall we call him the Terrier for sake of illustration?—that the Terrier would shoot the girl when he got right down to it. Even when he shoved her ahead, into that small knot of trees, she turned at the last to face him, probably to plead for her life." Callum realized that his voice sounded raspy. He noticed that Hugh Fraser had lowered his head and was trembling.

"I think then, at that last moment, the older woman realized in a flash that the Terrier would indeed shoot her friend. In her moment of unthinking panic she lunged for him." Callum bent over. "Look at the pattern of prints here, the long space between the two scuffled impressions. She lunged, perhaps intending to knock the gun from his hands. Instead—well, instead she simply shoved his arm upward and redirected his aim—and, therefore, the bullet."

He needed to go no further. In the brief silence that followed he could feel Fraser's trembling.

"Look, man," he said to the forester. "Do me a favor and take this lad to his car. Then join me back here and we'll see about the body."

His words seemed to come in slow motion. Hugh Fraser made no objection but allowed the older man to lead him along. Callum turned so that he faced the gully, with its burden of horror. He was generally good at forcing his mind to shut down, to maintain a screen of blankness whereon nothing registered. Not so tonight. He felt weak and shaky as he took a few steps forward and peered into the gloom. Merciful heavens! What a job was this for his hands and his mind.

He moved forward gently through the tangle of crushed bushes and bent branches, darkened here and there with stains of blood. He was relieved when he heard steps behind him and turned to see the forester coming steadily on.

Eddie buttoned his overcoat up to his neck and pulled his hat over his eyes. There were enough people milling about the scene of the crime now that he could fit in with no trouble. He took care to stay on the fringes, every sense fine-tuned to catch the least thing that might come his way.

He watched the forester walk Hugh back to his car, where he sat bent over the steering wheel, his head buried in his hands. He watched the inspector and the forester lift the body from the gully and bring it up to where others—gingerly and with gray faces—wrapped it in blankets and placed it in the ambulance. The big inspector with the deep-set, sad eyes was quite obviously in charge of the operation. Eddie recognized him and chuckled under his breath. "Well, I'll be boiled in hot oil," he muttered.

He backed away, out of the light of the torches. He'd seen enough. He'd even heard the name the forester called the big, quiet man. "Chief Inspector MacGregor," he'd said. Now, that would work to their purposes! He chuckled again as he rolled the truck in neutral down the steep incline. Just as soon as he rounded that first bend he'd start up the engine. He intended to head straight for the earl's house. If he knew his business, that's where all the fireworks would begin.

———•◦•———

Lord Forbes had received word that Laura Poulson would return to his house sometime the next morning. The women had experienced car troubles, and Penelope would stay until the repairs were completed and then drive down to join them.

The earl sat hunched up, staring into the embers of the fire, feeling chilled to the bone. The police believed with good reason that the older woman was present when the younger was shot. Did this mean that the gentle woman who had sat by his hearth—and shared such lovely moments with him—had watched her beautiful young daughter be murdered before her own eyes?

There was a chance, an outside chance, that the other person of the threesome in the woods had been a small-footed man, not a woman. But no one believed that was true. Yet if it was, he would be the first to inform Laura that her daughter was dead! How in the world could he do that?

He sat mulling over the dilemma until the fire was ashes, and his hands, numb with cold, felt like stones in his lap.

———————

Hugh had allowed MacGregor to drive him home, because the inspector had insisted and because he felt limp as a dishrag and could not stop the shaking that wrenched his body. Even now, after a cup of hot tea laced with whiskey and with the bedclothes piled over him, he still could feel the trembling. He hadn't gone close to the body at all. Perhaps it was simply because he was unwell, a little off balance, that this business could disturb him so deeply, that this girl—No! He would not think of it. He must forget it, he must get some sleep. He closed his eyes but the nightmare remained, and only sheer exhaustion of mind and body brought him eventual release.

———————

Corker, stuck by himself in Fort William, spent most of his night at a pub. He knew where his ladies were, and he knew they wouldn't be going anywhere before morning. He was bored and cold, and tired of this whole business. Once or twice he had nearly gone up to the women, normal-like, prepared to present his dilemma and appeal to their own reason; they seemed reasonable creatures, the both of them. But the boss had said that would not do. He was probably right. Even in their ignorance they could be a threat to him. And therefore this cat-and-mouse game. He thought longingly of New York City: the lights and glitter, the constant noise. It was so quiet here! He remembered the parties and the beautiful women, and decided that Eddie was right. They must take care of this thing, get it over with; no matter what happened, no matter what way it went.

Penny was restless that night and had trouble sleeping. Knowing she would be stuck in this place most of the next day did nothing to lighten her thoughts. Somehow everything seemed wrong, starting with when they first left Oban on her mother's wild scheme. She did not like this discontent, this sense almost of depression that clouded her. The trip had been wonderful, nearly ideal for her, before now. What was she feeling? Why was she so agitated? She could not understand it at all. She didn't like this lack of inner harmony, this lack of control. She didn't like it one bit.

Laura stayed up late talking with Andrew Ross in his library, a small, intimate room, paneled in dark woods and hung with carefully chosen and well-framed prints. It was nothing like the cavernous library at Forbes House, as she believed the earl's home was called. Yet this night reminded her of that other she had spent with the earl. She was strangely drawn to the large, quiet stranger. And now here, this man—intense, eager to please, and charming in his own little ways. *How narrow my life has been,* she chided herself. *And it is all my own fault. There is so much beauty to discover in the people around one!* She had the unpleasant thought that perhaps she had bored Gerald with her narrowness; her fixed, provincial ways. *It is too late,* her heart cried. *Too late to change any of that!*

Mr. Ross was smiling at her. The night outside their curtained windows was wet and black. She was aware of the bleak loneliness of the night; the strange, almost haunted feeling clung to her still, and she shuddered for any who were out in the damp and the loneliness. She lifted her book and followed along as Andrew Ross read Tennyson in his rich, solemn voice.

15

Laura sat in the large touring car beside the stranger; she was growing accustomed to this, being among strangers and handling it all right. Mr. Perkins was a colleague of Andrew Ross's and seemed a very nice man. She kissed her hand to Penelope and admonished her to drive safely once she got her small Morris repaired and running.

The day was mild after the storms of the previous evening, with an autumn glow in the sky and the scent of crushed leaves and apples carried on the crisp air. The road was uncrowded and the roadside trees a glory of bronze and russet, with here and there the startling yellow of a tall, leaning elm. Laura relaxed back against the cushioned seat with a sigh. This loveliness crooned to her soul like an ancient lullaby. She breathed in the hush of it, unaware of any other spirit or influence in the world.

———◆———

Corker followed at a distance. This was not the proper time nor were these the proper circumstances to take any action; besides, he felt a bit muddled after last night's heavy drinking. He guessed the stranger was driving Mrs. Poulson back to the earl's place, so he'd best find Eddie and compare notes. Then he wondered, if the girl was alone, perhaps they ought to nab her as a hostage of sorts, a way of getting at the mother. That ought to work well enough. And she was alone—would be driving the lonely, half-deserted road back to Oban by herself.

About two miles before the turnoff to the earl's estate Corker spied the old, paint-cracked truck parked alongside the road. He pulled off behind it. Sure enough, Eddie came round the side of the truck. His face wore a faint hint of his well-known cold, Cheshire cat grin. Perhaps for once there would be good news awaiting Corker. He liked the idea of that.

The earl heard Laura enter the house. He was waiting in the library. He listened to the sound of her voice as she greeted Janet in the front hall.

"As soon as possible, the earl would like to see you, ma'am," he heard Janet say. "He's waiting in the library."

"All right, Janet. Thank you. I suppose I can go in right now."

Her voice sounded puzzled and a bit tired. As she walked toward him he thought she looked tired as well. She smiled hesitantly. "Did you need me, sir?" she asked. "I'm so glad to be back. We've been through a little ordeal since the last time we saw you."

What was she trying to do?

"Madame," Lord Forbes began, "I regret that I must bring up such an unpleasant—" What the deuce was he saying? "—such a tragic matter. But—"

Did she know, or didn't she? Had she been there last

night? Her gaze was so open, so seemingly free of guile that it smote him like a physical blow.

"A young woman has been found dead in a ravine in the hills—a young blonde woman whom the police believe to be your daughter."

There. The dreadful words were out. But before he had half spoken them Laura Poulson swayed on her feet, her face deathly pale. The earl caught her just as her knees buckled under her. He laid her on the couch in the far corner and sat next to her, rubbing her hands. When she opened her eyes they were so filled with misery that he turned his own gaze away.

"How could this be? When—?" She could not form her words properly. Her mouth trembled and twisted all out of shape. "I can't—I don't see—"

"Last night, or rather very early this morning," Thomas Forbes explained gently. "A forester found the body and reported—"

Laura sat bolt upright, a pink spot on each white cheek. "This makes no sense at all. Penny was with me all night!" Her fingers dug into his wrist. "I saw her this morning—we said good-bye when I left Fort William about nine o'clock!"

An inexplicable relief, real and palpable, coursed through the earl's body. He grasped the hand that was closed round his wrist. "Are you sure?"

"Of course I am sure!" Laura's fingers were cold and trembling. "Who is this dead girl, and why did they think it was Penny?" The mingling of shock and relief had excited her system to a high pitch. And still there remained a dread thrill of doubt, of distorted possibility.

The earl leaned close. "Would you go look at the body? It is imperative that you identify it"—he paused a little awkwardly—"as that of a stranger."

Laura's eyes were wide. "I suppose. I suppose I could, if I must."

The earl had forgotten himself. He stood, lifting her with him. "Let us go now, before your courage fails you."

He helped her out of the room and into his car, which was waiting under the canopy. They rode in silence awhile.

"Where are we going?" she asked at length.

"To the city morgue, my dear. They've taken the poor girl there." He drew a deep breath. "She was terribly disfigured, I fear." He glanced at the quiet woman who sat watching him with large, woeful eyes. "She was shot in the face, and of course—"

Laura cried out and covered her own face with her hands.

"Yes. Don't think of it." Lord Forbes drew her hands from her face and held them tightly in his. The horror in her expression was easy to read. *A sweet young girl, some woman's daughter. What if! what if . . .*

The earl had his man drive round to the back of the building, where they could enter and exit discreetly. Laura walked woodenly, obediently beside him. If the glaring lights and the clinical, antiseptic atmosphere distressed her, she showed no signs. A man in a white coat, who had been told they were coming, led them into a room where, behind a curtained enclosure, the body lay beneath a white sheet.

Lord Forbes stood beside her and held her hand as they drew back the covering. Laura gasped and pressed his hand so tight he thought her small bones might melt into his.

"This is not my daughter," she said.

"Are you certain?" the coroner asked, with absolutely no expression in his voice or his face.

Laura swallowed. The color had drained from her face again, but she stood ramrod straight. "I am certain. The proportions of the body, the clothing she is wearing, the shape of her hands . . ." She reached out her fingers as if to touch the frozen white hands where they lay folded over the girl's breast. A tear slid down her cheek.

"Are there any distinguishing marks on your daughter that would identify her positively?" The coroner was calm and unhurried.

"Yes. She has a small birthmark inside the bend of her left arm."

The coroner stepped between them and the girl and bent over the body for a moment. Then he straightened and moved back. "If you would be good enough to sign a statement to the effect of your words, ma'am, I believe that is all we shall need."

He left the room. Lord Forbes pressed Laura's arm gently, but she stood staring down at the stark, frigid features. "Who is this girl you thought was my daughter? What is her name?"

"I haven't the slightest idea."

She glanced at him sharply, her eyes dark. "That seems impossible. Someone must know. Someone must care what happens to her." She murmured the words and extended her fingers so that they just brushed the girl's hand.

"Come," the earl said. He put his arm firmly round her shoulder and led her out of the room.

He saw her safely to the car, where his driver waited. "I must go back inside and make one very important phone call," he apologized. "I'll not be more than a minute or two."

As he dialed Hugh Fraser's number his sense of frustration mounted. When the young man picked up the receiver he identified himself and stated bluntly, "I thought you might like to know, young man, the dead girl is not Penelope."

He heard nothing on the other end but a long, trembling sigh of relief.

"Yes, I believe I know what you're feeling. But where in the deuce does this leave us?"

Hugh understood his distress. "It doesn't seem possible. Could we have been so wrong?" He understood the man's annoyance; he was mortified himself. This placed them in a deplorable situation, MacGregor especially, and he had no wish to see that.

"Miss Poulson should return by midafternoon. She's having her car repaired at Grant's Garage in Fort William, her mother says. I think when she returns we had better all meet together and sort this thing out."

"Capital idea." Hugh nearly said, *I'll look forward to it,* but thought better of that.

"I'll let you know then, Fraser. You stay close to your telephone."

"I'll do that, sir. Yes."

But when the earl had rung off, Hugh bolted for the door. He had already made up his mind. It was not much more than an hour from here to Fort William, not if he took the ferry and drove at his usual speed. He wasn't taking any more chances with this woman! He could hardly wait. To be with her—to drink in her charm and beauty without the pressing weight he had lived with these past days, without the gnawing awareness that she was a fraud, an imposter, something different from that which she seemed.

My instincts were right! he thought triumphantly. The gray Healey responded to his urgings like the fine-tuned machine that she was. He soared over the road, gaining more strength with each whizzing turn of the wheels. He found it difficult to concern himself with the terrible affair that yet faced them. For the moment he was free, and so was the gentle young woman who had so haunted his days and his nights.

———•◦•———

Eddie had rejected Corker's idea.

"If we take just the girl," he explained, as though speaking to a dull and tedious child, "then the whole police community will be alerted. The mother is still under the protection of that duke."

"Earl," Corker corrected.

"What difference does it make? Fact is, we gotta arouse no suspicions whatsoever. And the way we do that is to nab both those fool women at the same time. Then we head up into the hills, to that place we scouted out, you remember."

Corker nodded, but his face was a blank still. Eddie grabbed the tall, thin man by the shoulders.

"They do what we want, and we let 'em go, with the promise that they leave Scotland on the next boat out and talk to nobody who knows them—especially not the duke."

"If they break their word?"

"If they break their word, it don't matter much to us. We've got what we want and we're on our way home. They don't know nothin' 'bout us, and we'll make it plain to them that we know everything about them."

Corker grinned. "That's right. We can go back to that dump neighborhood in Salt Lake and do more than trash their house next time."

Eddie released his hold with a short shove. "Now yer catchin' on. Besides, I got other ways, much more effective, to convince them two not to talk."

"I know all that, Eddie," Corker protested.

"Yeah, well, we've done it your way for a couple weeks now, mamby-pambyin' across the country. I tell you, Corker, I've had enough."

"So have I," Corker rejoined, suddenly serious. "It's time and past. I'm with you all the way, Eddie."

Corker thought of the Prince Charlie, his favorite pub in Oban. That was one place he'd miss. Maybe he could finagle a couple cases of Skye whiskey on board the ship home; that shouldn't prove too hard to do.

––––––⋅•⋅––––––

Hugh arrived at the earl's house with Penelope on his arm. When Lord Forbes saw them enter together he arched an eyebrow in disapproval.

"I've told her nothing, sir. Not a bit. It's all your game." Hugh lifted his hands palm up in a gesture of mock helplessness. But his eyes belied the pretense. They were dark and serious, and the muscles on his face were drawn tight.

Lord Forbes sent for Laura and then saw them all seated in comfortable chairs before he began.

"May I see your passports, ladies?" he asked, astonishing all of them.

Laura and Penelope complied, digging them out of their pocketbooks and passing them round to the earl.

"Oh, and your American driver's licenses as well, and any other forms of identification you might have with you. Please."

His voice was firm, with a no-nonsense ring to it, and they did as he said. Hugh caught his eye once, questioning silently, but the earl paid him no heed.

"I shall need to retain these for a few days," he said curtly.

"Detain them where? And for what reason?" Penelope asked, her own voice a bit sharp.

"We meant to leave soon, you see," Laura added. Her voice was low and soft, so much the voice of a woman that the earl felt himself shudder. He avoided her eyes.

"Are you not even curious about all that's been happening to you, and around you, these past days?" He spoke the words with a passion, and a broad Scots accent, heavily rolling his *r*s and pronouncing "about" as "aboot." And his voice had that weakening effect on Laura which she was unable to help.

Penny leaned forward in her chair, her face taut with eagerness. "Yes. Yes, I have. I've been far more than curious, far more than interested. I've been frightened to death."

Her words brought a hush to the room, a hush that tingled.

"You have answers for us, don't you?" she asked.

The earl replied, with an almost painful air, "Yes, I have."

Penelope fixed her intense gaze on him. "Then go ahead."

It was not so simple as that. After all the thought he had given it, the earl did not know how best to begin.

"A strange thing has occurred," he said, "a series of coincidences, really."

"That involve us?" Penelope questioned.

"Most definitely, yes. You see, your arrival in this country coincided with a crime, a robbery of a most valuable painting from the home of a wealthy and influential Englishwoman, Catherine Allen, Marchioness of Huntingdon, by name. This was not an isolated crime, but one of a series—"

"And this one caused an uproar because of the lady's position."

The earl inclined his head slightly. "You have the rights of it, Miss Poulson. Now, where you come in is in the fact that these robberies were committed by two clever and highly skilled women."

Penelope perked up at that. Laura sat quietly, her hands in her lap, her face that of an unruffled Madonna. Lord Forbes could do no more than glance at her.

"And these women were masters of disguise. Usually they played off each other; the one masquerading as a bent and wrinkled old man, the other his young apprentice or perhaps a delivery boy. They had posed as cleaning ladies and upstairs maids to get into a household—"

"And case the joint!" Penelope's expression was sobering a little.

"That's right. They work, we're certain, with a professional network that has fences who market the stolen goods, our 'lovely ladies' getting only a modest cut."

"'Lovely ladies'—is that what you called them?" The words were velvet in Laura's mouth, laced with a touch of amusement that the earl could feel.

"In our frustration and"—he hesitated—"admiration, yes, we did call them that. They went as sisters; as a young man and his mother; as two old, black-toothed crones." He could sense their frustration, so he cut to the heart of the matter. "When we stumbled across you two we were convinced that this time they were posing as mother and daughter."

Penelope sucked in her breath. "Where did you 'stumble across' us?" she demanded.

"In Edinburgh, following the trail of the women who we believed had fled to the north, to Scotland."

"That soon? So you mean all of this time—" Her eyes were filling with an overwhelming comprehension. "You mean, clear through to Stirling and Loch Lomond—all the little churchyards and ruined castles—the lakes and the islands—" She shook her head at the thought.

"Yes, we were watching, we were following you."

"Who exactly is 'we'?" Laura asked the question softly, but all eyes turned to her.

"Yes. Well . . ." The earl glanced helplessly at Hugh Fraser, who gave him as encouraging a smile as he could.

"'We' was actually myself. And my name is Callum MacGregor."

Both women stared at him numbly.

"I am a chief inspector out of London on undercover assignment. I am the one who has followed you—who mistook you for our 'lovely ladies.' I am not Thomas Forbes, Earl of Seafield and Lochmont."

No one spoke, not even Penelope. Hugh could not read her expression.

"There is a real earl," Callum continued, to cover the awkwardness. "He is fifteen years older than I am, and he has graciously accommodated us by spending these past days at his country estate—"

"And allowing you to impersonate him!" Penelope cried.

Callum winced. This was something he had not wished to do. It had been his idea to place Hugh Fraser as the earl's handsome, playboy son. But everyone else thought this plan the stronger. Even his good friend the commissioner, back in London, had preferred it this way.

"You have the maturity the lad lacks," he had told Callum during their phone conversation. "He would get in over his head and slip up and not even know it."

"He *is* such a creature," Callum had argued. "His father is titled, he's led the life of the gentry. . . ."

Thomas had waved him aside. Callum could picture him, sitting behind his long desk; his small eyes, set deep in his broad face, lit by the ideas inside his own mind; and his index finger rubbing his hairless eyebrows.

"No, Callum, this is right up your alley. And it keeps you in charge! Important consideration!" He barked out the words. Then he added, more persuasively, "You're a natural, man. Your love of music, your knowledge of the classics, of poetry—your knowledge of people!"

He rambled on for a bit, and Callum had known the decision was out of his hands. It had terrified him, the thought of impersonating gentry—that pompous and privileged class he had always disdained. But the experience—how different it had been from his anticipations!

"You did well."

Callum looked up to see Laura's eyes watching him.

"Just the proper balance of firmness and kindness . . ." She seemed to be musing. "Of gentleness and strength."

His brow was dark and troubled, but she smiled at him. "It was a brave thing to do. And you did it so . . ." She was searching for the right word. "So . . . graciously."

She still held him with her gaze. He could feel his discomfort rising to color his broad face, to betray him.

"Sir, you have a call on the telephone. The gentleman said it was very important."

Janet stood at the door.

Callum jumped to his feet. This was a timely means of escape, and he took it.

"I shall return as soon as possible," he promised.

With long, grateful strides he crossed the length of the library. As he passed the chair where Laura Poulson sat he paused briefly and, on a sudden impulse, stooped and placed his hand over hers where they lay folded quietly in her lap. A brief touch only, then his back was to her, and he was gone from the room.

16

THERE WERE COUNTLESS QUESTIONS IN PENELOPE'S MIND, and after the stillness of Callum's departure they came tumbling forth.

"We met Lord Forbes at the pub," she told Hugh, "while we were staying with that sweet Mrs. Brodie."

"Mrs. Brodie knew," Hugh smiled. "As did the men at the pub."

"And, of course, all these people—these servants—"

"Are in the employ of the real earl. So they're in on the game."

"They did splendidly!" It seemed a bit of a lark to Penelope. "Poor little Janet; it must have been trying for her."

"The auction," Hugh explained, "was a setup. We hoped to entice you to do one more job."

"I don't believe it!" Penny sat back in her chair with a little gasp of astonishment. "So much trouble to go to. Did the auctioneer know?"

"Yes, all the principals were informed, especially Rob—

Baronet Hailes, who purchased the Rembrandt. He was an awfully good sport."

"Then it wasn't a real sale?"

"No, no, it wasn't. Just a setup all the way through."

"And was there a robbery?" Penelope blinked at him. "This is just like an Agatha Christie adventure! Really." She smiled across at her mother, not noticing that her face had gone pale.

Hugh hesitated. "There was an attempted robbery. But the police were in place and waiting. The thieves escaped—but without the painting."

"Two women?"

Hugh nodded. "We think so."

"Did anyone see them? Do you have any idea where they are?"

"Yes, we know where they are now." Callum filled up the doorway, looking somehow larger than he had before. His eyes turned to Hugh.

"Maggie Simpson—do you recognize that name, Fraser?—was picked up at Greenock. One of our lads spotted her on the ferry—" His mouth twisted into an enigmatic expression. "Well, he spotted someone who appeared suspicious; she didn't look much like herself at the time. Apparently she was heading for a rendezvous of some sort at Glasgow." He sighed. His eyes were warm with relief and an expression very much like joy.

"And the other?"

Callum turned to Penelope. Something in his gaze went right through her. He did not answer her question at once, but continued along his same vein.

"Maggie's talked already, Fraser. And I believe she'll talk more, especially if we cut her a deal. She has no tolerance left for the Terrier after what he did to her friend."

Callum lifted his eyes and sought Laura's tranquil face. Then he looked at Penny again.

"Maggie's friend was a young woman by the name of Glenda Bates."

Hugh shrugged his shoulders. "That name is not familiar. Does she have other aliases?"

"I don't know. She's the other one you were asking about, Penelope. She was shot and killed late last night."

Penelope put her hand to her throat and grew very still.

"She was meant to be shot nice and clean through the heart, but as it happened . . ."

Callum felt the warm pressure on his arm before he realized that Laura had risen and come to stand beside him.

"Don't," she said. "Please." Her face was very close to his; her voice was a whisper against his cheek. "It is not necessary. Why should her young mind be haunted?"

He turned to face her and bent his large frame over her frail one. "She will never know," he said, into her ear alone, "what torment you went through."

"And why should she?" Her voice was trembling a little. "What are mothers for?"

Callum encircled her with his long arms until she was resting lightly against his chest. He brushed her fragrant hair with his lips, then he released her again.

Penelope's thoughts were elsewhere. During this strange scene between her mother and the "earl" a thought had worked itself to the surface of her mind; a bleak, intruding thought. She turned to Hugh directly and forced him to look back at her.

"There's more to this 'we' than you've told me, isn't there?"

When he did not reply at once, she continued.

"The way he's been talking to you—you know all about this. You're one of them, aren't you? You're a 'plant,' too?"

Hugh struggled to remain calm. "I'm a police inspector. I live here in Oban. I was called in on the job."

He gave himself no quarter. Penelope glared at him, her eyes like bright chips of blue glass. "I was an assignment! You thought I was a common tart and a thief."

He smiled, though he tried hard not to. "Where did you learn language like that? Reading those murder mysteries, I'll wager."

He was so wretchedly charming when he smiled! His mouth went down at one corner and he looked like a mischievous little boy.

"That's what it was, all right. That's how it started out." Hugh decided all at once to be blunt, to put his cards on the table. "But I've been in pure hell. I tell you, Penelope, I knew you were different from what I was told to think that you were."

"That's right." Callum looked over at the two wretched young people. "It took more strength of will than I like to remember. The more we came to know you, the more we were certain that you couldn't be the girls we were after. And yet, everything pointed that way— everything! And we knew the 'lovely ladies' were master deceivers—"

"Oh, dear." Penelope laughed; the light, tinkling laughter of girlhood, which was like a breath of fresh air.

The afternoon was waning. Hugh glanced at his wristwatch and rose reluctantly. "I've work that must be done before this day's over. And so does his lordship, the inspector." He grinned at Callum.

"Could we four meet here, say at seven, for a late dinner and make a night of it?" Callum turned toward Laura. "Ladies, would you be so kind . . . ?

" 'Lovely ladies,' " Penelope chanted.

"Aye, you'll torment us with this now," Callum protested. "We'll never hear the end of it!"

"That's right." Penelope winked at her mother, but Callum's words had caught her abruptly. He had said, "We'll never hear the end of this," and it had such a pleasant ring. "Never" implied time, and a long, ongoing relationship. But now the whole adventure was over, and they very likely would be heading back home. How empty and dismal that prospect was.

"I shall have a long list of questions for you when you come back," she assured the departing Hugh.

Hugh smiled at her; his slow, mirthful smile. "At your service, lass."

Callum was tempted to stay, to draw Laura aside, but just then Janet notified him of a telephone call. He knew he must see to his duties.

Laura and Penelope walked arm in arm to their rooms.

"It doesn't seem possible, does it, Mother?" Penny murmured. "We had no idea at all. If we had known I would have been even more frightened than I was."

"I was beginning to be frightened myself," Laura admitted.

Penny laughed softly. "Mother, you've been terrified all along."

Laura laughed with her, but her face grew serious again. "You know, Penny, that isn't quite true. In the beginning even this trip itself overwhelmed me; I was frightened of my own shadow, remember?"

Penelope nodded, still watching her mother's sweet, serious face.

"But lately something's been happening inside me, something I can't even explain to myself."

"That's true," Penelope agreed. "I've noticed little changes myself."

"Some of the change shows, then," Laura responded thoughtfully. "Well, they say everything that happens has some good tucked in it. And this . . . this has . . ."

She tried, but she was forced to leave the sentence unfinished, her feelings unspoken. She did not know how to clothe with words the deep forces that were moving within her soul.

Callum was frustrated by the stranger on the phone who claimed to be the earl's factor and begged his kind offices, since he was yet legally authorized to act in his place. Just a little matter down at the stables, signing a few papers, straightening out a few matters. It should take less than an hour of the constable's time. Callum fumed inwardly, but he dare not say no; the earl had been gracious with them and required little in return. And his lordship was in the country still, out of reach of his factor and the day-to-day workings of his estate.

"I shall be there directly," Callum promised, and hastened out the back way to where his own comfortable Magnette was parked in His Lordship's garage.

Hugh left the earl's house feeling lighthearted, perhaps even a bit lightheaded. He had laid his heavy burden aside and could envision bright new prospects before him. He meant to motor past his own small cottage on his way back into Oban, but he noticed, out of the corner of his eye, a strange car in the drive—an old, lumpy-looking vehicle pulled past the gravel onto the grass, nearly up to his door. He slowed, then eased the Healey down the narrow side road upon which the house fronted and approached the scene with a sense of misgiving.

Surely something was wrong. There appeared to be no one in the truck, yet both the doors stood open wide on their hinges. As he got out of his car to investigate he noticed that the front door to his cottage was open as well. He walked cautiously, looking about him a bit as he went, fighting the impulse to call out.

He gave the open door a small push and took a few steps inside. Eddie walked out from behind him and repeated the process of two days before. If Hugh heard or sensed anything, he didn't have time to respond. Eddie dragged him into the bedroom and, with some effort, worked his limp body onto the bed. He tied him securely, then closed the door behind him and locked up the house. It looked good and proper when he was through with it and climbed into the rattletrap truck he'd been driving these past few days.

If his trigger finger was itching, it was no matter. He could not kill that lad back there because that lad was a copper, and killing a copper, be it here or in the states, was taboo. He didn't want the kind of trouble that would get him into. He would have to satisfy himself with the women. If they refused to cooperate, if they posed any problem at all, that would be the end of it, and he'd be the happier.

He backed the noisy truck out of the drive. If Corker had done his work it would be a matter of minutes before they'd be on their way. And none too soon, for the dim sun was fading and the sky turning drab. He wanted to be well up into those mountains before darkness fell. Anything else would be taking chances, and he didn't like taking chances the way Corker did.

———•—•———

Janet brought news of the call that had just come in from the constabulary.

"Local inspector says would you both please come down and sign some papers?"

"Papers?" Laura looked up from her reading.

"I don't know what for. Said Hugh Fraser would meet you there and explain it all to you. Just a few questions. I think he called it 'routine.' "

Laura sighed lazily. "Well, I suppose we must go."

Penelope, more eager at the prospect of seeing Hugh again, jumped up from her chair. "It shouldn't take long, Mother," she encouraged. "Just give me a minute to check my makeup and run a brush through this hair."

Laura smiled to herself. Penelope's energy and eagerness were endearing, but they wore Laura out, especially now, after all they had been through. Yet she looked forward to tonight, to talking easily and without restraint to this Callum MacGregor, this man who shared a common family name and who, no matter what his deceptions, had proven to be her friend.

She rose at Penelope's urgings, picked up her jacket against the chill air, and headed down to the car.

———◦—◦———

It was less than five miles from the earl's house to the village of Oban. Penelope had learned the back ways and could make it there in a little over ten minutes. Since they had last been outside the sky had turned stormy, with the grayness of night coming on. She took the steep curves in the road with the ease of practice. But just around one turn that lay in a dark stretch of forest, she gasped as she saw a stopped car straddling both lanes. She stepped hard on the brake and brought the Morris to a stop several feet from the rear door of the offending vehicle.

She rolled down her window and called out, a little impatiently, "Is anything wrong?"

There was no answer. She shrugged her shoulders at her mother.

"Do you suppose someone is hurt?" Laura asked. "Perhaps there's been some kind of trouble—besides an accident."

She could not bring herself to say "heart attack." But the thought of a man or woman lying crumpled and helpless in the seat of that automobile, the way Gerald must have done, made her tremble inside.

Reluctantly Penelope opened her door and got out. She walked slowly toward the place where the deserted car stood. At first she saw nothing at all. When the man stepped out from behind the front fender she let out a small cry. There was something about him that made her skin go cold and clammy.

"Remember me, sweetheart?" he leered.

Penelope did remember. She remembered his voice and the bruising pressure of his fingers over her mouth.

She had no time to move, to defend herself. His fist came down hard on the back of her neck, and with a little gasp, she slumped into his arms.

———•◆•———

Eddie had walked out from the trees that skirted the roadside, one eye on Corker and the girl as he made his way for the passenger's side of the Morris where Laura waited. He closed his fingers over the handle and opened the unlocked door swiftly. Laura didn't even get a proper look at his face. One moment she was blinking at him, at the blur of his strange and startling features; the next she knew nothing at all.

Minutes later the solitary car climbed the narrow twist of road into the higher ground which would eventually lead to the dark, ghost-shadowed fastnesses of the pass of Glencoe.

17

CALLUM'S MIND AND SENSES WERE LULLED A LITTLE. AFTER
that session in the earl's library he felt a great burden lift
from his chest, and he felt it lift from his confused heart
as well. He was tired and tranquillized a bit by the sheer
exaltation of relief, yet he smelled something wrong as
he strode toward the stables. Lord Forbes's factor, Albert
Stevensen, glanced up from his work with a mild, surprised air, which told Callum at once that he was not ex-
pecting him.

"Did you no' ring the great house and send for me?"
he cried out, lapsing into the broad Scots with ease.

Albert shook his head. "No, sir, I did not. Nor do I
know of anyone who did."

The man rose from his stooped position and con-
ferred for a while with the inspector. The longer they
spoke, the darker grew Callum's features, until his expression made Albert shudder. There was a fierceness to
him that looked all too natural there.

As Callum walked back to the car he struggled to sort his thoughts and feelings and to decide which move to take first. A cold, nagging fear played at the back of his mind. He decided to retrace his steps to the temporary office fixed up for the earl's factor during Callum's own occupation of the great house. He entered the small room, which smelled pleasantly of wax, leather, and horseflesh, and dialed the earl's number.

Janet picked up the phone. "No, they're not here, sir," she said in reply to his terse question. "A call came from the constabulary for them. I took the message myself."

Callum's face grew pinched and pale as he listened.

"Thank you." Callum slowly replaced the receiver. He drove his mind to the point of distraction. Who would be after his ladies still? His men had Maggie in custody, and Glenda was dead. The Terrier would not be hanging around these parts in search of revenge. There was no possible motive his mind could discover.

He dialed the Oban Constabulary and asked for the chief inspector. The man made a few inquiries, then assured Mr. MacGregor that no one from his office had placed a call to the earl's house for any reason whatsoever that day, much less to request the presence of Laura Poulson and her daughter. No, neither had they seen nor heard from Hugh Fraser since early that afternoon.

With the cold fear creeping further and further inside him Callum thanked the man and rang off. Next he dialed Hugh Fraser's cottage, but no one answered, though he let the blasted thing ring off the hook. That would be his first step: discover where Fraser was. Perhaps together they could . . .

He let his thoughts go no further. One little step at a time. Otherwise, what would happen to his sanity?

———•—•——

Despite himself, Callum felt relief when he saw the low gray Healey parked outside Fraser's house. That could be a good sign; dare he hope that it was?

He walked to the door and pounded upon its hard, unyielding surface. There was no response; not the slightest sound came from within. He tried the windows, banging a few. Everything here was locked up tight. A building sense of urgency tightened his muscles and made his fingers clumsy. At last he picked up a stone lying near his feet and sent it through one small pane, shattering the glass and making a noise that rattled his nerves in the stillness.

Reaching carefully through he loosened the handle that secured the window and pushed the entire frame inward. With surprising agility considering the size and bulk of him, he let himself through the opening and found he was standing in the dining room. On his left was the sitting room, and directly behind him was the kitchen with a hall leading off from it to the small room where Fraser slept.

He made his way there in a matter of seconds. Hugh Fraser lay stretched out on the bed, tied hand and foot to the bedposts, eyes closed and face white as a sheet. When Callum bent over him he saw the spread of clotted blood matting his hair on one side.

"Not again," he moaned, sitting on the edge of the bed beside the motionless body. The realization behind his words was weighty. This meant someone had been keeping a pretty careful watch on his ladies and knew of the very similar role that young Fraser had played. This was the second time he had been forcibly got rid of—and how many close calls might there have been?

He found the bathroom and wet a towel in cold

water, returning to daub Fraser's face and neck, then to clean the wound. It was less ugly than the blood had made it appear. *Which brings up another question,* Callum thought. *Why hasn't the lad simply been bumped off, and have done with it? What is going on here?*

He paced the narrow room in his agitation until a sound from the bed drew him back to the pale, stiffened figure. Fraser groaned and opened his eyes. "What happened?" He mouthed the words more than he spoke them.

Callum laughed shortly. "Come, lad, why don't you tell me? What kind of crazed person have you got yourself on the wrong side of?"

Hugh attempted a smile. Callum placed his hand on the boy's arm. "Lie still and listen to me," he directed.

In brief, succinct phrases he outlined what had happened. As he spoke he watched fear and anger play in Fraser's hot gaze.

"Call your men in!" Fraser croaked. "You have dozens posted."

"And alert them to what?"

Hugh put his hand to his forehead. "Most of the men know Laura and Penny's descriptions by heart!"

"Yes, down to that pretty little mole on Penelope's left cheek. And if we do that, if we call in a search, we'll cause one of two things: our chaps will go underground and take the ladies with them, or else leave them behind somewhere—neatly dead."

Fraser's pain showed in a weakening around his sensitive mouth. His blue eyes were blurred with it.

"In heaven's name, sir, what can we do?"

Callum leaned close. "Just the two of us, lad. But I don't think you're up to it now."

Hugh grabbed Callum's wrist. "I can do it, MacGregor. Just stick a bandage on this blasted head of mine."

Callum smiled, a half-formed yet indulgent smile. "Ach, well, I need your brains and your good aim more than I need the brawn of you. But there may be some walking to do."

Hugh struggled to a sitting position, wincing at the spasms of pain that shot through his head, but not flinching. Callum's expression was uncertain. "I don't know, lad . . ."

"What have you in mind?" Hugh needed to divert the inspector's sharp attention from his person. Out of the dullness of his bruised mind he dragged a question that was nagging at him. "Why did you say chaps? Do you believe there is more than one, then?"

"Yes, I do. It's a hunch, really, though it makes more sense that way."

"The night Penny was attacked in the street outside the chemist's; there was only one man that night."

"One man you saw!" Callum's eyes were clear, and Hugh could feel the piercing strength of them. "That morning by the ferry when you were struck behind in like manner; it was two men that time. There were two sets of footprints, one on either side of the scuffle marks that showed where they dragged you."

He stood and paced the room again, speaking with slow, studied care. "Even today, lad, the way they played us against each other; it would take two men to do that. If they have Laura and Penelope . . ." The muscles of Callum's jaw worked, and his eyes grew terrible. "Well, I believe if they have Laura and Penelope, that would require two men as well."

He wants to get them. It's obvious how he's chafing to get his hands on the brutes, Hugh thought. *After all these weeks of constraint, of constant manipulation, of groping in our blindness—here lies an outlet for the man's fury.* Hugh felt himself shrink back from MacGregor's anger and pain. *I'm only glad he's on my side,* he thought, straining against the dizziness that made his forehead feel light, as though it were stuffed full of cotton, and not much else besides.

"Where would you go? Where would you take the ladies if you had them and wanted to get out of man's way, maybe even dispose of them where no eyes could see you?" Callum's voice was tight, but in no other way did it betray him.

"One of the islands, perhaps?"

The two had spent over an hour at the hospital surgery, where Hugh's head was properly stitched and bandaged. He was reinforced with some relatively potent pain pills, MacGregor with half a dozen cups of black coffee that left an unpleasant taste in his mouth.

"No, the islands are too accessible, too traveled, even this time of year. Ferries and docksides? No, they'd avoid all such places."

Hugh had no suggestions at all. He glanced up at the sky, darkened by the approach of night and ominous with a burden of heavy black clouds.

"It's getting terribly late, sir. What can we do—"

"In the darkness?" Callum growled out the words. "You'll see."

They were driving back toward the earl's mansion, along the stretch of road that had become so familiar to them. Perhaps that was why Hugh spotted the car, little more than an incongruous splash of color along a stretch of brown, dun-shaded meadow. Callum pulled to a screeching halt that left the chassis of the M.G. Magnette shuddering long after the engine was still.

They waded through the leaves and dense brush to

investigate. There it was, big as life, the green Morris Oxford, driven helter-skelter off the roadway. Callum could sense the urgency of the last acts that had taken place here. He sniffed around the deserted car much the way a trained bloodhound would, and with the same solemn, long-faced air.

He dug about in his satchel of tools, which was commonly called "the murder bag." "Dust these door handles for fingerprints, will you?" He handed the powder to Hugh. "Start with the passenger's door."

While Fraser was at work Callum nosed around the road and the loose, soft earth at the shoulder, studying tire impressions and any marks or signs that were left him. In his mind he needed to reconstruct what had happened here, at least as far as he could.

When Hugh was finished Callum called him over. "See these skid marks?" He pointed with his finger. "They stretch vertically along the entire width of the road. I believe our roughs stopped their car over the roadway so as to block all passage. Perhaps they pretended to be in need of assistance. Look—these could be the marks of Penelope's tires. She probably got out of the car on her own accord—"

"Then one nabbed her, and it was a simple matter for the other to take care of Laura."

Callum nodded. "But where have they taken them?" He asked for a second time, "Fraser, where would you go?"

Hugh stared ahead of him at the lowering sky and the ragged outline of black mountains that rose to meet it. Callum followed his gaze.

"The most uninhabitated, forsaken place you can think of." Callum spoke the words slowly, not waiting for Hugh's reply. "Twenty miles from here as the crow flies— not much further by car. Just enough distance . . ." His eyes sought Fraser's. "I believe they've gone up to Glencoe!"

"What, man! Why would they?"

"It's away from ports, from major cities, from all the places where they know police may be posted."

Hugh nodded slowly. "You're right. I think you may be right, sir."

"We'll follow the hunch, tonight only. If we come up with nothing, I'll organize a search by the books first thing in the morning." Callum sounded almost elated.

"What can we accomplish tonight?"

Callum disdained to reply. He got his companion securely into the Magnette and drove the bleached, empty road at less than a circumspect speed.

As a lad living near Glasgow, imbued with a natural restlessness, he had often explored this terrain. He and his boyhood companions had trapped in the wilds of the mountains and fished in the streams. If these culprits, whoever they might be, were unfamiliar with the area, that would give Callum an advantage they lacked. An advantage he intended to improve upon with skill and precision.

After some thirty minutes of driving the road narrowed, nosed up a sharp incline, and was immediately swallowed in shadow. If night had not yet blanketed the valleys, it had spread its inky veil here. Hugh shuddered at the eerie solitude that seemed to close in on him. He felt like his head was splitting in two, and even his vision still seemed strained and blurred.

I'll be no help at all to MacGregor, he thought bitterly. He did not let himself think of the girl, confused and frightened, perhaps in more pain than he was. No, that would not do! He'd manage somehow. He could not let either the chief inspector or Penelope down.

18

W HEN LAURA REGAINED CONSCIOUSNESS IT TOOK HER SEVERAL long, painful minutes to figure out where she was. When she first turned her head and saw Penelope huddled beside her in the backseat of the car she began to cry out, but stifled the sound with her hand. She tried to think back to what had happened . . . the car blocking their way . . . Penelope walking out to see what was wrong. In horror she recalled the broad, rough-skinned face of the man who had dragged her out of the car. The fear she felt had choked her throat and frozen her reflexes. Then there had been nothing at all.

As an awareness of what was taking place spread through her, Laura's fear returned with a force that astonished her and made her insides go weak. Why in the world was this happening to them? Who would want to hurt them? Did it have to do with this horrid thievery business and that poor dead girl she had seen at the morgue, her shattered face hidden by a sheet, her small hands with their fine, slender fingers folded so delicately across her chest?

Unaccountably the words of the old groundskeeper from the kirk at Ettrick Bridge came to her from some recess of her subconscious. *"We never say of a person that he has died. Rather, he has changed—or he has traveled."* To where had the murdered girl traveled? To where had her slain son traveled from the faraway, foreign place where his death had found him? Would death find her here? The thought had no substance, no frame of reality in her mind.

She dug her nails into her hands. She must keep from screaming. She must keep her wits about her. She rode along in silence, the heads of the men in front of her merely dark, sinister shapes in the gloom. At length she became aware of the landscape through which they were passing: high, rugged cliffs and dark, brutal clefts in the rocks, stunted trees perched on raw, windblown heights. Unaccountably, she found herself mesmerized by the wild beauty as they sped along.

When the car stopped abruptly she lurched forward, hitting her forehead against the seat in front of her. She heard Penelope stir and whimper, and a flood of tenderness flowed through her. She moved close to her daughter and caught up both her cold little hands, rubbing them briskly. "Penelope—Penny, dear, can you hear me?"

Suddenly the car door opened, releasing a flood of white light that blinded her gaze for a moment. Rough hands pulled her outside. She stood trembling beneath the cold moonlight. Close beside her the dark cliffs were fractured and bare. High above, caught in some narrow recess, the night wind whined, like a lost child. With a chill, lonely sensation raising the hairs on her arms, Laura knew. . . . The sadness . . . the sense of oppression around her . . . she stood in the pass of Glencoe. Here, where so many scenes of horror and nightmare had been enacted—these cruel strangers had taken her here!

"Nobody'll hurt you if you just do what we tell you. Ya understand?" Corker's voice sounded peevish; he was tired and his head hurt. He took up the lead, with the two women following after and Eddie trailing behind. Every now and again he would play his flashlight over the bushes or jump it in weird patterns along the stark rock. It wasn't far to the small cottage they'd found tucked under a ledge of boulders and partly hidden by a cluster of stunted trees.

Penelope stumbled along, as much on the path as off it, not fully awake yet and only dimly aware of what was happening and where she was going. Corker half pushed, half dragged her through the low, narrow cottage door. A dank, musty smell assaulted her nostrils and worked in part as a restorative. She shook her head and blinked her eyes. In the murk of the unlit room she could make out the dim shapes of a low iron bedstead and ladder-back wooden chair, and a stove of some kind in one of the corners. The room was very small and very square in shape, and very dirty. Penelope picked up her heavy feet with care.

"All right, the two of you."

Someone pushed her down, and she found herself sitting hard on the thin, dirty mattress that covered the springs of the bed. Her mother was beside her and reached for her hand. How cool and reassuring her mother's grip felt.

What do you want with us? Why have you brought us here? Penelope wanted to demand. But she had not the energy for it. She felt very weak, very faint. She had to continue blinking her eyes to keep the two men in focus.

"It's late, ladies, and we're all tired, and all we got is a little matter of business that needs attending to." The cheerful, pleasant note in Corker's voice fooled no one, not even himself.

Laura sat with her hands folded serenely in her lap, her eyes wide and watchful. Eddie had thought both dames would blubber like babies. But the young one was too out of it still, and the mother—the widow, the one who most mattered—was she going to be a hard egg to crack?

Laura refused to lower herself to ask these men questions, though curiosity raged in her like a thirst. Beneath it an anger was building, such an anger as she had never felt before in her life.

"To make a long story short," Corker began again, "your old man got himself in a heap of trouble before he kicked the bucket."

"What kind of trouble?" Laura's voice was as brittle as ice.

"It's like this. He started to dabble around in the stock market, got in over his head." He watched Laura's face as he talked, and he saw that his words had got to her. A wariness, even an uncertainty, dulled the fire of her eyes. Most people were like that; most ordinary people, wives in particular, didn't know the first thing about stocks and bonds. And what's more, the whole subject frightened them. It seemed mysterious, beyond them. That was the way the boss got where he was, playing upon some people's fears, other people's ignorance.

"Listen, lady, your husband made certain investments that didn't pan out; let's say they weren't wise choices. When he suffered huge losses, when he was threatened with ruin, my boss bailed him out."

"Who is your boss?" The voice, though frightened, was icy still.

"That ain't no business of yours."

"Oh yes it is, obviously it is, if he's come all this way in search of me. What is it he wants?"

"He wants his rightful property returned to him, that's what. The portfolio your husband had at the time of his death he signed over to you and to her." He indicated Penelope with a jerk of his thumb. "But he had no right to do that. Most of those properties belong to my boss—he signed them over to your old man temporarily to help him out of his bind."

"That doesn't make sense."

"Well, it would if you understood Wall Street, honey."

"So just what is it that you say my husband has done?"

"He's messed things up!" Corker shouted the words. Their echo rang through the sour, dusty air of the close room. Laura felt Penelope shrink.

Eddie stepped forward, a short, wide bulk beside Corker, whose sharp face and long nose made him look like a lean, hungry predator. Eddie looked like a squat, stumpy mole. But as soon as he spoke, Laura realized he was the mean one, the one she should really be afraid of.

"Your husband should have stayed with his small-town broker, but he got greedy"—Eddie spoke the word as though it was some loathsome disease—"as most men do. He started playing hardball with the big guys who were out of his league. He got himself in trouble."

"Are you saying my husband was dishonest?"

Eddie stared hard at the woman whose stubborn position could not be swayed.

"That's another way of saying it, yes, ma'am. And he let our boss befriend him. Then, when he was afraid he was going to die, it appears he transferred all his holdings into joint tenancy held by you and the girl there."

Afraid he was going to die! "How did you know my husband was afraid he was going to die?" Laura spoke the words very slowly.

"He had an attack when he was in New York four months ago. Tried to cover it up, but the boss knew the signs. His old man kicked the bucket the same way."

Laura sat quite still. Her mind was in agony. So, Gerald had been frightened. He had been frightened of death—had waited for it in the loneliness of his own soul. But why hadn't he shared that fear with her? Shared more of his final, precious days with her? No wonder he had been in such a frenzy those last months!

"He was only trying to protect us, to provide for us!" Penelope spat out the words. For the first time Eddie turned his gaze to her. "Shut up," he said. He nodded curtly at Corker, who produced from somewhere a sheaf of papers. He thrust them out to Eddie, who took them in his chubby stump of a hand. "All you have to do is sign these," he said.

"I will not." Laura spoke the words softly, yet they sang through the air. "I will not implicate my husband and destroy the fine reputation he left behind."

"Lady, the guy's dead! What difference can it make to him? Use your head."

"I don't believe a word of what you've been telling me. And besides, if I signed those papers, what would I have left?"

"Your life. Try that for starters."

"Oh, Mother, please!" Penny placed her thin, slight hand on Laura's arm. Her voice held a note of pleading Laura had never heard there before.

"This is ridiculous!" Penelope's weakness, her seeming capitulation, so unlike her, stirred the anger Laura had been feeling. "Who are you, and what are you doing here? Have you been following us?" As she asked the question, it was as though a light went on in her mind. These men had nothing to do with Mr. MacGregor's ladies or the thefts of fine paintings. These men were New York gangsters, and they must be in deadly earnest to have followed her here.

"We want what's ours. You sign your names on the dotted lines here and you go free. It's that simple."

"Why should I believe you? What's to prevent you from killing us after we've signed?"

"The sense of the thing." Corker crowded out Eddie's bulk and came to stand right before Laura. "Use your head, all right? Eddie here likes to shoot holes into people, but I'm not so keen on the risk of murdering someone, at least if I don't have to. You sign the boss's property back to him and you can go on your way. You try to be brave or stubborn or noble—" He shrugged his thin, narrow shoulders, and his whole lanky frame shifted. "You try that, and you're dead. You see, the boss's name is still on these deeds as legal beneficiary after yours." He bent down with his hands on his knees, his face on a level with Laura's. "Figure it out for yourself, lady. With you two out of the picture entirely, there'd be nothing to stand in his way." He laughed, an ugly, gravelly sound far back in his throat. "He'll get what he wants from you one way or another. Remember that."

"Awright, so you got it now?" Eddie thrust the papers at Laura. She touched them with reluctant fingers. "I want a light. I want to read these."

Eddie stuck a flashlight right up against her cheek and pushed the "on" button. The searing brightness blinded her. She leaned back and turned her face aside, but Eddie grabbed her by the hair and shoved her face into the glare again. "Look, lady, I'm losing patience! Just sign."

"Leave her alone, you stupid bully!"

Laura was only vaguely aware of her daughter's protest and the stout man's ugly reply. She had no intentions of signing these papers, at least not now. Far back in her mind she had the nagging impression that she must play for time. She knew the small, ugly man who smelled of stale perspiration was watching her.

"Let me talk to my daughter for a few minutes—alone," she tried.

The blow took her off guard. She felt her cheek sting so hard that it brought tears to her eyes. Eddie thrust a pen under her nose, then grabbed her wrist and forced it between her fingers. "Just sign!"

"Mother, please."

She realized that Penelope was crying softly. She reached over and placed her hand on her daughter's knee. Eddie turned on his heel. "I'm gonna have to rough 'em up a little," he said under his breath to Corker.

Corker pulled him aside to one of the murky corners. "I don't think that would be wise. They either don't walk out of here at all or they walk out on their own two feet, with no cuts or bruises that show—nothin' awkward they might have to explain to somebody. You get my drift?"

Corker couldn't help it. He was proud of his reasoning, after weeks of Eddie always throwing up his stupidity to him. He wasn't stupid, he just wasn't ruthless like Eddie was.

"Let me try one more thing. Tie 'em face down on the bed and leave 'em here in the dark. Tell 'em we'll come back in the morning and let them think they'll be stuck here all night."

"And?"

Eddie was listening, and that pleased Corker. "We'll go out for a drink and mosey back in an hour or so."

"And if that doesn't do it . . ." Eddie touched the gun where it bulged in his pocket.

"Yeah, we do it your way and get the heck out of here."

———•◆•———

The cords bit deep into Laura's wrists and ankles, and she fought the smothering sensation caused by a cloth tied over her mouth and her face shoved into the rancid mattress. She wished she could talk to Penelope, comfort her, explain to her somehow. Fear was taunting her, sparring with the resolve that had served her for courage and seemed to be disintegrating and leaving her with nothing to cling to. She could not hold out for long. She saw that now.

Her muscles ached, and the cold was deep and terrible. The long minutes crawled by. Would the men really leave them here for hours in this tortured position? She felt the muscles of her leg cramp, and cried out in pain.

When the men came back she would have to sign and take her chances. In the darkness that surrounded her she prayed to God to protect her beloved Penny—Penny first. In some ways what happened to her no longer mattered. She thought of Gerald. Was he waiting somewhere for her? Would death take her to him? But, oh, she was such a coward! Death, perhaps—but not pain. She could not bear the contemplation of suffering, suffering beyond her endurance.

The cruel hours wore on, and Laura fancied she could hear the whispers of lost spirits out in the night, haunting the ground where their blood had been spilled and their hearts outraged, mourning endlessly the terrible brutality and hardness of man.

19

THE DEEP, HOLLOW CRY OF THE NIGHT OWL HOVERED OVER the loneliness of the dark mountain pass. Callum drove not much faster than a crawl, and with the windows rolled down. There were other strange sounds besides the flutter of the owl's call, sounds that belonged to the gloom, that were past man's identifying.

"If they came this way," Callum reasoned out loud to Fraser, "I don't believe they'd come far."

Hugh gave a short laugh. "I'd say you're right there. If they don't know this ground, they'd hesitate to venture too deep into this dread cavern."

"We'd better walk from here," Callum decided suddenly, steering the car off the road.

"And if your car's spotted?"

"It will soon be dark as the pit here, and the Magnette's as black as any night." He gave one fender an affectionate pat as he gathered his things.

The narrow road, insubstantial in the moonlight, led straight up the glen. But at several points, foot-hardened paths veered off from it.

"You take this first one on the left," Callum instructed. "I'll take that one on the right. Walk for fifteen minutes and, if you've found nothing, then trace your way back. Carefully, mind you. Keep a careful eye both ways."

Hugh stared at him. "And you mean to do this all night?"

"If need be." The uneasiness Callum was feeling ate at him like a bad toothache, but he knew he must will it aside. His judgment must be clear and unhampered.

He took the trail that forked off to the left, working his way around stones and boulders that seemed to have been tossed down by some giant hand. He could have filled this whole cavity with men, and that might flush his game out. But what of the safety of the two innocent women? He wondered suddenly, for the first time, if they were waiting for him. Did they pin any hope to the fact that he might be able to rescue them, or did the thought seem impossible to their minds?

Who were these men, and what were they after? Callum wished he could roar out his fears like the Highlanders of old, coming down on their enemies from the hills, the clan battle cries thick in their throats and their swords in their hands.

He played his torch carefully over the ground, along the low ferns and bracken that lined the path. Fraser was right; this could take all night and go nowhere. He stood stock-still. He must not give place to the panic that threatened to engulf him. He closed his eyes for a moment and tried to think back to the days when he had roamed here as a lad. That was so long ago! He plucked at the memories. Was there some little suggestion or reminder, some recognition . . .

Slowly, dimly, he saw in his mind a steep hillside where white sheep grazed and a black and white collie ran. And then the kindly, whiskered face of the old shepherd standing in front of his low stone cottage, and at his feet, a basket full of wriggling, mewling collie puppies.

He drew a deep breath of the moist night air, trying to steady his mind; relax it—keep it back in the past. He would ride his bicycle up the steep path to where the cliffs began to close in on both sides. Not much further. Around one bend, then a second—no, perhaps there were three. He could feel himself trembling. He could feel the rapid pump of his heart pounding against his chest.

He opened his eyes. In the soft moonlight he saw it: a thin mountain ash leaned against three round boulders that were piled right on top of each other, snowman style. That was the marker! There ran the path to the old "but and ben" where the shepherd slept with his dogs; there the stream ran deep through the long mountain grass.

He retraced his footsteps in no time at all and caught sight of Fraser just making his way back to the main stretch of road. "Get back in the car," he called as he ran toward him. "I think I might know where to go."

He explained as they drove further up between rock walls and overhanging ledges that shut out all light. The lad seemed a bit dubious. "We've passed half a dozen turnoffs," he informed MacGregor. But Callum kept pressing on.

Then, directly beyond a steep, sharp curve in the road, Callum slammed on the brakes. The M.G. shuddered and squealed a little in protest. In front of their eyes a slender ash, gray and weathered, leaned against three rocks that rose as a round pillar into the sky.

"This is the place," Callum pronounced. His voice sounded solemn, unsubstantial. He flipped on his torch and, nodding for Fraser to follow him, started up the steep path.

Corker and Willie had gotten a little sidetracked with their smokes and the fiery whiskey that warmed their insides. They sat against a great rock, away from the bite of the cold air. It was too dark to read a wristwatch; they had no idea of the time. Nearly two hours had passed when they stumbled back into the cottage. Reinforced by the liquor, they were in no mood for nonsense. Willie called out to the darkness, "All right, we're here. Let's get this thing over and done with. Quick!"

It was raven-black here and a cold wind fretted at the cracks in the cliffs. "This is as good a spot to begin as any," Callum said, reading Hugh's thoughts. "Look at it that way. Those half-dozen trails could have kept us walking around in a maze of our own making all night."

"If this is the place, why don't we see a car about somewhere? They must have driven in as we did."

"They could be parked off in one of those side tracks. But most probably they pulled on ahead and left their car beyond the mark, where it wouldn't be discovered."

"Yes," Hugh replied glumly. "Yes, you're probably right."

The eerie wind stayed close to their side, noisy in the glow of the torches, restless in the dried, brown bracken through which they walked. After a few yards, without any warning Callum stopped dead in his tracks. He pointed wordlessly to a long, trailing branch of an elderberry bush. At first Hugh saw nothing at all. He moved his face and his light a bit closer. Clinging there like a live thing was a torn bit of cloth, frail, almost gossamer. It looked very much like a butterfly perched on a twig.

"It *is* a butterfly," Callum said. "Look at the colors." He reached out and pinched the thin substance between two fingers. "It's part of a butterfly, actually." His voice had a strange note to it. "And I've seen it before. This is Penelope's scarf." He smiled at Hugh's amazed face. "Don't you see? That means we're on the right track!"

After that they made their way without the aid of torch light. But after a few tortuous feet they were able to discern the bulk of the cottage a few feet above them. Up this high a bit of moonlight found its way through, and the gloom, so heavy, so ghastly to Hugh, was softened enough that he could make out the shapes of things and find his way by something beyond touch alone.

They crept round to the back of the building. There was only one low door in the front. But there was a single square window back here. If they could work their way close to it, they could perhaps get a glimpse inside.

———•◦•———

When Corker at last snapped on a flashlight he held it close to his side, with the light trained down at the floor. Eddie untied the women, none too gently.

"You gals look a bit worse for wear," Corker leered. He gathered the papers from the chair where he had left them. "Here we go. Let's be good girls, now."

Laura found the documents thrust into her hands again, but her fingers were almost too stiff to move. Her muscles ached from the strained position they had been forced into, and from the wet, piercing cold.

"I'll go first." Penelope reached for the papers. Eddie gave her the pen. She was hoping her mother would not try any heroics. During the long, torturous hours she had tried to think, and she felt that for some crazy reason her mother believed that the earl—or rather, Inspector MacGregor—would find them, would make this all go away. Penelope had no such illusions. She did not want to die, she did not want to be hurt. She didn't care what the papers said or what these men were after; she just wanted to get out of here!

In the stiff silence Laura could hear the scratch of Penelope's pen over the paper. The sound made her feel sick. *What are we doing? Should I still try to stall them?*

Penelope handed the papers to Corker. She could at least stand to look into his face. Eddie frightened her; Eddie made her skin crawl.

"All right, tie her again."

Laura had lifted the pen. It remained poised in her clumsy grip while she watched Eddie tie Penny's arms, already bruised and aching, behind her back.

"We'll leave you here, ladies. Get a good night's sleep." Eddie chuckled. "By the time some one finds you, we'll be far enough away from here that it just won't matter."

Laura knew what his vulgar tone implied. There was an ugly, lewd expression in his eyes as he looked at Penelope, and for the first time Laura knew terror. Perhaps that terror unbalanced her. She found herself ripping the pages she held, her fingers shaking.

With a curse Corker lunged for her. But something went awry. There was a great crashing sound as the door of the cottage collapsed inward, and the heavy edge of the wood caught Corker's heel. He fell face down, hard against the packed-earth floor. He felt the press of a foot into the small of his back. When he cried out the foot pressed harder.

"Shut up and lie still." Hugh wrenched the man's long arms behind his back and tied them with a length of twine from his pocket.

Corker had no chance to see what was happening, but Eddie had. With a low, animal-like growl he turned to the big man who had burst in, filling the door frame, looking as fierce as the night. The small pistol was cradled in Eddie's palm. Even as he raised his arm, Callum couldn't see it. But he knew what the motion meant. Instinctively he dodged and then crouched, eluding the bullet. In the next moment he lunged for Eddie's middle, but the small, soft-looking man was stronger than he appeared. He caught Callum with a heavy blow in the shoulder, his hand and the hard steel of the weapon connecting with a force that sent Callum staggering.

As he struggled to right himself Eddie was on top of him, pummeling him with a cold precision that seemed incongruous with the looks of the man. But Callum was the stronger. Bringing his skills to bear, he wove his fingers together and, with the palms of his hands under Eddie's chin, gave a shove that sent the man sprawling. He followed his lead with a series of blows that disabled the wretch and left him little more than a quivering mass of flesh.

"On your feet!" Callum rasped, dragging him up by the collar. In a few deft moves he had both his hands and feet bound. "Hugh, walk this one out of here. I'll take the scarecrow. I think he has more spunk left."

For the first time since entering he turned his attentions on the women. Laura had untied Penny's hands, and they both sat quiet and wide-eyed on the edge of the bed. Callum walked close to Laura and bent down beside her.

"Are you hurt?" he asked. "Did these men harm you?" He thought he would know not so much by her reply but by what he saw in her eyes.

"Not enough to matter," Laura answered evenly. "Yes, we're all right."

"Mother was certain you'd come for her." Penelope's

voice was very small, like the voice of a child. Callum did his best to restrain the pleasure and wonder that her words brought.

"Laura, is this true?" He caught up her hands and held them against his lips. "Thank heaven I came!"

———•◦•———

It was decided that Callum would drive into town with the culprits and Hugh would escort the women to the earl's house. But Laura didn't want that.

"You may need Hugh's assistance," she protested. "Penelope and I can manage very well by ourselves."

Penny didn't share her mother's sense of the noble; she longed for the company and protection of the young man who gazed at her with such yearning eyes. But she acquiesced to her mother's wishes, though Hugh walked them down the hill to the Magnette which she would drive.

"Where did those two leave the car they brought you in?"

"Further on, up the hill. We walked back down to the path through the mountains."

Hugh nodded at her response but said nothing.

Laura, trailing a few steps behind, was in her own world, surrounded by the whispered memories of Glencoe. She was not frightened. She did not mind the lurid light and the shadows from the mottled clouds overhead. She felt one with the sufferers, who were men and women of her own blood. She had survived her ordeal when every fear, every weakness had been exposed. She had come through it well—and she would know that for the rest of her life.

20

IT HAD WRENCHED CALLUM TO TURN HIS BACK ON LAURA AND leave her in Fraser's care. A spell existed in Glencoe. However wild and terrifying it might be, it held Callum MacGregor in its clutches. And yet, well he knew that such enchantments are too frail to survive the harsh realities of the ordinary.

He drove down the mountain to the constabulary and turned his two prisoners over to the chief constable's care. Then he took Fraser, who was drooping and in more pain than he would admit to, home to bed. By this time the sun was up and the world in gear again. And Laura and Penelope, Janet assured him, were safe in their beds. Wearily he stumbled to his own room for a few hours' rest.

When he awoke in the late afternoon they had not stirred yet, and he had a call from the city; not Oban, but Edinburgh, where Maggie had been taken. It was imperative that he go there at once. Feeling cruelly torn, he left a note for Laura, dialed Fraser and gave orders, then climbed into the Magnette—mud-splattered and tired—and headed southwest through a gray drizzle toward the capital, nearly a hundred miles off.

———— ·•·•· ————

Hugh felt stiff and achy still, but the prospects of the day were too enticing for him to be down-spirited. With MacGregor off to the city, the questioning of the kidnappers would be under his own direction. He felt uneasy at first. He had never dealt with a crime of such a serious nature before. What's more, he had never been personally involved in a criminal case.

He walked into the room where the two were being held for questioning, rubbing the back of his head and grinning wickedly. "Seems I have a score or two to settle with you fellows," he said.

Eddie was surly and would not even raise his eyes to him. But Corker tried the smooth act. "We'll make a deal," he offered. "Everyone come out feeling better."

"I'd tear your eyes out if my hands were free," Eddie menaced.

But, as it was, Corker didn't have much to offer. He was pretty well caught between a rock and a hard place, fearing the authorities but perhaps fearing the man that he worked for more.

Hugh pored over the papers the two had tried to threaten the women into signing. He was educated and had a little experience of his own in buying stocks, but they were beyond him. With permission from the chief he called his father's solicitor, who came down to the station. He got further in a few minutes than Hugh had in an hour.

"This New York shyster appears to be a very clever man," the solicitor pronounced, raising a long, tapered eyebrow and pointing to the documents with long, tapered fingers. "From what I can tell after a quick once-over, he's playing several ends against the middle, as the saying goes. He's involved in power struggles in a number of major companies, I'll wager, and needs to control a majority of the stock. Therefore, he cons unsophisticated, inexperienced investors such as your Mr. Poulson here into allowing him to represent them and to recommend certain investments, some of which are legitimate, some of which are not. Then he also does some very illegal juggling." He knit his brow in frustration. "It's difficult to explain this in lay terms"—he smiled dryly—"and in ten minutes or less. I suspect he puts investors' names on stocks that actually belong to him, but only temporarily, until he can shuffle certain conditions to his liking. Then he can readjust the paperwork, and all will be legal again. Unfortunately for him, Mr. Poulson died before the culprit had a chance to reclaim his investments."

Hugh was astonished. When he stopped at the earl's place and explained his findings to Laura and Penelope, his gratification grew.

"So your father is vindicated," he said softly, seeing the fine glaze in Penelope's eyes.

"Are we poverty-stricken?" Penelope wanted to know.

"Not at all," Laura assured her. "There was enough that was legitimately your father's." She trembled, thinking of Gerald's high sense of responsibility and the price it must have cost him.

While the young people sat close and talked low in the library, Laura walked in the sleeping garden beneath a fine mist of rain. She felt strangely calm and at peace—and unhurried. Her life wasn't waiting for her at some point in the future; her life was happening now. And how rich a life it was! She was beginning to see that, to feel it inside.

The biggest regret she grappled with was that Gerald had missed this whole side of her. As she blossomed, as she strengthened, she would have been of so much more value to him. *"Of all sad words of tongue or pen . . ."* She thought of Whittier's words with a sigh. *"The saddest are these: 'It might have been!'"*

It was no use thinking of things that were past her control, that would do her no good. Gerald was gone for the time being, and so was Peter. But she and Penny were here. And their lives were good—their lives were the vital ones now.

———•◦•———

MacGregor was gone indefinitely. And he had strongly requested Laura not to leave the earl's house until his return. Hugh and Penelope spent long, unhurried days together. In this tranquil aftermath, and with the resilience of youth, they were able to laugh at the ironies of their past adventures. They had much at which to marvel, much that held them in common. Hugh, in his somewhat disdainful aloofness of womankind, let down his defenses for the first time and enjoyed the freedom of really being himself.

The fall colors faded to more somber shades, and the winds from the north began to blow in. They did not notice. They had other to explore than the landscapes of Scotland just now.

———•◦•———

Callum spent three days in Edinburgh, tying up the loose ends of the case. His old friend, Thomas Howe, was well pleased with the outcome. The thieves had been apprehended, and Willie "the Terrier" had been picked up outside the train station in Paris. As if that were not enough, Maggie had supplied them with names that supported the suspicions of the Edinburgh art dealer, Mr. Grant. The men he had overheard talking about stolen art in Prague had now been positively identified; a conviction would not be long in following.

"I do believe we'll nab the whole lot of them, MacGregor!" Callum could hear Thomas smack his lips in satisfaction, even over the phone. "Well, my good man, you can come home any time now."

Home. Strange how the earl's great house in Oban had come to mean that. "I've a wee bit of unfinished business of my own to take care of yet, sir, if it's all the same to you."

"Yes, Callum. Somehow I'd expected that. Well then, come as soon as you can. The waterfront will still be waiting."

These were words Callum had been anticipating, almost from the very beginning of this assignment. Why did they leave him feeling cold and deflated now?

The one mystery that yet remained unsolved was the whereabouts of the ring, the costly emerald that Glenda had pinched from the dead woman's hand. Callum decided to pay one last visit to Maggie, and while they were chatting quite comfortably he casually asked, "What did Glenda do with the old lady's ring, anyway?"

Maggie hesitated; he watched a resentful stubbornness flash in her eyes.

"I've given you the cake and the icing! Do you want the cherry on top of it, too?"

"We've found it, Maggie," Callum bluffed. "I thought you might be interested in filling in some details, that's all."

"The little fool!" Maggie's voice was harsh, but the softness in her eyes betrayed her. "She never should have taken it in the first place—like a child grabbing for a fancy bauble. It was partly my fault. I told her to get rid of it, any way she could manage. And she did." Maggie grinned, showing wide, uneven teeth. "So, if you know where it is, gov', you've got one better 'n me!"

Stumped and frustrated as he was, Callum felt inclined to believe her. "Tell me this one thing. Was it you and Glenda who followed me that night in Edinburgh?"

"Naw, it wasn't us. The Terrier was there, and he heard you'd been spotted at some nightclub. He was sure you were on to him; that's why he laid low."

While all the time it was you I was on to"—Callum chuckled softly—"or thought I was on to."

"I can't believe that Glennie," Maggie said in a haunted voice. "Bless her, she figured it out."

"What?" Callum's senses jolted to attention.

"She saw them two ladies on the street in Inverary. Figured out she looked a bit like the young one and thought it a grand coincidence that they was mother and daughter—like us."

Callum was watching her closely.

"Well, like we pretended, you know. She wasn't really my kin. Anyways, she was convinced that you blokes were on the path of those two, thought we ought to help you along a little. But I never paid her no mind."

There were tears in Maggie's eyes. She wiped at them with her sleeve.

"Well, aren't we all the blind ones," Callum mused. He stood and placed his large, warm hand on Maggie's shoulder. "I'm sorry, Maggie, truly I am."

"And you'll do all you can for me?"

"I have," he assured her, "and will continue to do."

He walked out into a day that was leaden and a sky that was weeping. He felt like weeping himself. There was only one place he wanted to go to right now. There was only one person he wanted to see.

———•—•——

The ferry was nearly deserted, but the wind that blew in off the sea had a gentle touch and a taste of faraway places.

"Thank you for coming," Callum said.

"What need is there to thank me," Laura smiled, "for doing something I wanted to do?"

He had been telling her some of the things he had learned from Maggie, clearing up certain obscure points for her. Now he remembered one more.

"It was I who first invaded your privacy. Back on Loch Lomondside—I broke into your room there."

Laura's eyes widened. "You did?"

He gave her the details, not sparing himself in the telling.

"I did not even know," she confessed. "I remember Penelope acting a bit strange one evening; perhaps she suspected something, but she didn't tell me."

Callum thought of the other time, when Penelope was accosted on the dark streets of Oban; she had kept that incident from Laura as well.

"You two are cut out of much the same cloth, you know," he said gently. "You do a good job of taking care of one another."

Laura saw in his eyes deep loneliness, the hunger for tenderness that only a lone man can know. She stared into the white, churning water and thought of the silkie with his deep, luminous eyes, and wondered.

They, too, in their conversations noted the ironies.

"If you had not been trying to trap us, you would not have been there to protect us," Laura marveled. Then she brightened noticeably, looking as winsome as a girl. "You must promise me you will straighten things out with young Donald. I can't bear to have him thinking of Penelope and me as two common thieves."

"He never has that, I fear," Callum chuckled. "He had been charmed too entirely."

The day was theirs, an interval apart from both their realities. They spent it well, with the wind and the sea and the solitude—beyond the reaches of memory, beyond the reaches of that confinement which men call time.

———•◆•———

The day came for leaving; they could no longer postpone it. The four of them stood in the earl's immense library, close to the cheerful fire, feeling, if not awkward, at least ill at ease.

Penelope reached into the pocket of the tweed jacket which Janet had cleaned for her. "Ouch," she cried out. "I've pricked my finger on something."

"Let me see." Laura put her hand in and pulled out the ring. Penelope gasped.

"Let me see that!" Callum's voice held a note of authority that made Laura hand the ring over before having a proper view of it herself. The emerald danced and spun in the lights from the fire. It was the largest jewel Laura had ever seen.

"Where did it come from?" she breathed. "Do you know anything about this, Penny?"

"I certainly don't. I wish I could claim it as mine; believe me, I do."

"This is the ring Glenda Bates stole from the Ferguson house." Callum's voice was grave.

"The one she took from the hand of a dead woman?"

"Yes, that's right. The one that dropped off the edge of the earth, as far as anyone knew." He held it up and twisted it around in his fingers. It appeared to have a shimmering, pulsing life of its own.

"Poor Glenda," Laura murmured. Her eyes met Callum's and held for a moment.

"What will you do with it now?" Penelope asked.

"Return it to the daughter, the rightful owner." Callum smiled a bit mischievously. "I'm sorry, Penelope. I can imagine how you must feel."

"And to think that I had it and didn't even realize it!"

"Yes, and I'd like to know how. When did she plant it in your jacket?"

"And why?" Hugh added.

"I can tell you the why," Callum said. "Both Maggie and the Terrier told her she had to get rid of it; it was too hot to hang on to, too hot to fence in the circumstances. She panicked; she didn't know what to do. But she'd seen you before—in Inverary, Maggie told me."

Penelope put her fingers to her temples and tried to remember any encounter with a young woman.

"Could she be the girl I bumped into outside the recorder's office?"

"Yes, Mother! Yes!" Penny was excited now, and her face was flushed. "The one who said nasty things to you that you didn't quite hear."

"Well, she was convinced that the police had confused you with them. So perhaps she planted the ring in your jacket on purpose, even hoping it might be discovered and transfer the suspicion to you."

"Do you recall the last time you wore the jacket, Penny?" Hugh was getting a little intense himself now. "Try to remember."

"I have been. I think it must have been on the ferry, because I remember it being splashed with mud and water and I asked Janet if she would set it out somewhere to dry. But instead she took it to the cleaners for me, which I thought very nice."

Callum was already across the room, calling from the entrance for Janet. When she walked in with an understandable air of uncertainty, they all bombarded her with questions at once. Finally Callum held his hand up for silence. "Just answer one thing, my dear. Do you remember at any time admitting a stranger—or seeing a stranger within this house?"

She began to say no, but Callum moved closer and, staring directly into her eyes, asked her a second time. "Think about it, Janet. Anything unusual? The slightest thing out of the ordinary?"

"A stranger is a stranger. You either know folk or you don't," she began indignantly. Then she stopped. "There was a time, one of the days you went off touring, and Miss Penelope came back to the house alone—just popped in out of nowhere. I remember, 'cause I called to her when I saw her on the stair but she just kept on goin'. That wasn't like her. She's most times so friendly and thoughtful. I do recall that . . . and yes, I ran after her, clear out on the porch, but she'd disappeared. And it seemed a bit strange, there being no car in sight, and her suddenly here for no reason."

Janet could not understand the pleasure on the four faces that were watching her.

"That was Glenda, all right." Hugh was triumphant, but Callum was thoughtful.

"She was trying to retrieve the treasure—trying desperately," Callum said. "It was her failure to come up with this ring that cost her her life."

His words had a subduing effect. He thanked Janet and sent her away. A palpable silence settled over the big room, interrupted only by the sounds of the fire as it hissed and roared in the grate.

"Come now, we must not part on such a solemn note," Callum urged. "I'll bring out my surprise for Laura and that will revive us again."

"Surprise?" Laura had no idea what to expect, but she could not resist a thrill of anticipation.

The package he brought out was large and unwieldy, but narrow, and wrapped all round in brown paper. Penelope knew it at once, recognizing the shape and remembering the auction. "You bought it for her!" she whispered. And Callum nodded and winked.

Callum held the frame while Laura tore at the paper, which fell away to reveal the Whistler landscape the "earl" had purchased at the auction. Laura's eyes filled with tears.

"I couldn't possibly . . . it is too dear a present . . ."

Callum knelt down beside her. "It is yours. Take it to help you remember—everything."

"I need no help remembering," she said, meeting his gaze. "But I shall cherish it." She reached out with the tips of her fingers and touched his cheek.

———·◆·———

The four of them, looking somewhat forlorn, walked out to the Morris. Callum helped Laura into her seat and, bending over her, kissed her cheek.

"Haste ye back." His voice was no more than a murmur against her hair.

The two men stood in the gravel drive and watched the car pull away. A cold rain began to fall, and a lone rook wheeled overhead. *There is no more mournful sound in the world,* Callum thought, *than a raven's cry.*

He would go back to London, but the waterfront would never be quite the same. He had always been well aware of the many risks of his trade. But this was one he had never encountered—never even imagined before. Many things would be different for him now, and for the rest of his life.

———·◆·———

There was a silence within the green Morris Oxford. At last Penelope spoke. "It's raining, Mother."

"Yes, it is fitting that we leave Scotland when it is raining, don't you think?"

"It's too much, Mother. It's been too overwhelming."

Laura placed her hand over Penelope's slender fingers where they curved round the steering wheel. "Indeed it has, my darling. We will both need some time."

"Are you in pain, Mother?" Penelope asked outright, though she had to watch the road and could not see Laura's face.

"Yes, I am. But it's all right, Penny. This time it's all right."

———•◆•———

The wind blew the rain in horizontal slashes across the black strip of road. The trees in the unprotected heaths had lost nearly all of their leaves and raised thin, beseeching branches into the wet expanse. And high above, a solitary raven swooped and soared, his graceful wings gleaming ebony against the long stretch of silver sky.

ABOUT THE AUTHOR

Susan Evans McCloud's previously published writings include poems, a children's book, local newspaper feature articles, narratives for tapes and filmstrips, screenplays, and lyrics—including two hymns found in the 1985 Church hymnbook. She is listed in several international biographies of writers of distinction, and she currently teaches creative writing. Her many novels include *For Love of Ivy; By All We Hold Dear; My Enemy, My Love; Anna; Jennie; Ravenwood; A Face in the Shadows;* and *The Heart That Truly Loves.*

The author and her husband, James, are the parents of six children and have three grandchildren. The family resides in Provo, Utah.